Mary Elizabeth Braddon

THE GOLDEN CALF

In two volumes

Elibron Classics
www.elibron.com

COLLECTION

OF

BRITISH AUTHORS

TAUCHNITZ EDITION.

VOL. 2133.

THE GOLDEN CALF BY M. E. BRADDON.

IN TWO VOLUMES.

VOL. I.

THE GOLDEN CALF.

A NOVEL.

BY

M. E. BRADDON,

AUTHOR OF "LADY AUDLEY'S SECRET,"
ETC. ETC.

COPYRIGHT EDITION.

IN TWO VOLUMES.

VOL. I.

LEIPZIG

BERNHARD TAUCHNITZ

1883.

CONTENTS

OF VOLUME I.

THE GOLDEN CALF.

CHAPTER I.

THE ARTICLED PUPIL.

"Where is Miss Palliser?" inquired Miss Pew, in that awful voice of hers, at which the class-room trembled, as at unexpected thunder. A murmur ran along the desks, from girl to girl, and then some one, near that end of the long room which was sacred to Miss Pew and her lieutenants, said that Miss Palliser was not in the class-room.

"I think she is taking her music lesson, ma'am," faltered the girl who had ventured diffidently to impart this information to the schoolmistress.

"Think?" exclaimed Miss Pew, in her stentorian voice. "How can you think about an absolute fact? Either she is taking her lesson, or she is not taking her lesson. There is no room for thought. Let Miss Palliser be sent for this moment."

At this command, as at the behest of the Homeric Jove himself, half a dozen Irises started up to carry the ruler's message; but again Miss Pew's mighty tones resounded in the echoing class-room.

"I don't want twenty girls to carry one message. Let Miss Rylance go."

There was a grim smile on the principal's coarsely-featured countenance as she gave this order. Miss Rylance was not one of the six who had started up to do the schoolmistress's bidding. She was a young lady who considered her mission in life anything rather than to carry a message—a young lady who thought herself quite the most refined and elegant thing at Mauleverer Manor, and so entirely superior to her surroundings as to be absolved from the necessity of being obliging. But Miss Pew's voice, when fortified by anger, was too much even for Miss Rylance's calm sense of her own merits, and she rose at the lady's bidding, laid down her ivory penholder on the neatly-written exercise, and walked out of the room quietly, with the slow and stately deportment imparted by a long course of instruction from Madame Rigolette, the fashionable dancing-mistress.

"Rylance won't much like being sent on a message," whispered Miss Cobb, the Kentish brewer's daughter, to Miss Mullins, the Northampton carriage-builder's heiress.

"And old Pew delights in taking her down a peg," said Miss Cobb, who was short, plump, and ruddy, a picture of rude health and unrefined good looks—a girl who bore "beer" written in unmistakable characters across her forehead, Miss Rylance had observed to her own particular circle. "I will say that for the old lady," added Miss Cobb, "she never cottons to stuckupish-ness."

Vulgarity of speech is the peculiar delight of a schoolgirl off duty. She spends so much of her life under the all-pervading eye of authority, she is so drilled, and lectured, and ruled and regulated, that, when the eye of authority is off her, she seems naturally to degenerate into licence. No speech so interwoven with slang as the speech of a schoolgirl—except that of a schoolboy.

There came a sudden hush upon the class-room after Miss Rylance had departed on her errand. It was a sultry afternoon in late June, and the four rows of girls seated at the two long desks in the long bare room, with its four tall windows facing a hot blue sky, felt almost as exhausted by the heat as if they had been placed under an air-pump. Miss Pew had a horror of draughts, so the upper sashes were only lowered a couple of inches, to let out the used atmosphere. There was no chance of a gentle west wind blowing in to ruffle the loose hair upon the foreheads of those weary students.

Thursday afternoons were devoted to the study of German. The sandy-haired young woman at the end of the room furthest from Miss Pew's throne was Fräulein Wolf, from Frankfort, and it was Fräulein Wolf's mission to go on eternally explaining the difficulties of her native language to the pupils at Mauleverer Manor, and to correct those interesting exercises of Ollendorff's which ascend from the primitive simplicity of golden candlesticks and bakers' dogs, to the loftiest themes in romantic literature.

For five minutes there was no sound save the scratching of pens, and the placid voice of the Fräulein demonstrating to Miss Mullins that in an exercise of twenty lines, ten words out of every twenty were wrong, and then the door was opened suddenly—not at all in the manner so carefully instilled by the teacher of deportment. It was flung back, rather, as if with an angry hand, and a young woman, taller than the generality of her sex, walked quickly up the room to Miss Pew's desk, and stood before that bar of justice, with head erect, and dark flashing eyes, the incarnation of defiance.

"*Was für ein Mädchen!*" muttered the Fräulein, blinking at that distant figure, with her pale gray-green eyes.

Miss Pew pretended not to see the challenge in the girl's angry eyes. She turned to her subordinate, Miss Pillby, the useful drudge who did a little indifferent teaching in English grammar and geography, looked after the younger girls' wardrobes, and toadied the mistress of the house.

"Miss Pillby, will you be kind enough to show Ida Palliser the state of her desk?" asked Miss Pew, with awe-inspiring politeness.

"She needn't do anything of the kind," said Ida coolly. "I know the state of my desk quite as well as she does. I daresay it's untidy. I haven't had time to put things straight."

"Untidy!" exclaimed Miss Pew, in her appalling baritone, "untidy is not the word. It's degrading. Miss Pillby, be good enough to call over the various articles which you have found in Ida Palliser's desk."

Miss Pillby rose to do her employer's bidding. She was a dull piece of human machinery to which the idea of resistance to authority was impossible. There was no dirty work she would not have done meekly, willingly even, at Miss Pew's bidding. The girls were never tired of expatiating upon Miss Pillby's meanness; but the lady herself did not even know that she was mean. She had been born so.

She went to the locker, lifted the wooden lid, and proceeded in a flat, drawling voice to call over the items which she found in that receptacle.

"A novel, 'The Children of the Abbey,' without a cover."

"Ah!" sighed Miss Pew.

"One stocking, with a rusty darning-needle sticking in it. Five apples, two mouldy. A square of hard-bake. An old neck-ribbon. An odd cuff. Seven letters. A knife, with the blade broken. A bundle of pen-and-ink—well, I suppose they are meant for sketches."

"Hand them over to me," commanded Miss Pew.

She had seen some of Ida Palliser's pen-and-ink sketches before to-day—had seen herself represented in every ridiculous guise and attitude by that young person's facile pen. Her large cheeks reddened in anticipation of her pupil's insolence. She took the sheaf of crumpled paper and thrust it hastily into her pocket.

A ripple of laughter swept over Miss Palliser's resolute face; but she said not a word.

"Half a New Testament—the margins shamefully scribbled over," pursued Miss Pillby, with implacable monotony. "Three Brazil nuts. A piece of slate-pencil. The photograph of a little boy——"

"My brother," cried Ida hastily. "I hope you are not going to confiscate that, Miss Pew, as you have confiscated my sketches."

"It would be no more than you deserve if I were to burn everything in your locker, Miss Palliser," said the schoolmistress.

"Burn everything except my brother's portrait. I might never get another. Papa is so thoughtless. Oh, please, Miss Pillby, give me back the photo."

"Give her the photograph," said Miss Pew, who was not all inhuman, although she kept a school, a hardening process which is supposed to deaden the instincts of womanhood. "And now, pray, Miss Palliser, what excuse have you to offer for your untidiness?"

"None," said Ida, "except that I have no time to be tidy. You can't expect tidiness from a drudge like me."

And with this cool retort, Miss Palliser turned her back upon her mistress and left the room.

"Did you ever see such cheek?" murmured the irrepressible Miss Cobb to her neighbour.

"She can afford to be cheeky," retorted the neighbour. "She has nothing to lose. Old Pew couldn't possibly treat her any worse than she does. If she did, it would be a police case."

When Ida Palliser was in the little lobby outside the class-room, she took the little boy's photograph from her pocket, and kissed it passionately. Then she ran upstairs to a small room on the landing, where there was nothing but emptiness and a worn out old square piano, and sat down for her hour's practice. She was always told off to the worst pianos in the house. She took out a book of five-finger exercises, by a Leipsic professor, placed it on the desk, and then, just as she was beginning to play, her whole frame was shaken like a bulrush in a sudden gust of wind; she let her head fall forward on the desk, and burst into tears, hot, passionate tears, that came like a flood, in spite of her determination not to cry.

What was the matter with Ida Palliser? Not much, perhaps. Only poverty, and poverty's natural corollary, a lack of friends.

She was the handsomest girl in the school, and one of the cleverest—clever in an exceptional way, which claimed admiration even from the coldest. She occupied the anomalous position of a pupil teacher, or an articled pupil. Her father, a military man, living abroad on his half pay, with a young second wife, and a five-year old son, had paid Miss Pew a lump sum of fifty pounds, and for those fifty pounds Miss Pew had agreed to maintain and educate Ida Palliser during the space of three years, to give her the benefit of instruction from the masters who attended the school, and to befit her for the brilliant and lucrative career of governess in a gentleman's family. As a set-off against these advantages, Miss Pew had full liberty to exact what services she pleased from Miss Palliser, stopping short, as Miss Green had suggested, of a police case.

Miss Pew had not shown herself narrow in her ideas of the articled pupil's capacity. It was her theory that no amount of intellectual labour, including some manual duties in the way of assisting in the lavatory on tub-nights, washing hair-brushes, and mending clothes, could be too much for a healthy young woman of nineteen. She always talked of Ida as a young woman. The other pupils of the same age she called girls; but of Ida she spoke uncompromisingly as a "young woman."

"Oh, how I hate them all!" said Ida, in the midst of her sobs. "I hate everybody, myself most of all!"

Then she pulled herself together with an effort,

dried her tears hurriedly, and began her five-finger exercises, *tum*, *tum*, *tum*, with the little finger, all the other fingers pinned resolutely down upon the keys.

"I wonder whether, if I had been ugly and stupid, they would have been a little more merciful to me?" she said to herself.

Miss Palliser's ability had been a disadvantage to her at Mauleverer Manor. When Miss Pew discovered that the girl had a knack of teaching she enlarged her sphere of tuition, and from taking the lowest class only, as former articled pupils had done, Miss Palliser was allowed to preside over the second and third classes, and thereby saved her employers forty pounds a year.

To teach two classes, each consisting of from fifteen to twenty girls, was in itself no trifling labour. But besides this Ida had to give music lessons to that lowest class which she had ceased to instruct in English and French, and whose studies were now conducted by Miss Pillby. She had her own studies, and she was eager to improve herself, for that career of governess in a gentleman's family was the only future open to her. She used to read the advertisements in the governess column of the *Times* supplement, and it comforted her to see that an all-accomplished teacher demanded from eighty to a hundred a year for her services. A hundred a year was Ida's idea of illimitable wealth. How much she might do with such a sum! She could dress herself handsomely, she could save enough money for a summer holiday in Normandy with her neglectful father and her weak little vulgar stepmother, and the half-brother, whom she loved better than anyone else in the world.

The thought of this avenue to fortune gave her
fortitude. She braced herself up, and set herself
valourously to unriddle the perplexities of a nocturne
by Chopin.

"After all I have only to work on steadily," she
told herself; "there will come an end to my slavery."

Presently she began to laugh to herself softly:

"I wonder whether old Pew has looked at my cari-
catures," she thought, "and whether she'll treat me
any worse on account of them?"

She finished her hour's practice, put her music
back into her portfolio, which lived in an ancient
canterbury under the ancient piano, and went to the
room where she slept, in company with seven other
spirits, as mischievous and altogether evilly disposed
as her own.

Mauleverer Manor had not been built for a school,
or it would hardly have been called a manor. There
were none of those bleak, bare dormitories, specially
planned for the accommodation of thirty sleepers—none
of those barrack-like rooms which strike desolation to
the soul. With the exception of the large class-room
which had been added at one end of the house, the
manor was very much as it had been in the days of
the Mauleverers, a race now as extinct as the Dodo.
It was a roomy, rambling old house of the time of the
Stuarts, and bore the date of its erection in many unmistakable peculiarities. There were fine rooms on
the ground floor, with handsome chimney-pieces and
oak panelling. There were small low rooms above,
curious old passages, turns and twists, a short flight of
steps here, and another flight there, various levels, ir-
regularities of all kinds, and, in the opinion of every

servant who had ever lived in the house, an unimpeachable ghost. All Miss Pew's young ladies believed firmly in that ghost; and there was a legend of a frizzy-haired girl from Barbadoes who had seen the ghost, and had incontinently gone out of one epileptic fit into another, until her father had come in a fly—presumably from Barbadoes—and carried her away for ever, epileptic to the last.

Nobody at present located at Mauleverer Manor remembered that young lady from Barbadoes, nor had any of the existing pupils ever seen the ghost. But the general faith in him was unshaken. He was described as an elderly man in a snuff-coloured, square-cut coat, knee-breeches, and silk stockings rolled up over his knees. He was supposed to be one of the extinct Mauleverers; harmless and even benevolently disposed; given to plucking flowers in the garden at dusk; and to gliding along passages, and loitering on the stairs in a somewhat inane manner. The bolder-spirited among the girls would have given a twelvemonth's pocket-money to see him. Miss Pillby declared that the sight of that snuff-coloured stranger would be her death.

"I've a weak 'art, you know," said Miss Pillby, who was not mistress of her aspirates,—she managed them sometimes, but they often evaded her,—"the doctors said so when I was quite a little thing."

"Were you ever a little thing, Pillby?" asked Miss Rylance with superb disdain, the present Pillby being long and gaunt.

And the group of listeners laughed, with that frank laughter of schoolgirls, keenly alive to the ridiculous in other people.

There was as much difference in the standing of the various bedrooms at Mauleverer Manor as in that of the London squares, but in this case it was the inhabitants who gave character to the locality. The five-bedded room off the front landing was occupied by the stiffest and best behaved of the first division, and might be ranked with Grosvenor Square or Lancaster Gate. There were rooms on the second floor where girls of the second and third division herded in inelegant obscurity, the Bloomsbury and Camden Town of the mansion. On this storey, too, slept the rabble of girls under twelve—creatures utterly despicable in the minds of girls in their teens, and the rooms they inhabited ranked as low as St. Giles's.

Ida Palliser was fortunate enough to have a bed in the butterfly-room, so called on account of a gaudy wall paper, whereon Camberwell Beauties disported themselves among roses and lilies in a strictly conventional style of art. The butterfly-room was the most fashionable and altogether popular dormitory at the Manor. It was the May Fair—a district not without a shade of Bohemianism, a certain fastness of tone. The wildest girls in the school were to be found in the butterfly-room.

It was a pleasant enough room in itself, even apart from its association with pleasant people. The bow-window looked out upon the garden and across the garden to the Thames, which at this point took a wide curve between banks shaded by old pollard willows. The landscape was purely pastoral. Beyond the level meadows came an undulating line of low hill and woodland, with here and there a village spire dark against the blue.

Mauleverer Manor lay midway between Hampton and Chertsey, in a land of meadows and gardens which the speculating builder had not yet invaded.

The butterfly-room was furnished a little better than the common run of boarding-school bedchambers. Miss Pew had taken a good deal of the Mauleverer furniture at a valuation when she bought the old house; and the Mauleverer furniture being of a *rococo* and exploded style, the valuation had been ridiculously low. Thus it happened that a big wainscot wardrobe, with doors substantial enough for a church, projected its enormous bulk upon one side of the butterfly-room, while a tall, narrow, cheval glass stood in front of a window.

That cheval was the glory of the butterfly-room. The girls could see how their skirts hung, and if the backs of their dresses fitted. On Sunday mornings there used to be an incursion of outsiders, eager to test the effect of their Sabbath bonnets, and the sets of their jackets, by the cheval.

And now Ida Palliser came into the butterfly-room, yawning wearily, to brush herself up a little before tea, knowing that Miss Pew and her younger sister, Miss Dulcibella — who devoted herself to dress and the amenities of life generally—would scrutinize her with eyes only too ready to see anything amiss.

The butterfly-room was not empty. Miss Rylance was plaiting her long flaxen hair in front of the toilet table, and another girl, a plump little sixteen-year-old, with nut-brown hair, and a fresh complexion, was advancing and retiring before the cheval, studying the effect of a cherry-coloured neck-ribbon with a gray gown.

"Cherry's a lovely colour in the abstract," said this damsel, "but it reminds one too dreadfully of bar-maids."

"Did you ever see a barmaid?" asked Miss Rylance languidly, slowly winding the long flaxen plait into a shining knob at the back of her head, and contemplating her reflection placidly with large calm blue eyes which saw no fault in the face they belonged to.

With features so correctly modelled, and a complexion so delicately tinted, Miss Rylance ought to have been lovely. But she had escaped loveliness by a long way. There was something wanting, and that something was very big.

"Good gracious, yes; I've seen dozens of barmaids," answered Bessie Wendover, with her frank voice. "Do you suppose I've never been into an hotel, or even into a tavern? When I go for a long drive with papa he generally wants brandy and soda, and that's how I get taken into the bar and introduced to the bar-maid."

"When you say introduced, of course you don't mean it," said Miss Rylance, fastening her brooch. "Calling things by their wrong names is your idea of wit."

"I would rather have a mistaken idea of wit than none at all," retorted Miss Wendover, and then she pirouetted on the tips of her toes, and surveyed her image in the glass from head to foot, with an aggravated air. "I hope I'm not vulgar looking, but I'm rather afraid I am," she said. "What's the good of belonging to an old Saxon family if one has a thick waist and large hands?"

"What's the good of anything at Mauleverer Manor?"

asked Ida, coming into the room, and seating herself on the ground with a dejected air.

Bessie Wendover ran across the room and sat down beside her.

"So you were in for it again this afternoon, you poor dear thing," she murmured, in a cooing voice. "I wish I had been there. It would have been "Up Guards, and at 'em!" if I had. I'm sure I should have said something cheeky to old Pew. The idea of over-hauling your locker! I should just like her to see the inside of mine. It would make her blood run cold."

"Ah!" sighed Ida, "she can't afford to make an example of you. You mean a hundred and fifty pounds a year. I am of no more account in her eyes than an artist's lay figure, which is put away in a dark closet when it isn't in use. She wanted to give you girls a lesson in tidiness, so she put me into her pillory. Fortunately I'm used to the pillory."

"But you are looking white and worried, you dear lovely thing," exclaimed Bessie, who was Ida Palliser's bosom friend. "It's too bad the way they use you. Have this neck-ribbon," suddenly untying the bow so carefully elaborated five minutes ago. "You must, you shall; I don't want it; I hate it. Do, dear."

And for consolation Miss Wendover tied the cherry-coloured ribbon under her friend's collar, patted Ida's pale cheeks, and kissed and hugged her.

"Be happy, darling, do," she said, in her loving half-childish way, while Miss Rylance looked on with ineffable contempt. "You are so clever and so beautiful; you were born to be happy."

"Do you think so, pet?" asked Ida, with cold

scorn; "then I ought to have been born with a little more money."

"What does money matter?" cried Bessie.

"Not very much to a girl like you, who has never known the want of it."

"That's not true, darling. I never go home for the holidays that I don't hear father grumble about his poverty. The rents are so slow to come in; the tenants are always wanting drain-pipes and barns and things. Last Christmas his howls were awful. We are positive paupers. Mother has to wait ages for a cheque."

"Ah, my pet, that's a very different kind of poverty from mine. You have never known what it is to have only three pairs of wearable stockings."

Bessie looked as if she were going to cry.

"If you were not so disgustingly proud, you horrid thing, you need never feel the want of stockings," she said discontentedly.

"If it were not for what you call my disgusting pride, I should degenerate into that loathsome animal a sponge," said Ida, rising suddenly from her dejected attitude, and standing up before her admiring little friend,

"A daughter of the gods, divinely tall,
And most divinely fair."

That fatal dower of beauty had been given to Ida Palliser in fullest measure. She had the form of a goddess, a head proudly set upon shoulders that were sloping but not narrow, the walk of a Moorish girl, accustomed to carrying a water-jug on her head, eyes dark as night, hair of a deep warm brown rippling naturally across her broad forehead, a complexion of creamiest white and richest carnation. These were but

the sensual parts of beauty which can be catalogued.
But it was in the glorious light and variety of expression that Ida shone above all compeers. It was by the
intellectual part of her beauty that she commanded the
admiration — enthusiastic in some cases, in others
grudging and unwilling — of her schoolfellows, and
reigned by right divine, despite her shabby gowns and
her cheap ready-made boots, the belle of the school.

CHAPTER II.
"I AM GOING TO MARRY FOR MONEY."

WHEN a schoolgirl of sixteen falls in love with one
of her schoolfellows there are no limits to her devotion.
Bessie Wendover's adoration of Miss Palliser was
boundless. Ida's seniority of three years, her beauty,
her talent, placed her, as it were, upon a pinnacle in
the eyes of the younger girl. Her poverty, her inferior
position in the school, only made her more interesting
to the warm-hearted Bessie, who passionately resented
any slight offered to her friend. It was in vain that
Miss Rylance took Bessie to task, and demonstrated
the absurdity of this childish fancy for a young person
whose future sphere of life must be necessarily remote
from that of a Hampshire squire's daughter. Bessie
despised this worldly wisdom.

"What is the use of attaching yourself to a girl
whom you are never likely to see after you leave school?"
argued Miss Rylance.

"I shall see her. I shall ask her home," said Bessie,
sturdily.

"Do you think your people will let you?"

"Mother will do anything I ask her, and father will do anything mother asks him. I am going to have Ida home with me all the summer holidays."

"How do you know that she will come?"

"I shall make her come. It is very nasty of you to insinuate that she won't."

"Palliser has a good deal of pride — pride and poverty generally go together, don't you know. I don't think she'll care about showing herself at the Grange in her old clothes and her three pairs of stockings, one on, one off, and one at the laundress's," said Miss Rylance, winding up with a viperish little laugh, as if she had said something witty.

She had a certain influence with Bessie, whom she had known all her life. It was she who had inspired Bessie with the desire to come to Mauleverer Manor, to be finished, after having endured eight years of jogtrot education from a homely little governess at home—who grounded the boys in Latin and mathematics before they went to Winchester, and made herself generally useful. Miss Rylance was the daughter of a fashionable physician, whose head-quarters were in Cavendish Square, but who spent his leisure at a something which he called "a place" at Kingthorpe, a lovely little village between Winchester and Romsey, where the Wendovers were indigenous to the soil, whence they seemed to have sprung, like the armed men in the story; for remotest tradition bore no record of their having come there from anywhere else, nor was there record of a time when the land round Kingthorpe belonged to any other family.

Dr. Rylance, whose dainty verandah-shaded cottage stood in gardens of three and a half acres, and who rented a paddock for his cow, was always lamenting that he could not buy more land.

"The Wendovers have everything," he said. "It is impossible for a new man to establish himself."

It was to be observed, however, that when land within a reasonable distance of Kingthorpe came into the market, Dr. Rylance did not put himself forward as a buyer. His craving for more territory always ended in words.

Urania Rylance had spent much of her girlhood at Kingthorpe, and had always been made welcome at The Knoll; but although she saw the Wendovers established upon their native soil, the rulers of the land, and revered by all the parish, she had grown up with the firm conviction that Dr. Rylance, of Cavendish Square, and Dr. Rylance's daughter were altogether superior to these country bumpkins, with their narrow range of ideas and their strictly local importance.

The summer days wore on at Mauleverer Manor, not altogether unpleasantly for the majority of the girls, who contrived to enjoy their lives in spite of Miss Pew's tyranny, which was considered vile enough to rank that middle-aged, loud-voiced lady with the Domitians and Attilas of history. There was a softening influence, happily, in the person of Miss Dulcibella, who was slim and sentimental, talked about sweetness and light, loved modern poetry, spent all her available funds upon dress, and was wonderfully girlish in her tastes and habits at nine-and-thirty years of age.

It was a splendid summer, a time of roses and sunshine, and the girls were allowed to carry on their studies in the noble old garden, in the summer-houses and pleasure domes which the extinct Mauleverers had made for themselves in their day of power. Grinding at history, grammar, and geography did not seem so oppressive a burden when it could be done under the shade of spreading cedars, amid the scent of roses, in an atmosphere of colour and light. Even Ida's labours seemed a little easier when she and her pupils sat in a fast decaying old summer-house in the rose-garden, with a glimpse of sunlit river flashing athwart the roses.

So the time wore on until the last week in July, and then all the school was alive with excitement, and every one was looking forward to the great event of the term, "breaking up." "Old Pew," had sent out her invitations for a garden party, an actual garden party—not a mere namby-pamby entertainment among the girls themselves, in which a liberal supply of blancmange and jam tarts was expected to atone for the absence of the outside world. Miss Pew had taken it into her head that Mauleverer Manor ought to be better known, and that a garden party would be a good advertisement. With this idea, she had ordered a hundred invitation cards, and had disseminated them among the most eligible of her old pupils, and the parents and guardians of those damsels now at the Manor. The good old gardens, where velvet greensward and cedars of Lebanon cost little labour to maintain in perfect order, were worthy to be exhibited. The roses, Miss Dulcibella's peculiar care, were, in that lady's opinion, equal to anything outside Chatsworth or Trentham. A garden party, by all means, said Miss Dulcibella, and she gave the young ladies to understand that the whole thing was her doing.

"I waited till Sarah was in a good temper," she

told her satellites, half a dozen or so of the elder girls who worshipped her, and who, in the slang phraseology of the school, were known as Miss Dulcie's "cracks," "and then I proposed a garden party. It required a great deal of talking to bring her even to think about such a thing. You see the expense will be enormous! Ices, tea and coffee, cakes, sandwiches, claret-cup. Thank goodness it's too late in the year for people to expect strawberries. Yes, my dears, you may thank me for your garden party."

"Dear Miss Dulcibella," exclaimed one.

"You too delicious darling," cried another.

"What will you wear?" asked a third, knowing that Miss Dulcie was weak about dress, and had a morbid craving for originality.

"Well dears," began Miss Dulcie, growing radiant at the thrilling question, "I have been thinking of making up my art needlework tunic—the pale green, you know, with garlands of passion flowers, worked in crewels—over a petticoat of the faintest primrose."

"That will be quite too lovely," exclaimed four enthusiasts in a chorus.

"You know how fond I am of those delicate tints in that soft Indian cashmere, that falls in such artistic folds."

"Heavenly," sighed the chorus, and Miss Dulcie went on talking for half-an-hour by Chertsey clock, in fact till the tea-bell broke up the little conclave.

What was Ida Palliser going to wear at the garden party? The question was far more serious for her than for Miss Dulcibella, who had plenty of money to spend upon her adornment. In Ida the necessity for a new gown meant difficulty, perhaps mortification.

"Why should I not spend the day in one of the garrets, darning stockings and packing boxes?" she said bitterly, when a grand discussion about the garden party was being held in the butterfly-room; "nobody will want me. I have no relations coming to admire me."

"You know you don't mean what you say," said Miss Rylance. "You expect to have half a dozen prizes, and to lord it over all of us."

"I have worked hard enough for the prizes," answered Ida. "I don't think you need grudge me them."

"I do not," said Miss Rylance, with languid scorn. "You know I never go in for prizes. My father looks upon school as only a preliminary kind of education. When I am at home with him in the season I shall have lessons from better masters than any we are favoured with here."

"What a comfort it is for us to know that!" retorted Ida, her eyes dancing mischievously.

It was now within a week of the garden party. Miss Pew was grimmer of aspect and louder of voice than usual, and it was felt that, at the slightest provocation, she might send forth an edict revoking all her invitations, and the party might be relegated to the limbo of unrealized hopes. Never had the conduct of Miss Pew's pupils been so irreproachable, never had lessons been learned, and exercises prepared, so diligently.

Ida had received a kind little note from Mrs. Wendover, asking her to spend her summer holidays at Kingthorpe, and at Bessie's earnest desire had accepted the cordial invitation.

"You don't know what a foolish thing you are

doing, Bess," said Miss Palliser, when—reluctant to the last—she had written her acceptance, Bessie looking over her shoulder all the while. "Foolish for you, foolish for me. It is a mistake to associate yourself with paupers. You will feel ashamed of me half a dozen times a day at Kingthorpe."

"No, no, no!" cried the energetic Bessie; "I shall never feel anything but pride in you. I shall be proud to show my people what a beautiful, brilliant, wonderful friend I have chosen for myself."

"Ardent child!" exclaimed Ida, with a touch of sadness even in her mockery. "What a pity you have not a bachelor brother to fall in love with me!"

"Never mind the brother. I have two bachelor cousins."

"Of course! The rich Brian, and the poor Brian, whose histories I have heard almost as often as I heard the story of 'Little Red Ridinghood' in my nursery days. Both good-looking, both clever, both young. One a man of landed estate. All Kingthorpe parish belongs to him, does it not?"

"All except the little bit that belongs to papa."

"And Dr. Rylance's garden and paddock; don't forget that."

"Could I forget the Rylances? Urania says that although her father has no land at Kingthorpe, he has influence."

"The other cousin dependent on his talents, and fighting his way at the Bar. Is not that how the story goes, Bess?"

"Yes, darling. I am afraid poor Brian has hardly begun fighting yet. He is only eating his terms. I have no idea what that means, but it sounds rather low."

"Well, Bess, if I am to marry either of your cousins, it must be the rich one," said Ida, decisively.

"Oh, Ida, how can you say so? You can't know which you will like best."

"My likes and dislikes have nothing to do with it. I am going to marry for money."

Miss Rylance had brought her desk to that end of the table where the two girls were sitting, during the latter part of the conversation. It was evening, the hour or so of leisure allowed for the preparation of studies and the writing of home letters. Miss Rylance unlocked her desk, and took out her paper and pens; but, having got so far as this, she seemed rather inclined to join in the conversation than to begin her letter.

"Isn't that rather a worldly idea for your time of life?" she asked, looking at Ida with her usual unfriendly expression.

"No doubt. I should be disgusted if you or Bessie entertained such a notion. But in me it is only natural. I have drained the cup of poverty to the dregs. I thirst for the nectar of wealth. I would marry a soap-boiler, a linseed-crusher, a self-educated navvy who had developed into a great contractor—any plebeian creature, always provided that he was an honest man."

"How condescending!" said Miss Rylance. "I suppose, Bessie, you know that Miss Pew has especially forbidden us all to indulge in idle talk about courtship and marriage?"

"Quite so," said Bessie, "but as old Pew knows that we are human, I've no doubt she is quite aware that this is one of her numerous rules which we diligently set at naught."

Urania began her letter, but although her pen moved swiftly over her paper in that elegant Italian hand which was, as it were, a badge of honour at Mauleverer Manor, her ears were not the less open to the conversation going on close beside her.

"Marry a soap-boiler, indeed!" exclaimed Bessie, indignantly; "you ought to be a duchess!"

"No doubt, dear, if dukes went about the world like King Cophetua, on the look out for beggar-maids."

"I am so happy to think you are coming to King-thorpe! It is the dearest old place! We shall be so happy!"

"It will not be your fault if we are not, darling," said Ida, looking tenderly at the loving face, uplifted to hers. "Well, I have written to my father to ask him for five pounds, and if he send the five pounds I will go to Kingthorpe. If not, I must invent an excuse —mumps, or measles, or something—for staying away. Or I must behave so badly for the last week of the term that old Pew will revoke her sanction of the intended visit. I cannot come to Kingthorpe quite out at elbows."

"You look lovely even in the gown you have on," said Bessie.

"I don't know anything about my loveliness, but I know that this gown is absolutely threadbare."

Bessie sighed despondently. She knew her friend's resolute temper, and that any offer of clothes or money from her would be worse than useless. It would make Ida angry.

"What kind of man is your father, darling?" she asked, thoughtfully.

"Very good-natured."

"Ah! Then he will send the five pounds."

"Very weak."

"Ah! Then he may change his mind about it."

"Very poor."

"Then he may not have the money."

"The lot is in the urn of fate, Bess. We must take our chance. I think, somehow, that the money will come. I have asked for it urgently, for I do want to come to Kingthorpe." Bessie kissed her. "Yes, dear, I wish with all my heart to accept your kind mother's invitation; though I know, in my secret soul, that it is foolishness for me to see the inside of a happy home, to sit beside a hospitable hearth, when it is my mission in life to be a dependent in the house of a stranger. If you had half a dozen small sisters, now, and your people would engage me as a nursery governess——"

"You a nursery governess!" cried Bessie, "you who are at the top of every class, and who do everything better than the masters who teach you?"

"Well, if my perfection prove worth seventy pounds a-year when I go out into the world, I shall be satisfied," said Ida.

"What will you buy with your five pounds?" asked Bessie.

"A black cashmere gown, as plain as a nun's, a straw hat, and as many collars, cuffs, and stockings as I can get for the rest of the money."

Miss Rylance listened, smiling quietly to herself as she bent over her desk. To the mind of an only daughter, who had been brought up in a supremely correct manner, who had had her winter clothes and summer clothes at exactly the right season, and of the best that money could buy, there was a piteous depth of poverty and degradation in Ida Palliser's position. The girl's beauty and talents were as nothing when weighed against such sordid surroundings.

The prize-day came, a glorious day at the beginning of August, and the gardens of Mauleverer Manor, the wide reach of blue river, the meadows, willows, the distant woods, all looked their loveliest, as if Nature was playing into the hands of Miss Pew.

"I am sure you girls ought to be very happy to live in such a place!" said one of the mothers, as she strolled about the velvet lawn with her daughters, "instead of being mewed up in a dingy London square."

"You wouldn't say that if you saw the bread and scrape and the sloppy tea we have for breakfast," answered one of the girls. "It's all very well for you, who see this wretched hole in the sunshine, and old Pew in her best gown and her company manners. The place is a whited sepulchre. I should like you to have a glimpse behind the scenes, ma."

"Ma" smiled placidly, and turned a deaf ear to these aspersions of the schoolmistress. Her girls looked well fed and healthy. Bread and scrape evidently agreed with them much better than that reckless consumption of butter and marmalade which swelled the housekeeping bills during the holidays.

It was a great day. Miss Pew the elder was splendid in apple-green moiré antique; Miss Pew the younger was elegant in pale and flabby raiment of cashmere and crewel-work. The girls were in that simple white muslin of the *jeune Meess Anglaise*, to which they were languishing to bid an eternal adieu. There were a great many pretty girls at Mauleverer Manor, and on this day, when the white-robed girlish forms were flitting to and fro upon the green lawns, in the sweet summer air and sunshine, it seemed as if the old manorial mansion were a bower of beauty. Among the parents of existing pupils who had accepted the Misses Pew's invitation was Dr. Rylance, the fashionable physician, whose presence there conferred distinction upon the school. It was Miss Rylance's last term, and the doctor wished to assist at those honours which she would doubtless reap as the reward of meritorious studies. He was not blindly devoted to his daughter, but he was convinced, that like everything else belonging to him, she was of the best quality; and he expected to see her appreciated by the people who had been privileged to educate her.

The distribution of prizes was the great feature of the day. It was to take place at four o'clock, in the ball-room, a fine old panelled saloon, in which the only furniture was a pair of grand pianos, somewhat the worse for wear, a table at the end of the room on which the prizes were arranged, and benches covered with crimson cloth for the accommodation of the company.

There was to be a concert before the distribution. Four of the best pianoforte players in the school were to hammer out an intensely noisy version of the overture to *Zampa*, arranged for eight hands on two pianos. The crack singer was to sing "Una voce," and Ida Palliser was to play the "Moonlight Sonata."

Dr. Rylance had come early, on purpose to be present at this ceremonial. He was the most important guest who had yet arrived, and Miss Pew devoted herself to his entertainment, and went rustling up and down the terrace in front of the ball-room windows in her armour of apple-green moiré, listening deferentially to the physician's remarks.

Dr. Rylance was a large fair-complexioned man, who had been handsome in his youth, and who at seven-and-forty was still remarkably good-looking. He had fine teeth, good hair, full blue eyes, capable of the hardest, coldest stare that ever looked out of a human countenance. Mr. Darwin has told us that the eyes do not smile, that the radiance we fancy we see in the eye itself is only produced by certain contractions of the muscles surrounding it. Assuredly there was no smile in the eyes of Dr. Rylance. His smile, which was bland and frequent, gave only a vague impression of white teeth and brown whiskers. He had a fine figure, and was proud of his erect carriage. He dressed carefully and well, and was as particular as Brummell about his laundress. His manners were considered pleasing by the people who liked him: while those who disliked him accused him of an undue estimate of his own merits, and a tendency to depreciate the rest of humanity. His practice was rather select than extensive, for Dr. Rylance was a specialist. He had won his reputation as an adviser in cases of mental disease; and as, happily, mental diseases are less common than bodily ailments, Dr. Rylance had not the continuous work of a Gull or a Jenner. His speciality paid him remarkably well. His cases hung long on hand, and when he had a patient of wealth and standing Dr. Rylance knew how to keep him. His treatment was soothing and palliative, as befitted an enlightened age. In an age of scepticism no one could expect Dr. Rylance to work miraculous cures. It is in no wise to his discredit to say that he was more successful in sustaining and comforting the patient's friends than in curing the patient.

This was Laurence Rylance, a man who had begun life in a very humble way, had raised himself by his own efforts, if not to the top of the medical tree, certainly to a very comfortable and remunerative perch among its upper branches; a man thoroughly satisfied with himself and with what destiny had done for him; a man who, to be a new Cæsar, would hardly have foregone the privilege of being Laurence Rylance.

"My daughter has done well during this last term, I hope, Miss Pew?" he said, interrogatively, but rather as if the question were needless, as he walked beside the rustling moiré.

"She has earned my entire approval," replied Miss Pew, in her oiliest accents. "She has application." Dr. Rylance nodded assentingly. "She has a charming deportment. I know of no girl in the school more thoroughly ladylike. I have never seen her with a collar put on crookedly, or with rough hair. She is a pattern to many of my girls."

"That is all gratifying to my pride as a father; but I hope she has made progress in her studies."

Miss Pew coughed gently behind a mittened hand.

"She has not made quite so great an advance as I should have wished. She has talent, no doubt; but it is hardly of a kind that comes into play among other girls. In after-life, perhaps, there may be de-

3*

velopment. I am sorry to say she is not in our roll-call of honour to-day. She has won no prize."

"Perhaps she may have hardly thought it worth her while to compete," said Dr. Rylance, hurt in his own individual pride by the idea that his daughter had missed distinction, just as he would have been hurt if anybody had called one of his pictures a copy, or made light of his blue china. "With the Rylances it has always been Cæsar or nothing."

"I regret to say that my three most important prizes have been won by a young woman whom I cannot esteem," said Miss Pew, bristling in her panoply of apple-green, at the thought of Ida Palliser's insolence. "I hope I shall ever be just, at whatever sacrifice of personal feeling. I shall to-day bestow the first prize for modern languages, for music, and for English history and literature, upon a young person of whose moral character I have a very low opinion."

"And pray who is this young lady?" asked Dr. Rylance.

"Miss Palliser, the daughter of a half-pay officer residing in the neighbourhood of Dieppe—for very good reasons, no doubt."

"Palliser; yes, I have heard my daughter talk of her. An insolent, ill-bred girl. I have been taught to consider her somewhat a disgrace to your excellent and well-managed school."

"Her deportment is certainly deplorable," admitted Miss Pew; "but the girl has remarkable talents."

More visitors were arriving from this time forward, until everyone was seated in the ball-room. Miss Pew was engaged in receiving people, and ushering them to their seats, always assisted by Miss Dulcibella—an

image of limp gracefulness—and the three governesses
—all as stiff as perambulating blackboard. Dr. Rylance
strolled by himself for a little while, sniffed at the
great ivory cup of a magnolia, gazed dreamily at the
river—shining yonder across intervening gardens and
meadows—and ultimately found his daughter.

"I am sorry to find you are not to be honoured
with a prize, Ranie," he said, smiling at her gently.

In no relation of life had he been so nearly perfect
as in his conduct as a father. Were he ever so disappointed in his daughter, he could not bring himself
to be angry with her.

"I have not tried for prizes, papa. Why should I
compete with such a girl as Ida Palliser, who is to get
her living as a governess, and who knows that success
at school is a matter of life and death with her?"

"Do you not think it might have been worth your
while to work as hard as Miss Palliser, for the mere
honour and glory of being first in your school?"

"Did you ever work for mere honour and glory,
papa?" asked Urania, with her unpleasant little air of
cynicism.

"Well, my love, I confess there has been generally
a promise of solid pudding in the back-ground. Pray,
who is this Miss Palliser, whom I hear of at every
turn, and whom nobody seems to like?"

"There you are mistaken, papa. Miss Palliser has
her worshippers, though she is the most disagreeable
girl in the school. That silly little Bessie raves about
her, and has actually induced Mrs. Wendover to invite
her to The Knoll!"

"That is a pity, if the girl is ill-bred and unpleasant," said Dr. Rylance.

"She's a horror," exclaimed Urania, vindictively.

Five minutes later Dr. Rylance and his daughter made their entrance into the ball-room, which was full of people, and whence came the opening crash of an eight-handed "Zampa." Father and daughter went in softly, and with a hushed air, as if they had been going into church; yet the firing of a cannon or two more or less would hardly have disturbed the performers at the two pianos, so tremendous was their own uproar. They were taking the overture in what they called orchestral time; though it is doubtful whether even their playing could have kept pace with the hurrying of excited fiddles in a presto passage, or the roll of the big drum, simulating distant thunder. Be that as it may, the four performers were pounding along at a breathless pace; and if their pianissimo passages failed in delicacy, there was no mistake about their fortissimo.

"What an abominable row!" whispered Dr. Rylance. "Is this what they call music?"

Urania smiled, and felt meritorious in that, after being chosen as one of the four for this very "Zampa," she had failed ignominiously as a timist, and had been compelled to cede her place to another pupil.

"I might have toiled for six weeks at the horrid thing," she thought, "and papa would have only called it a row."

"Zampa" ended amidst polite applause, the delighted parents of the four players feeling that they had not lived in vain. And now the music mistress took her place at one of the pianos, the top of the instrument was lowered, and Miss Fane, a little fair girl with a round face and frizzy auburn hair, came simpering forward to sing "Una voce," in a reedy soprano, which had been attenuated by half-guinea lessons from an Italian master, and which frequently threatened a snap.

Happily on this occasion the thin little voice got through its work without disaster; there was a pervading sense of relief when the crisis was over, and Miss Fane had simpered her acknowledgments of the applause which rewarded a severely conscientious performance.

"Any more singing?" inquired Dr. Rylance of his daughter, not with the air of a man who pants for vocal melody.

"No, the next is the 'Moonlight Sonata.'"

Dr. Rylance had a dim idea that he had heard of this piece before. He waited dumbly, admiring the fine old room, with its lofty ceiling, and florid cornice, and the sunny garden beyond the five tall windows.

Presently Ida Palliser came slowly towards the piano, carrying herself like an empress. Dr. Rylance could hardly believe the evidence of his eyes. Was this the girl whose deportment had been called abominable, whom Urania had denounced as a horror? Was this the articled pupil, the girl doomed to life-long drudgery as a governess, this superb creature, with her noble form and noble face, looking grave defiance at the world which hitherto had not used her too kindly?

She was dressed in black, a sombre figure amidst the white muslins and rainbow sashes of her comrades. Her cashmere gown was of the simplest fashion, but it became the tall full figure to admiration. Below her linen collar she wore a scarlet ribbon, from which hung a silver locket, the only ornament she possessed. It was Bessie Wendover who had insisted on the scarlet ribbon, as a relief to that funereal gown.

"I was never so surprised in my life," whispered Dr. Rylance to his daughter. "She is the handsomest girl I ever saw."

"Yes, she is an acknowledged beauty," said Urania, with a contraction of her thin lips; "nobody disputes her good looks. It is a pity her manners are so abominable."

"She moves like a lady."

"She has been thoroughly drilled," sneered Urania. "The original savage in her has been tamed as much as possible."

"I should like to know more of that girl," said Dr. Rylance, "for she looks as if she has force of character. I'm sorry you and she are not better friends."

Ida seated herself at the piano and began to play, without honouring the assembly with one glance from her dark eyes. She sat looking straight before her, like one whose thoughts are far away. She played by memory, and at first her hands faltered a little as they touched the keys, as if she hardly knew what she was going to play. Then she recollected herself in a flash, and began the firm, slow, legato movement with the touch of a master hand, the melody rising and falling in solemn waves of sound, like the long, slow roll of a calm sea.

The "Moonlight Sonata" is a composition of some length. Badly, or even indifferently performed, the "Moonlight Sonata" is a trial; but no one grew weary of it to-day, though the strong young hands which

gave emphasis to the profound beauties of that wonderful work were only the hands of a girl. Those
among the listeners who knew least about music,
knew that this was good playing; those who cared
not at all for the playing were pleased to sit and
watch the mobile face of the player as she wove her
web of melody, her expression changing with every
change in the music, but unmoved by a thought of
the spectators.

Presently, just as the sonata drew to its close, an
auburn head was thrust between Dr. Rylance and his
daughter, and a girl's voice whispered,

"Is she not splendid? Is she not the grandest
creature you ever saw?"

The doctor turned and recognized Bessie Wendover.

"She is, Bessie," he said, shaking hands with her.
"I never was so struck by anyone in my life."

Urania grew white with anger. Was it not enough
that Ida Palliser should have outshone her in every
accomplishment upon which school-girls pride themselves? Was it not enough that she should have taken
complete possession of that foolish little Bessie, and
thus ingratiated herself into the Wendover set, and
contrived to get invited to Kingthorpe? No. Here
was Urania's own father, her especial property, going
over to the enemy.

"I am glad you admire her so much, papa," she
said, outwardly calm and sweet, but inwardly con-
sumed with anger; "for it will be so pleasant for you
to see more of her at Kingthorpe."

"Yes," he said, heartily, "I am glad she is coming
to Kingthorpe. That was a good idea of yours, Bessie."

"Wasn't it? I am so pleased to find you like her. I wish you could get Ranie to think better of her."

Now came the distribution of prizes and accessits. Miss Pew took her seat before the table on which the gaudily-bound books were arranged, and began to read out the names. It was a hard thing for her to have to award the three first prizes to a girl she detested; but Miss Pew knew the little world she ruled well enough to know that palpable injustice would weaken her rule. Ninety-nine girls who had failed to win the prize would have resented her favouritism if she had given the reward to a hundredth girl who had not fairly won it. The eyes of her little world were upon her, and she was obliged to give the palm to the real victor. So, in her dull, hard voice, looking straight before her, with cold, unfriendly eyes, she read out—

"The prize for modern languages has been obtained by Miss Palliser!" and Ida came slowly up to the table and received a bulky crimson volume, containing the poetical works of Sir Walter Scott.

"The prize for proficiency in instrumental music is awarded to Miss Palliser!"

Another bulky volume was handed to Ida. For variety the binding was green, and the inside of the book was by William Cowper.

"The greatest number of marks for English history and literature have been obtained by Miss Palliser."

Miss Palliser was now the happy possessor of a third volume, bound in blue, containing a selection from the works of Robert Southey.

With not one word of praise nor one smile of approval did Miss Pew sweeten the gifts which she bestowed upon the articled pupil. She gave that which justice, or rather policy, compelled her to give. No more. Kindliness was not in the bond.

Ida came slowly away from the table, laden with her prizes, her head held high, but not with pride in the trophies she carried. Her keenest feeling at this moment was a sense of humiliation. The prizes had been given her as a bone might be flung to a strange dog, by one whose heart held no love for the canine species. An indignant flush clouded the creamy whiteness of her forehead, angry tears glittered in her proud eyes. She made her way to the nearest door, and went away without a word to the crowd of younger girls, her own pupils, who had crowded round to congratulate and caress her. She was adored by these small people, and it was her personal influence as much as her talent which made her so successful a teacher.

Dr. Rylance followed her to the door with his eyes. He was not capable of wide sympathies, or of projecting himself into the lives of other people; but he did sympathize with this girl, so lonely in the splendour of her beauty, so joyless in her triumph.

"God help her, poor child, in the days to come!" he said to himself.

CHAPTER III.

AT THE KNOLL.

BETWEEN Winchester and Romsey there lies a region of gentle hills and grassy slopes shadowed by fine old yew trees, a land of verdure, lonely and exceeding fair; and in a hollow of this undulating district nestles the village of Kingthorpe, with its half-dozen handsome old houses, its richly cultivated gardens, and quaint old square-towered church. It is a prosperous, well-to-do little settlement, where squalor and want are unknown. Its humbler dwellings belong chiefly to the labourers on the Wendover estate, and those are liberally paid and well cared for. An agricultural labourer's wages at Kingthorpe might seem infinitely small to a London mechanic; but when it is taken into account that the tiller of the fields has a roomy cottage and an acre of garden for sixpence a-week, his daily dole of milk from the home farm, as much wood as he can burn, blankets and coals at Christmas, and wine and brandy, soup and bread from the great house, in all emergencies, he is perhaps not so very much worse off than his metropolitan brother.

There was an air of comfort and repose at Kingthorpe which made the place delightful to the eye of a passing wanderer—a spot where one would gladly have lain down the burden of life and rested for awhile in one of those white cottages that lay a little way back from the high road, shadowed by a screen of tall elms. There was a duck-pond in front of a low red brick inn which reminded one of Birkett Foster, and made the central feature of the village; a spot of busy life where all else was stillness. There were accommodation roads leading off to distant farms, above which the tree-tops interlaced, and where the hedges were rich in blackberry and sloe, dog-roses and honey-suckle, and the banks in spring-time dappled with violet and primrose, purple orchis and wild crocus, and all the flowers that grow for the delight of village children.

Ida Palliser sat silent in her corner of the large landau which was taking Miss Wendover and her schoolfellows from Winchester station to Kingthorpe. Miss Rylance had accepted a seat in the Wendover landau at her father's desire; but she would have preferred to have had her own smart little pony-carriage to meet her at the station. To drive her own carriage, were it ever so small, was more agreeable to Urania's temper than to sit behind the overfed horses from The Knoll, and to be thus, in some small measure, indebted to Bessie Wendover.

Ida Palliser's presence made the thing still more odious. Bessie was radiant with delight at taking her friend home with her. She watched Ida's eyes as they roamed over the landscape. She understood the girl's silent admiration.

"They are darling old hills, aren't they, dear?" she asked, squeezing Ida's hand, as the summer shadows and summer lights went dancing over the sward, like living things.

"Yes, dear, they are lovely," answered Ida, quietly.

She was devouring the beauty of the scene with her eyes. She had seen nothing like it in her narrow wanderings over the earth—nothing so simple, so beautiful, and so lonely. She was sorry when they left that open hill country and came into a more fertile scene, a high road which was like an avenue in a gentleman's park, and then the village duck-pond and red homestead, the old gray church, with its gilded sundial marking the hour of six, the gardens brimming over with roses, and as full of sweet odours as those spicy islands which send their perfumed breath to greet the seaman as he sails to the land of the Sun.

The carriage stopped at the iron gate of an exquisitely kept garden, surrounding a small Gothic cottage of the fanciful order of architecture,—a cottage with plate-glass windows, shaded by Spanish blinds, a glazed verandah sheltering a tesselated walk, sloping banks and terraces, on a very small scale, stone vases full of flowers, a tiny fountain sparkling in the afternoon sun.

This was Dr. Rylance's country retreat. It had been a yeoman's cottage, plain, substantial, and homely as the yeoman and his household. The doctor had added a Gothic front, increased the number of rooms, but not the general convenience of the dwelling. He had been his own architect, and the result was a variety of levels and a breakneck arrangement of stairs at all manner of odd corners, so ingenious in their peril to life 'and limb that they might be supposed to have been designed as traps for the ignorant stranger.

"Don't say good-bye, Ranie," said Bessie, when Miss Rylance had alighted, and was making her adieux at the carriage door; "you'll come over to dinner, won't you, dear? Your father won't be down till Saturday. You'll be dreadfully dull at home."

"Thanks, dear, no; I'd rather spend my first evening at home. I'm never dull," answered Urania, with her air of superiority.

"What a queer girl you are!" exclaimed Bessie, frankly. "I should be wretched if I found myself alone in a house. Do run over in the evening, at any rate. We are going to have lots of fun."

Miss Rylance shuddered. She knew what was meant by lots of fun at The Knoll; a romping game at croquet, or the newly-established lawn-tennis, with girls in short petticoats and boys in Eton jackets, a raid upon the plum-trees on the crumbling red brick walls of the fine old kitchen-garden; winding up with a boisterous bout at hide-and-seek in the twilight; and finally a banquet of sandwiches, jam tarts, and syllabub in the shabby old dining-room.

"I'll come over to see Mrs. Wendover, if I am not too tired," she said, with languid politeness, and then she closed the gate, and the carriage drove on to The Knoll.

Colonel Wendover's house was a substantial dwelling of the Queen Anne period, built of unmixed red brick, with a fine pediment, a stone shell over the entrance, four long narrow windows on each side of the tall door, and nine in each upper story, a house that looked all eyes, and was a blaze of splendour when the western sun shone upon its many windows. The house stood on a bit of rising ground at the end of the village, and dominated all meaner habitations. It was the typical squire's house, and Colonel Wendover was no bad representative of the typical squire.

A fine old iron gate opened upon a broad gravel drive, which made the circuit of a well-kept *parterre*, where the flowers grew as they only grow for those who love them dearly. This gate stood hospitably open at all times, and many were the vehicles which drove up to the tall door of The Knoll, and friendly the welcome which greeted all comers.

The door, like the gate, stood open all day long—indeed, open doors were the rule at Kingthorpe. Ida saw a roomy old hall, paved with black and white marble, a few family portraits, considerably the worse for wear, against panelled walls painted white, a concatenation of guns, fishing-rods, whips, canes, cricket-bats, croquet-mallets, and all things appertaining to the out-door amusements of a numerous family. A large tiger skin stretched before the drawing-room door was one memorial of Colonel Wendover's Indian life; a tiger's skull gleaming on the wall, between a pair of elephant's ears, was another. One side of the wall was adorned with a collection of Indian arms, showing all those various curves with which oriental ingenuity has improved upon the straight simplicity of the western sword.

It was not a neatly kept hall. There had been no careful study of colour in the arrangement of things—hats and caps were flung carelessly on the old oak chairs—there was a licentious mixture of styles in the furniture—half old English, half Indian, and all the worse for wear; but Ida Palliser thought the house had a friendly look, which made it better than any house she had ever seen before.

Through an open door at the back of the hall she saw a broad gravel walk, long and straight, leading to a temple or summer-house built of red brick, like the mansion itself. On each side of the broad walk there was a strip of grass, just about wide enough for a bowling-green, and on the grass were orange-trees in big wooden tubs, painted green. Slowly advancing along the broad walk there came a large lady.

"Is that your mother?" asked Ida.

"No, it's Aunt Betsy. You ought to have known Aunt Betsy at a glance. I'm sure I've described her often enough. How good of her to be here to welcome us!" and Bessy flew across the hall and rushed down the broad walk to greet her aunt.

Ida followed at a more sober pace. Yes, she had heard of Aunt Betsy—a maiden aunt, who lived in her own house a little way from The Knoll. A lady who had plenty of money and decidedly masculine tastes, which she indulged freely; a very lovable person withal, if Bessy might be believed. Ida wondered if she too would be able to like Aunt Betsy.

Miss Wendover's appearance was not repulsive. She was a woman of heroic mould, considerably above the average height of womankind, with a large head nobly set upon large well-shaped shoulders. Bulky Miss Wendover decidedly was, but she carried her bulkiness well. She still maintained a waist, firmly braced above her expansive hips. She walked well, and was more active than many smaller women. Indeed, her life was full of activity, spent for the most part in the open air, driving, walking, gardening, looking after her cows and poultry, and visiting the labouring-classes round Kingthorpe, among whom she was esteemed an oracle.

Bessie hung herself round her large aunt like ivy on an oak, and the two thus united came up the broad walk to meet Ida, Bessie chattering all the way.

"So this is Miss Palliser," said Aunt Betsy heartily,

and in a deep masculine voice, which accorded well with her large figure. "I have heard a great deal about you from this enthusiastic child,—so much that I was prepared to be disappointed in you. It is the highest compliment I can pay you to say I am not."

"Where's mother?" asked Bessie.

"Your father drove her to Romsey to call on the new vicar. There's the phaeton driving in at the gate."

It was so. Before Ida had had breathing time to get over the introduction to Aunt Betsy, she was hurried off to see her host and hostess.

They were very pleasant people, who did not consider themselves called on to present an icy aspect to a new acquaintance.

The Colonel was the image of his sister, tall and broad of figure, with an aquiline nose and a commanding eye, thoroughly good-natured withal, and a man whom everybody loved. Mrs. Wendover was a dumpy little woman, who had brought dumpiness and a handsome fortune into the family. She had been very pretty in girlhood, and was pretty still, with a round-faced innocent prettiness which made her look almost as young as her eldest daughter. Her husband loved her with a fondly protecting and almost paternal affection, which was very pleasant to behold; and she held him in devoted reverence, as the beginning and end of all that was worth loving and knowing in the Universe. She was not an accomplished woman, and had made the smallest possible use of those opportunities which civilization affords to every young lady whose parents have plenty of money; but she was a lady to the marrow of her bones—benevolent, kindly, thinking no evil, rejoicing in the truth—an embodiment of domestic love.

Such a host and hostess made Ida feel at home in their house in less than five minutes. If there had been a shade of coldness in their greeting her pride would have risen in arms against them, and she would have made herself eminently disagreeable. But at their hearty welcome she expanded like a beautiful flower which opens its lovely heart to the sunshine.

"It is so good of you to ask me here," she said, when Mrs. Wendover had kissed her, "knowing so little of me."

"I know that my daughter loves you," answered the mother, "and it is not in Bessie's nature to love anyone who isn't worthy of love."

Ida smiled at the mother's simple answer.

"Don't you think that in a heart so full of love some may run over and get wasted on worthless objects?" she asked.

"That's very true," cried a boy in an Eton jacket, one of a troop that had congregated round the Colonel and his wife since their entrance. "You know there was that half-bred terrier you doted upon, Bess, though I showed you that the roof of his mouth was as red as sealing-wax."

"I hope you are not going to compare me to a half-bred terrier," said Ida, laughing.

"If you were a terrier, the roof of your mouth would be as black as my hat," said the boy decisively. It was his way of expressing his conviction that Ida was thoroughbred.

The ice being thus easily broken, Ida found herself received into the bosom of the family, and at

4*

once established as a favourite with all. There were
two boys in Eton jackets, answering to the names of
Reginald and Horatio, but oftener to the friendly ab-
breviations Reg. and Horry. Both had chubby faces,
liberally freckled, warts on their hands, and rumpled
hair; and it was not easy for a new comer to distinguish Horatio from Reginald, or Reginald from
Horatio. There was a girl of fourteen with flowing
hair, who looked very tall because her petticoats were
very short, and who always required some one to hug
and hang upon. If she found herself deprived of
human support she lolled against a wall.

This young person at once pounced upon Ida, as
a being sent into the world to sustain her.

"Do you think you shall like me?" she asked,
when they had all swarmed up to the long corridor,
out of which numerous bed-rooms opened.

"I like you already," answered Ida.

"Do thoo like pigs?" asked a smaller girl, round
and rosy, in a holland pinafore, putting the question
as if it were relevant to her sister's inquiry.

"I don't quite know," said Ida doubtfully.

"'Cos there are nine black oneths, tho pwutty.
Will thoo come and thee them?"

Ida said she would think about it: and then she
received various pressing invitations to go and see lop-
eared rabbits, guinea-pigs, a tame water-rat in the
rushes of the duck-pond, a collection of eggs in the
schoolroom, and the new lawn-tennis ground which
father had made in the paddock.

"Now all you small children run away!" cried
Bessie, loftily. "Ida and I are going to dress for
dinner."

The crowd dispersed reluctantly, with low mutterings about rabbits, pigs, and water-rats, like the murmurs of a stage mob; and then Bessie led her friend into a large sunny room fronting westward, a room with three windows, cushioned window-seats, two pretty white-curtained beds, and a good deal of old-fashioned and heterogeneous furniture, half English, half Indian.

"You said you wouldn't mind sleeping in my room," said Bessie, as she showed her friend an exclusive dressing-table, daintily draperied, and enlivened with blue satin bows, for the refreshment of the visitor's eye.

While the girls were contemplating this work of art the door was suddenly opened and Blanche's head was thrust in.

"I did the dressing-table, Miss Palliser, every bit, on purpose for you."

And the door then slammed to, and Bessie rushed across the room and drew the bolt.

"We shall have them all one after another," she said.

"Don't shut them out on my account."

"Oh, but I must. You would have no peace. I can see they are going to be appallingly fond of you."

"Let them like me as much as they can. Do you know, Bessie, this is my first glimpse into the inside of a home!"

"Oh, Ida dear, but your father," remonstrated Bessie.

"My father has never been unkind to me, but I have had no home with him. When my mother brought me home from India—she died very soon after we got home, you know"—Ida strangled a sob at this point—"I was placed with strangers, two elderly maiden ladies, who reared me very well, no doubt, in their stiff businesslike way, and who really gave me a very good education. That went on for nine years,—a long time to spend with two old maids in a dull little house at Turnham Green,—and then I had a letter from my father to say he had come home for good. He had sold his commission and meant to settle down in some quiet spot abroad. His first duty would be to make arrangements for placing me in a high-class school, where I could finish my education; and he told me, quite at the end of his letter, that he had married a very sweet young lady, who was ready to give me all a mother's affection, and who would be able to receive me in my holidays, when the expense of the journey to France and back was manageable."

"Poor darling!" sighed Bessie. "Did your heart warm to the sweet young lady?"

"No, Bess; I'm afraid it must be an unregenerate heart, for I took a furious dislike to her. Very unjust and unreasonable, wasn't it? Afterwards, when my father took me over to his cottage, near Dieppe to spend my holidays, I found that my stepmother was a kind-hearted, pretty little thing, whom I might look down upon for her want of education, but whom I could not dislike. She was very kind to me; and she had a baby boy. I have told you about him, and how he and I fell in love with each other at first sight."

"I am horribly jealous of that baby boy," protested Bessie. "How old is he now?"

"Nearly five. He was two years and a half old

when I was at Les Fontaines, and that was before I went to Mauleverer Manor."

"And you have been at Mauleverer Manor more than two years without once going home for the holidays," said Bessie. "That seems hard."

"My dear, poverty is hard. It is all of a piece. It means deprivation, humiliation, degradation, the severance of friends. My father would have had me home if he could have afforded it; but he couldn't. He has only just enough to keep himself and his wife and boy. If you were to see the little box of a house they inhabit, in that tiny French village, you would wonder that anybody bigger than a pigeon could live in so small a place. They have a narrow garden, and there is an orchard on the slope of a hill behind the cottage, and a long white road leading to nowhere in front. It is all very nice in the summer, when one can live half one's life out of doors, but I am sure I don't know how they manage to exist through the winter."

"Poor things!" sighed Bessie, who had a large stock of compassion always on hand.

And then she tied a bright ribbon at the back of Ida's collar, by way of finishing touch to the girl's simple toilet, which had been going on while they talked, and then, Bessie in white and Ida in black, like sunlight and shadow, they went downstairs to the drawing room, where Colonel Wendover was stretched on his favourite sofa reading a county paper. Since his retirement from active service into domestic idleness the Colonel had required a great deal of rest, and was to be found at all hours of the day extended at ease on his own particular sofa. During his intervals of activity he exhibited a large amount of energy. When he was indoors his stentorian voice penetrated from garret to cellar; when he was out of doors the same deep-toned thunder could be heard across a couple of paddocks. He pervaded the gardens and stables, supervised the home farm, and had a finger in every pie.

Mrs. Wendover was sitting in her own particular arm-chair, close to her husband's sofa—they were seldom seen far apart—with a large basket of crewel-work beside her, containing sundry squares of kitchen towelling and a chaos of many-coloured wools, which never seemed to arrive at any result.

The impression which Mrs. Wendover's drawing-room conveyed to a stranger was a general idea of homeliness and comfort. It was not fine, it was not æsthetic, it was not even elegant. A great bay window opened upon the garden, a large old-fashioned fire-place with carved wooden chimney-piece faced the bay. The floor was polished oak, with only an island of faded Persian carpet in the centre, and Indian prayer rugs lying about here and there. There were chairs and tables of richly carved Bombay blackwood, Japanese cabinets in the recesses beside the fire-place, a five-leaved Indian screen between the fire-place and the door. There was just enough Oriental china to give colour to the room, and to relieve by glowing reds and vivid purples the faded dead-leaf tint of curtains and chair-covers.

The gong began to boom as the two girls came into the room, and the rest of the family dropped in through the open windows at the same moment, Aunt Betsy bringing up the rear. There was no nursery dinner at The Knoll. Colonel Wendover allowed his children to dine with him from the day they were able to manage their knives and forks. Save on state occasions, the whole brood sat down with their father and mother to the seven o'clock dinner; as the young sprigs of the House of Orleans used to sit round good King Louis Philippe in his tranquil retirement at Claremont. Even the lisping girl who loved pigs had her place at the board, and knew how to behave herself. There was a subdued struggle for the seat next Ida, whom the Colonel had placed on his right, but Reginald, the elder of the Winchester boys, asserted his claim with a quiet firmness that proved irresistible. Grace was said with solemn brevity by the Colonel, whose sum total of orthodoxy was comprised in that brief grace, and in regular attendance at church on Sunday mornings; and then there came a period of chatter and laughter which might have been a little distracting to a stranger. Each of the boys and girls had some wonderful fact, usually about his or her favourite animal, to communicate to the father. Aunt Betsy broke in with her fine manly voice at every turn in the conversation. Ripples of laughter made a running accompaniment to everything. It was a new thing to Ida Palliser to find herself in the midst of so much happiness.

After dinner they all rushed off to play lawn tennis, carrying Ida along with them.

"It's a shame," protested Bessy. "I know you're tired, darling. Come and rest in a shady corner of the drawing-room."

This sounded tempting, but it was not to be.

"No she's not," asserted Blanche boldly.   "You're not tired, are you, Miss Palliser?"

"Not too tired for just one game," replied Ida. "But you are never to call me Miss Palliser."

"May I really call you Ida?   That's too lovely."

"May we all call you Ida?" asked Horatio. "Don't begin by making distinctions.   Blanche is no better than the rest of us."

"Don't be jealous," said Miss Palliser, laughing, "I am going to be everybody's Ida."

On this she was borne off to the garden as in a whirlwind.

There were some bamboo chairs and sofas on the grass in front of the bay window, and here the elder members of the family established themselves.

"I like that schoolfellow of Bessie's," said Aunt Betsy, with her decided air, whereupon the Colonel and his wife assented, as they always did to any proposition of Miss Wendover's.

"She is remarkably handsome," said the Colonel.

"She is good and thorough, and that's of much more consequence," said his sister.

"She takes to the children, and that is so truly nice in her," murmured Mrs. Wendover.

CHAPTER IV.

WENDOVER ABBEY.

THE next day was fine. The children had all been praying for fine weather, that they might entertain Miss Palliser with an exploration of the surrounding neighbourhood.   Loud whoops of triumph and sundry breakdown dances were heard in the top story soon after five o'clock, for the juvenile Wendovers were early risers, and when in high spirits made themselves distinctly audible.

The eight o'clock breakfast in the old painted dining-room — all oak panelling, but painted stone colour by generations of Goths and Vandals—was even more animated than the seven o'clock dinner.

Such a breakfast, after the thick bread and butter and thin coffee at Mauleverer. Relays of hot buttered cakes and eggs and bacon, fish, honey, fresh fruit from the garden, a picturesque confusion of form and colour on the lavishly-furnished table, and youthful appetites ready to do justice to the good cheer.

"What are you going to do with Miss Palliser?" asked the Colonel. "Am I to take her for a drive?"

"No, father, you can't have Miss Palliser to-day. She's going in the jaunting-car," said Reginald, talking of the lady as if she were a horse. "We're going to take her over to the Abbey."

The Abbey was the ancestral home of the Wendovers, now in possession of Brian Wendover, only son of the Colonel's eldest brother, and head of the house.

"Well, don't upset her oftener than you can help," replied the father. "I suppose you don't much mind being spilt off an outside car, Miss Palliser? I believe young ladies of your age rather relish the excitement."

"She needn't be afraid," said Reginald; "I am going to drive."

"Then we are very likely to find ourselves reposing in a ditch before the day is over," retorted Bessie. "I hope you—or the pony—will choose a dry one."

"I'll risk it, ditches and all," said Ida, good-naturedly. "I am longing to see the Abbey."

"The rich Brian's Abbey," said Bessie, laughing. "What a pity he is not at home for you to see him too! Do you think Brian will be back before Ida's holidays are over, father?"

"I never know what that young man is going to do," answered the Colonel. "When last I heard from him he was fishing in Norway. He doesn't care much about the sport, he tells me; indeed, he was never a very enthusiastic angler; but he likes the country and the people. He ought to stay at home, and stand for the county at the next election. A young man in his position has no business to be idle."

"Is he clever?" asked Ida.

"Too clever for my money," answered the Colonel. "He has too much book-learning, and too little knowledge of men and things. What is the good of a man being a fine Greek scholar if he knows nothing about the land he owns, or the cattle that graze upon it, and has not enough tact to make himself popular in his own neighbourhood? Brian is a man who would starve if his bread depended on his own exertions."

"He's a jolly kind of cousin for a fellow to have," suggested Horry, looking up from his eggs and bacon. "He lets us do what we like at the Abbey. By the way, Blanche, have you packed the picnic basket?"

"Yes."

"What have you put in?"

"That's my secret," answered Blanche. "Do you think I am going to tell you what you are to have for lunch? That would spoil all the fun."

"Blanche isn't half a bad caterer," said Reg. "I

place myself in her hands unreservedly; I will only venture to hint that I hope she hasn't forgotten the chutnee, Tirhoot, and plenty of it. What's the good of having a father who was shoulder to shoulder with Gough in the Punjab, if we are to run short of Indian condiments?"

At nine o'clock the young people were all ready to start. The jaunting-car held five, including the driver; Bessie and her friend were to occupy one side, Eva, the round child who loved pigs, was to have a seat, and a place was to be kept for Miss Rylance, who was to be invited to join the exploration party, much to the disgust of the Winchester lads, who denounced her as a stuck-up minx, and distinguished her with various other epithets of an abusive character selected from a vocabulary known only to Wykamites. Blanche and Horatio and a smaller boy, called Ernest, who was dressed like a gillie, and had all the wildness of a young Highlander, were to walk, with the occasional charity of a lift.

The jaunting-car was drawn by a large white pony, fat and pampered, overfed with dainties from the children's tables, and petted and played with until he had become almost human in his intelligence, and a match for his youthful masters in cunning and mischief. This impish animal had been christened Robin Goodfellow, a name that was shortened for convenience to Robin. Robin's eagerness to depart was now made known to the family by an incessant rattling of his bit.

Reginald took the reins, and got into his seat with the quiet grandeur of a celebrity in the four-in-hand club. Ida and Bessie were handed to their places by Horatio, the chubby Eva scrambled into her seat, with a liberal display of Oxford blue stocking, under the shortest of striped petticoats; and off they drove to the cottage, Dr. Rylance's miniature dwelling, where the plate-glass windows were shining in the morning sun, and the colours of the flower-beds were almost too bright to be looked at.

Bessie found Miss Rylance in the dainty little drawing-room, all ebonised wood and blue china, as neat as an interior by Mieris. The fair Urania was yawning over a book of travels—trying to improve a mind which was not naturally fertile—and she was not sorry to be interrupted by an irruption of noisy Wendovers, even though they left impressions of their boots on the delicate tones of the carpet, and made havoc of the cretonne chair-covers.

Miss Rylance had no passion for country life. Fields and trees, hills and winding streams, even when enlivened by the society of the lower animals, were not all sufficient for her happiness. It was all very well for her father to oscillate between Cavendish Square and Kingthorpe, avoiding the expense and trouble of autumn touring, and taking his rest and his pleasure in this rustic retreat. But her summer holidays for the last three years had been all Kingthorpe, and Miss Rylance detested the picturesque village, the busy duck-pond, the insignificant hills, which nobody had ever heard of, and the monotonous sequence of events.

"We are going to the Abbey for a nice long day, taking our dinner with us, and coming round to Aunt Betsy's to tea on our way home," said Bessie, as if she were proposing an entirely novel excursion; "and we want you to come with us, Ranie."

Miss Rylance stifled a yawn. She had been trying to pin her thoughts to a particular tribe of Abyssinians, who fought all the surrounding tribes, and always welcomed the confiding stranger with a shower of poisoned arrows. She did not care for the Wendover children, but they were better than those wearisome Abyssinians.

"You are very kind, but I know the Abbey so well," she said, determined to yield her consent as a favour.

"Never mind that. Ida has never seen it. We are going to show her everything. We want her to feel one of us."

"We shall have a jolly lunch," interjected Blanche. "There are some lemon cheesecakes that I made myself yesterday afternoon. Cook was in a good temper, and let me do it."

"I hope you washed your hands first," said Horatio. "I'd sooner cook had made the cheese-cakes."

"Of course I washed my hands, you too suggestive pig. But I should hope that in a general way my hands are cleaner than cook's. It is only schoolboys who luxuriate in dirt."

"You'll come, Ranie?" pleaded Bess.

"If you really wish it."

"I do, or I shouldn't be here. But I hope you wish it too. You ought to be longing to get out of doors on such a lovely morning. Houses were never intended for such weather as this. Come and join the birds and butterflies, and all the happiest things in creation."

"I must go for my hat and sunshade. I wasn't born full-dressed, like the birds and butterflies," replied Urania.

She ran away, leaving Bessie and Ida in the drawing-room. The younger children, having rushed in and left their mark upon the room, had now rushed out again to the jaunting-car.

"A pretty drawing-room, isn't it?" asked Bess. "It looks so neat and fresh and bright, after ours."

"It doesn't look half so much like home," said Ida.

"Perhaps not. But I believe it is just the exact thing a drawing-room ought to be in this latter part of the nineteenth century; or, at least, so Dr. Rylance says. How do you like the blue china? Dr. Rylance is an amateur of blue china. He will have no other. Dresden and Sèvres have no existence for him. He recognizes nothing beyond his own particular breed of ginger-jars."

Miss Rylance came back, dressed as carefully as if she had been going for a morning lounge in Hyde Park, hat and feather, pongee sunshade, mousquetaire gloves. The Wendovers all wore their gloves in the pockets, and cultivated blisters on the palms of their hands, as a mark of distinction, which implied great feats in rowing, or the pulling in of desperate horses.

Now they were all mounted on the car, just as the church clock struck ten. Reginald gave the reins a shake, cracked his whip, and Robin, who always knew where his young friends wanted to go, twisted the vehicle sharply round a corner and started at an agreeable canter, expressive of good spirits.

Robin carried them joltingly along a lovely lane till they came to a gentle acclivity, by which time, having given vent to his exuberance, the pony settled down into a crawl. Vainly did Reginald crack his whip—vain even stinging switches on Robin's fat sides. Out of that crawl nothing could move him. The sun was gaining power with every moment, and blazing down upon the occupants of the car; but Robin cared not at all. He was an animal of tropical origin, and had no apprehension of sunshine; his eyes were so constructed as to accommodate themselves to a superfluity of light.

"I think we shall be tolerably well roasted by the time we get to the Abbey," said Bessie. "Don't you think if we were all to get down and push the back of the car, Robin might go a little faster?"

"He'll go fast enough when he has blown a bit," said Reg. "Can't you admire the landscape?"

"We could, if we were not being baked," replied Ida.

Miss Rylance sat silent under her pongee umbrella, and wished herself in Cavendish Square; even though western London were as empty and barren as the great wilderness.

They were on the ridge of a hill, overlooking undulating pastures and quiet sheep-walks, fair hills on which the yew-trees cast their dark shadows, a broad stretch of pastoral country with sunny gleams of water shining low in the distance.

Suddenly the road dipped, and Robin was going downhill with alarming speed.

"This means that we shall all be in the ditch presently," said Bessie. "Never mind. It's only a dry bed of dock and used-up stinging nettles. We shan't be much hurt."

After two or three miraculous escapes they landed at the bottom of the hill, and Ida beheld the good old gates of Kingthorpe Abbey, low iron gates that stood open, between tall stone pillars supporting the sculptured escutcheon of the Wendovers. There was a stone lodge on each side of the gate, past which the car drove in triumph into an avenue of ancient yew-trees, low and wide-spreading, with a solemn gloom that would better have become a churchyard than a gentleman's park.

It was a noble old park, richly timbered with oaks as old as those immemorial trees that make the glory of Stoneleigh. There was a lake in a wooded hollow in front of the Abbey, a long low pile of stone, the newest part of which was as old as the days of the last Tudor. Nor had much money been spent on the restoration or decorative repair of that fine old house. It had been kept wind and weather proof. It had been protected against the injuries of time; and that was all. There it stood, a brave and solid monument of the remote past, grand in its stern simplicity and its historic associations.

"Oh, what a dear old house!" cried Ida, clasping her hands, as the car came out of the yew-tree avenue into the open space in front of the Abbey; a wide lawn, where four mighty cedars of Lebanon spread their dense shadows—grave old trees—which were in somewise impostors, as they looked older than the house, and yet had been saplings in the days of Queen Anne. "What a sweet old place!" repeated Ida; "and how I envy the rich Brian!"

"Don't you think the rich Brian's wife will be still more enviable?" sneered Miss Rylance.

"That depends. She may be a Vere-de-Vereish

kind of person, and pine amongst her halls and towers,"
said Ida.

"Not if she had been brought up in poverty. She
would revel in the advantages of her position as Mrs.
Wendover of the Abbey," asserted Miss Rylance.

"Would she? The Earl of Burleigh's wife had
been poor, and yet did not enjoy being rich and great,"
said Bessie. "It killed her, poor thing. And yet she
had married for love, and had no remorse of conscience
to weigh her down."

"She was a sensitive little fool," said Ida; "I have
no patience with her."

"Modern young ladies are not easily crushed,"
remarked Miss Rylance; "they make marrying for
money a profession."

"Is that your idea of life?" asked Ida.

"No; but I understand it is yours. I heard you
say you meant to marry for money."

"Then you must have been listening to a conversation in which you had no concern," Ida answered coolly.
"I never said as much to you."

The three girls, and the chubby Eva, had alighted
from the car, which was being conveyed to the stables
at a hand-gallop, and this conversation was continued
on the broad gravel sweep in front of the Abbey. Just
as the discussion was intensifying in unpleasantness,
the arrival of the pedestrians made an agreeable diversion. Blanche and her two brothers had come by a
short cut, across fields and common, had given chase
to butterflies, experimented with tadpoles, and looked
for hedge-bird's eggs in the course of their journey,
and were altogether in a state of dilapidation—perspiration running down their sunburnt faces—their hats

5*

anyhow—their hands embellished with recent scratches
—their boots coated with clay.

"Did ever anyone see such objects?" exclaimed
Bessie, who had imbibed certain conventional ideas
of decency at Mauleverer Manor: "you ought to be
ashamed of yourselves."

"I daresay we ought, but we aren't," retorted
Horatio. "I found a tadpole in an advanced stage
of transmutation, Miss Palliser, and it has almost con-
verted me to Darwinism. Given a single step and you
may accept the whole ladder. If from tadpoles frogs,
why not from monkeys man?"

"Go and be a Darwinite, and don't prose," said
Blanche, impatiently. "We are going to show Ida the
Abbey. How do you like the outside, darling?" asked
the too-affectionate girl, favouring Miss Palliser with
the full weight of her seven stone and three-quarters.

"I adore it. It is like a page out of an old
chronicle."

"Isn't it?" gasped Blanche; "and you can fancy
the fat old monks sitting on those stone benches, nod-
ding in the sunshine. The house is hardly altered a
bit since it was an actual abbey, except that half a
dozen cells have been knocked into one comfortable
bed-room. The long dark passages are just the same
as they were when those sly old monks went gliding
up and down them—such dear old passages, smelling
palpably of ghosts."

"Mice," said Horatio.

"No, sir, ghosts. Do you suppose my sense of
smell is of such inferior quality that I can't distinguish
a ghost from a mouse?"

"Now, how about luncheon?" demanded Horatio.

"I propose that we all go and sit under that prime old cedar and discuss the contents of the picnic basket before we discuss the Abbey."

"Why, it isn't half-past eleven," said Bessie.

"Ah," sighed Blanche, "I'm afraid it's too early for lunch. We should have nothing left to look forward to all the rest of the day."

"There'd be afternoon tea at Aunt Betsy's to build upon," said Horry. "I gave her to understand we were to have something good: blue gages from the south wall, cream to a reckless extent."

"Strawberry jam and pound-cake," suggested Eva.

"If you go on like that you'll make me distracted with hunger," said Blanche, a young person who at the seaside wanted twopence to buy buns directly after she had swallowed her dinner.

Bessie and Miss Rylance had been walking up and down the velvet sward beside the beds of dwarf roses and geraniums, with a ladylike stateliness which did credit to their training at Mauleverer. Ida was the centre of the juvenile group.

"Come and see the Abbey," exclaimed Horry, putting his arm through Miss Palliser's, "and at the stroke of one we will sit down to lunch under the biggest of the cedars—the tree which according to tradition was planted by John Evelyn himself, when he came on a visit to Sir Tristram Wendover."

They all trooped into the Abbey, the hall door standing open, as in a fairy tale. Bessie and Urania followed at a more sober pace; but Ida had given herself over to the children, and they did what they liked with her, Blanche hanging on her bodily all the time.

They were now joined by Reginald, who appeared

mysteriously from the back premises, where he had been seeing Robin eat his corn, having a fixed idea that it was in the nature of all grooms and stablemen to cheat horses.

The Abbey was furnished with a sober grandeur, in perfect tone with its architecture. Everything was solid and ponderous, save here and there, where in some lady's bower there appeared the spindle-legged tables and inlaid cabinets of the Chippendale period, which had an air of newness where all else was so old. The upper rooms were low and somewhat dark, the heavily mullioned windows, being designed to exclude rather than to admit light. There was much tapestry, subdued in hue, but in good condition, and as frankly uninteresting in subject as the generality of old English needlework.

Below, the rooms were large and lofty, rich in carved chimney pieces, well preserved panelling, and old oak furniture. There were some fine pictures, from Holbein downwards, and the usual array of family portraits, which the boys and girls explained and commented upon copiously.

"There's my favourite ancestor, Sir Tristram," cried Blanche pointing to a dark-eyed cavalier, with strongly-marked brow and bronzed visage. "He was middle-aged when that picture was painted, but I know he was handsome in his youth. The face is still in the family."

"Of course it is," said Horatio—"on my shoulders."

"Your shoulders!" ejaculated Blanche, contemptuously. "As if my Sir Tristram ever resembled you. He fought in all the great battles, from Edgehill to

Worcester," continued the girl; "and he was wounded seven times: and he was true to his master through every trial; and he had all the Wendover plate melted down; and he followed Charles the Second into exile; he mortgaged his estate to raise money for the King; and he married a very lovely French woman, who introduced turned-up noses into the family," concluded Blanche, giving her tip-tilted nose a complacent toss.

"I thought it was a mercy that we were spared the old housekeeper," said Urania, "but really Blanche is worse."

"Ida doesn't know all about our family, if you do," protested Blanche. "It is all new to her."

"Yes, dear, it is all new and interesting to me," said Ida.

"How much more deeply you would have been interested if Mr. Wendover had been here to expatiate upon his family tree," said Urania.

"That might have made it still more interesting," admitted Ida, with a frankness which took the sting out of Miss Rylance's remark.

The young Wendovers had shown Ida everything. They had opened cabinets, peered into secret drawers, sniffed at the stale *pot-pourri* in old crackle vases: they had dragged their willing victim through all the long slippery passages, by all the mysterious stairs and by-ways; they had obliged her to look at the interior of ghostly closets, where the ladies of old had stored their house linen or hung their mantuas and farthingales; they had made her look out of numerous windows to admire the prospect; they had introduced her to the state bedroom in which the heads of the Wendover race made a point of being born; they made her peep shuddering into the death-chamber where the family were laid in their last slumber. The time thus pleasantly occupied slipped away unawares; and the chapel clock was striking one as they all went trooping down the broad oak staircase for about the fifteenth time.

A gentleman was entering the hall as they came down. They could only see the top of his hat.

"It's father," cried Eva.

"You little idiot, did you ever see my father in a stove-pipe hat on a week-day?" cried Reg., with infinite scorn.

"Then it's Brian."

"Brian is in Norway."

The gentleman looked up and greeted them all with a comprehensive smile. It was Dr. Rylance.

"So glad I have found you, young people," he said blandly.

"Papa," exclaimed Urania, in a tone which did not express unmitigated pleasure, "this is a surprise. You told me you would not be down till late in the evening."

"Yes, my dear: but the fine morning tempted me. I found my engagements would stand over till Monday or Tuesday, so I put myself into the eight o'clock train, and arrived at The Cottage just an hour after you and your friends had left for your picnic. So I walked over to join you. I hope I am not in the way."

"Of course not," said Bessie. "I'm afraid you'll find us hardly the kind of company you are accustomed to; but if you will put up with our roughness and noise we shall feel honoured."

"We are going to get lunch ready," said Blanche.

"You grown-ups will find us under Evelyn's tree when
you're hungry, and you'd better accommodate yourselves
to be hungry soon."

"Or you may find a dearth of provisions," interjected Reg. "I feel in a demolishing humour."

The troop rushed off, leaving the three elder girls
and Dr. Rylance standing in the hall, listlessly contemplative of Sir Tristram's dinted breast-plate, hacked
by Roundhead pikes at Marston Moor.

CHAPTER V.

DR. RYLANCE ASSERTS HIMSELF.

THE luncheon under Evelyn's tree took a cooler
shade from Dr. Rylance's presence than from the far-
reaching branches of the cedar. His politeness made
the whole business different from what it would have
been without him.

Blanche and the boys, accustomed to abandon
themselves to frantic joviality at any outdoor feast of
their own contriving, now withdrew into the back-
ground, and established themselves behind the trunk
of the tree, in which retirement they kept up an insane
giggling, varied by low and secret discourse, and from
which shelter they issued forth stealthily, one by one,
to pounce with crafty hands upon the provisions.
These unmannerly proceedings were ignored by the
elders, but they exercised a harassing influence upon
poor little Eva, who had been told to sit quietly by
Bessie, and who watched her brothers' raids with
round-eyed wonder, and listened with envious ears to
that distracting laughter behind the tree.

"Did you see Horry take quite half the cake, just now?" she whispered to Bessie, in the midst of a polite conversation about nothing particular.

And anon she murmured in horrified wonder, after a stolen peep behind the tree, "Reg. is taking off Dr. Rylance."

The grown-up luncheon party was not lively. Tongue and chicken, pigeon-pie, cheese-cakes, tarts, cake, fruit —all had been neatly spread upon a tablecloth laid on the soft turf. Nothing had been forgotten. There were plates and knives and forks enough for everybody —picnicking being a business thoroughly well understood at The Knoll; but there was a good deal wanting in the guests.

Ida was thoughtful, Urania obviously sullen, Bessie amiably stupid; but Dr. Rylance appeared to think that they were all enjoying themselves intensely.

"Now this is what I call really delightful," he said, as he poured out the sparkling Devonshire cider with as stately a turn of his wrist as if the liquor had been Cliquot or Roederer. "An open air luncheon on such a day as this is positively inspiring, and to a man who has breakfasted at seven o'clock, on a cup of tea and a morsel of dry toast—thanks, yes, I prefer the wing if no one else will have it—such an unceremonious meal is doubly welcome. I'm so glad I found you. Lucky, wasn't it, Ranie?"

He smiled at his daughter, as if deprecating that stolid expression of hers, which would have been eminently appropriate to the funeral of an indifferent acquaintance,—a total absence of all feeling, a grave nullity.

"I don't see anything lucky in so simple a fact,"

answered Urania. "You were told we had come here, and you came here after us."

"You might have changed your minds at the last moment and gone somewhere else. Might you not, now, Miss Palliser?"

"Yes, if we had been very frivolous people; but as to-day's exploration of the Abbey was planned last night, it would have indicated great weakness of mind if we had been tempted into any other direction," answered Ida, feeling somewhat sorry for Dr. Rylance.

The coldest heart might compassionate a man cursed in such a disagreeable daughter.

"I am very glad you were not weak-minded, and that I was so fortunate as to find you," said the doctor, addressing himself henceforward exclusively to Ida and her friend.

Bessie took care of his creature-comforts with a matronly hospitality which sat well upon her. She cut thin slices of tongue, she fished out savouriest bits of pigeon and egg, when he passed, by a natural transition, from chicken to pie. She was quite distressed because he did not care for tarts, or cake. But the doctor's appetite, unlike that of the young. people on the other side of the cedar, had its limits. He had satisfied his hunger long before they had, and was ready to show Miss Palliser the gardens.

"They are fine old gardens," he said, approvingly. "Perhaps their chief beauty is that they have not a single modern improvement. They are as old-fashioned as the gardens of Sion Abbey, before the good queen Bess ousted the nuns to make room for the Percies."

They all rose and walked slowly away from the cedar, leaving the fragments of the feast to Blanche and her three brothers. Eva stayed behind, to make one of that exuberant group, and to see Reg. "take off" Urania and her father. His mimicry was cordially admired, though it was not always clear to his audience which was the doctor and which was his daughter. A stare, a strut, a toss, an affected drawl were the leading features of each characterization.

"I had no opportunity of congratulating you on your triumphs the other day, Miss Palliser," said Dr. Rylance, who had somehow managed that Ida and he should be side by side, and a little in advance of the other two. "But, believe me, I most heartily sympathized with you in the delight of your success."

"Delight?" echoed Ida. "Do you think there was any real pleasure for me in receiving a gift from the hands of Miss Pew, who has done all she could do to make me feel the disadvantages of my position, from the day I first entered her house to the day I last left it? The prizes gave me no pleasure. They have no value in my mind, except as an evidence that I have made the most of my opportunities at Mauleverer, in spite of my contempt for my schoolmistress."

"You dislike her intensely, I see."

"She has made me dislike her. I never knew unkindness till I knew her. I never felt the sting of poverty till she made me feel all its sharpness. I never knew that I was steeped in sinful pride until she humiliated me."

"Your days of honour and happiness will come," said the doctor, "days when you will think no more of Miss Pew than of an insect which once stung you."

"Thank you for the comforting forecast," answered Ida, lightly. "But it is easy to prophesy good fortune."

"Easy, and safe, in such a case as yours. I can sympathize with you better than you may suppose, Miss Palliser. I have had to fight my battle. I was not always Dr. Rylance, of Cavendish Square; and I did not enter a world in which there was a fine estate waiting for me, like the owner of this place."

"But you have conquered fortune, and by your own talents," said Ida. "That must be a proud thought."

Dr. Rylance, who was not utterly without knowledge of himself, smiled at the compliment. He knew it was by tact and address, smooth speech and clean linen, that he had conquered fortune, rather than by shining abilities. Yet he valued himself not the less on that account. In his mind tact ranked higher than genius, since it was his own peculiar gift: just as blue ginger-jars were better than Sèvres, because he, Dr. Rylance, was a collector of ginger-jars. He approved of himself so completely that even his littlenesses were great in his own eyes.

"I have worked hard," he said, complacently, "and I have been patient. But now, when my work is done, and my place in the world fixed, I begin to find life somewhat barren. A man ought to reap some reward —something fairer and sweeter than pounds, shillings, and pence, for a life of labour and care."

"No doubt," asserted Ida, receiving this remark as abstract philosophy, rather than as having a personal meaning. "But I think I should consider pounds, shillings, and pence a very fair reward, if I only had enough for them."

"Yes, now, when you are smarting under the insolence of a purse-proud schoolmistress—but years hence, when you have won independence, you will feel disappointed if you have won nothing better."

"What could be better?"

"Sympathetic companionship—a love worthy to influence your life."

Ida looked up at the doctor with naïve surprise. Good heavens, was this middle-aged gentleman going to drop into sentiment, as Silas Wegg dropped into poetry? She glanced back at the other two. Happily they were close at hand.

"What have you done with the children, Bessie?" asked Ida, as if she were suddenly distracted with anxiety about their fate.

"Left them to their own devices. I hope they will not quite kill themselves. We are all, to meet in the stable-yard at four, so that we may be with Aunt Betsy at five."

"Don't you think papa and I had better walk gently home?" suggested Urania; "I am sure it would be cruel to inflict such an immense party upon Miss Wendover."

"Nonsense," exclaimed Bessie. "Why, if all old Pew's school was to march in upon her, without a moment's notice, Aunt Betsy would not be put out of the way one little bit. If Queen Victoria were to drop in unexpectedly to luncheon, my aunt would be as cool as one of her own early cucumbers, and would insist on showing the Queen her stables, and possibly her pigs."

"How do you know that?" asked Ida.

"Because she never had a visitor yet whom she did not drag into her stables, from archbishops downwards; and I don't suppose she'd draw the line at a queen," answered Bessie, with conviction.

"I am going to drink tea with Miss Wendover, whatever Urania may do," said Dr. Rylance, who felt that the time had come when he must assert himself. "I am out for a day's pleasure, and I mean to drink the cup to the dregs."

Urania looked at her father with absolute consternation. He was transformed; he had become a new person; he was forgetting himself in a ridiculous manner; letting down his dignity to an alarming extent. Dr. Rylance, the fashionable physician, the man whose nice touch adjusted the nerves of the aristocracy, to disport himself with unkempt, bare-handed young Wendovers! It was an upheaval of things which struck horror to Urania's soul. Easy, after beholding such a moral convulsion, to believe that the Wight had once been part of the mainland; or even that Ireland had originally been joined to Spain.

They all roamed into the rose-garden, where there were alleys of standard rose-trees, planted upon grass that was soft and springy under the foot. They went into the old vineries, where the big bunches of grapes were purpling in the gentle heat. Dr. Rylance went everywhere, and he contrived always to be near Ida Palliser.

He did not again lapse into sentiment, and he made himself fairly agreeable, in his somewhat stilted fashion. Ida accepted his attention with a charming unconsciousness; but she was perfectly conscious of Urania's vexation, and that gave a zest to the whole thing.

"Well, Ida, what do you think of Kingthorpe Abbey?" asked Bessie, when they had seen everything, even to the stoats and weasels, and various vermin nailed flat against the stable wall, and were waiting for Robin to be harnessed.

"It is a noble old place. It is simply perfect. I wonder your cousin can live away from it."

"Oh, Brian's chief delight is in roaming about the world. The Abbey is thrown away upon him. He ought to have been an explorer or a missionary. However, he is expected home in a month, and you will be able to judge for yourself whether he deserves to be master of this old place. I only wish it belonged to the other Brian."

"The other Brian is your favourite."

"He is ever so much nicer than his cousin—at least, the children and I like him best. My father swears by the head of the house."

"I think I would rather accept the Colonel's judgment than yours, Bess," said Ida. "You are so impulsive in your likings."

"Don't say that I am wanting in judgment," urged Bessie, coaxingly, "for you know how dearly I love you. You will see the two Brians, I hope, before your holidays are over; and then you can make your own election. Brian Walford will be with us for my birthday picnic, I daresay, wherever he may be now. I believe he is mooning away his time in Herefordshire, with his mother's people."

"Is his father dead?"

"Yes, mother and father both, ages ago, in the days when I was a hard-hearted little wretch, and thought it a treat to go into mourning, and rather nice to be able to tell everybody, "Uncle Walford's dead. He had a fit, and he never speaked any more." It was news, you know, and in a village that goes for something."

After a lengthy discussion, and some squabbling, it was decided that the children were to have the benefit of the jaunting-car for the homeward journey, and that Dr. Rylance and the three young ladies were to walk, attended by Reginald, who insisted upon attaching himself to their service, volunteering to show them the very nearest way through a wood, and across a field, and over a common, and down a lane, which led straight to the gate of Aunt Betsy's orchard.

Urania wore fashionable boots, and considered walking exercise a superstition of medical men and old-fashioned people; yet she stoutly refused a seat in the car.

"No, thanks, Horatio, I know your pony too well. I'd rather trust myself upon my own feet."

"There's more danger in your high heels than in my pony," retorted Horatio. "I shouldn't wonder if you dropped in for a sprained ankle before you got home."

Urania risked the sprained ankle. She began to limp before she had emerged from the wood. She hobbled painfully along the rugged footpath between the yellow wheat. She was obliged to sit down and rest upon a furzy hillock on the common, good-natured Bess keeping her company, while Ida and Reginald were half a mile ahead with Dr. Rylance. Her delicate complexion was unbecomingly flushed by the time she and Bessie arrived wearily at the little gate opening into Miss Wendover's orchard.

There were only some iron hurdles between Aunt Betsy's orchard and the lawn before Aunt Betsy's drawing-room. The house was characteristic of the lady. It was a long red brick cottage, solid, substantial, roomy, eschewing ornament, but beautified in the eyes of most people by an air of supreme comfort, cleanliness, and general well-being. In all Kingthorpe there were no rooms so cool as Aunt Betsy's in summer —none so warm in winter. The cottage had originally been the homestead of a small grass-farm, which had been bequeathed to Betsy Wendover by her father, familiarly known as the Old Squire, the chief landowner in that part of the country. With this farm of about two hundred and fifty acres of the most fertile pasture land in Hampshire and an income of seven hundred a year from consols, Miss Wendover found herself passing rich. She built a drawing-room with wide windows opening on to the lawn, and a bed-room with a covered balcony over the drawing-room. These additional rooms made the homestead all-sufficient for a lady of Aunt Betsy's simple habits. She was hospitality itself, receiving her friends in a large-hearted, gentlemanlike style, keeping open house for man and beast, proud of her wine, still prouder of her garden and greenhouses, proudest of her stables; fond of this life, and of her many comforts, yet without a particle of selfishness; ready to leave her cosy fireside at a moment's notice on the bitterest winter night, to go and nurse a sick child, or comfort a dying woman; religious without ostentation, charitable without weakness, stern to resent an injury, implacable against an insult.

A refreshing sight, yet not altogether a pleasant one for Miss Rylance, met the eyes of the two young ladies as they neared the little iron gate opening from the orchard to the lawn. A couple of tea-tables had been brought out upon the grass before the drawing-room window. The youngsters were busily engaged at one table, Blanche pouring out tea, while her brothers and small sister made havoc with cake and fruit, homemade bread and butter, and jams of various hues. At the other table, less lavishly but more elegantly furnished, sat Miss Wendover and Ida Palliser, with Dr. Rylance comfortably established in a Buckinghamshire wickerwork chair between them.

"Does not that look a picture of comfort!" exclaimed Bessie.

"My father seems to be making himself very comfortable," said Urania.

She hobbled across the lawn, and sank exhausted into a low chair, near her parent.

"My poor child, how dilapidated you look after your walk," said Dr. Rylance; "Miss Palliser and I enjoyed it immensely."

"I cannot boast of Miss Palliser's robust health," retorted Urania contemptuously, as if good health were a sign of vulgarity. "I had my neuralgia all last night."

Whenever the course of events proved objectionable, Miss Rylance took refuge in a complaint which she called her neuralgia, indicating that it was a species of disorder peculiar to herself, and of a superior quality to everybody else's neuralgia.

"You should live in the open air, like my sunburnt young friends yonder," said the doctor, with a glance at the table where the young Wendovers were stuffing; "I am sure they never complain of neuralgia."

Urania looked daggers, but spoke none.

It was a wearisome afternoon for that injured

6*

young lady. Dr. Rylance dawdled over his tea, handed teacups and bread and butter, was assiduous with the sugar basin, devoted with the cream jug, talked and laughed with Miss Palliser, as if they had a world of ideas in common, and made himself altogether objectionable to his only child.

By-and-by, when there was a general adjournment to the greenhouses and stables, Urania contrived to slip her arm through her father's.

"I thought I told you that Miss Palliser was my favourite aversion, papa," she said, tremulous with angry feeling.

"I have some faint idea that you did express yourself unfavourably about her," answered the doctor, with his consulting-room urbanity, "but I am at a loss to understand your antipathy. The girl is positively charming, as frank as the sunshine, and full of brains."

"I know her. You do not," said Urania tersely.

"My dear, it is the speciality of men in my profession to make rapid judgments."

"Yes, and very often to make them wrong. I was never so much annoyed in my life. I consider your attention to that girl a deliberate insult to me; a girl with whom I never could get on—who has said the rudest things to me."

"Can I be uncivil to a friend of your friend, Bessie?"

"There is a wide distance between being uncivil and being obsequiously, ridiculously attentive."

"Urania," said the doctor in his gravest voice, "I have allowed you to have your own way in most things, and I believe your life has been a pleasant one."

"Of course, papa. I never said otherwise."

"Very well, my dear, then you must be good

enough to let me take my own way of making life pleasant to myself, and you must not take upon yourself to dictate what degree of civility I am to show to Miss Palliser, or to any other lady."

Urania held her peace after this. It was the first deliberate snub she had ever received from her father, and she added it to her lengthy score against Ida.

CHAPTER VI.

A BIRTHDAY FEAST.

IDA PALLISER'S holidays were coming to an end, like a tale that is told. There was only one day more left, but that day was to be especially glorious; for it was Bessie Wendover's birthday, a day which from time immemorial—or, at all events, ever since Bessie was ten years old—had been sacred to certain games or festivities—a modernised worship of the great god Pan.

Sad was it for Bessie and all the junior Wendovers when the seventh of September dawned with gray skies, or east winds, rain, or hail. It was usually a brilliant day. The clerk of the weather appeared favourably disposed to the warm-hearted Bessie.

On this particular occasion the preparations for the festival were on a grander scale than usual, in honour of Ida, who was on the eve of departure. A cruel, cruel car was to carry her off to Winchester at six o'clock on the morning after the birthday; the railway station was to swallow her up alive; the train was to rush off with her, like a fiery dragon carrying off the princess of fairy tale; and the youthful Wendovers were to be left lamenting.

In six happy weeks their enthusiasm for their young guest had known no abatement. She had realized their fondest anticipations. She had entered into their young lives and made herself a part of them. She had given herself up, heart and soul, to childish things and foolish things, to please these devoted admirers; and the long summer holiday had been very sweet to her. The open-air life—the balmy noontides in woods and meadows, beside wandering trout streams —on the breezy hill-tops—the afternoon tea-drinking in gardens and orchards—the novels read aloud, seated in the heart of some fine old tree, with her auditors perched on the branches round about her, like gigantic birds—the boating excursions on a river with more weeds than water in it—the jaunts to Winchester, and dreamy afternoons in the cathedral—all had been delicious. She had lived in an atmosphere of homely domestic love, among people who valued her for herself, and did not calculate the cost of her gowns, or despise her because she had so few. The old church was lovely in her eyes; the old vicar and his wife had taken a fancy to her. Everything at Kingthorpe was delightful, except Urania. She certainly was a drawback; but she had been tolerably civil since the first day at the Abbey.

Ida had spent many an hour at the Abbey since that first inspection. She knew every room in the house—the sunniest windows—the books in the long library, with its jutting wings between the windows, and cosy nooks for study. She knew almost every tree in the park, and the mild faces of the deer looking gravely reproachful, as if asking what business she had there. She had lain asleep on the sloping bank above

the lake on drowsy afternoons, tired by wandering far
a-field with her young esquires. She knew the Abbey
by heart—better than even Urania knew it; though
she had used that phrase to express utter satiety. Ida
Palliser had a deeper love of natural beauty, a stronger
appreciation of all that made the old place interesting.
She had a curious feeling, too, about the absent master
of that grave, gray old house—a fond, romantic dream,
which she would not for the wealth of India have revealed to mortal ear, that in the days to come Brian's
life would be in somewise linked with hers. Perhaps
this foolish thought was engendered of the blankness
of her own life, a stage on which the players had been
so few that this figure of an unknown young man as-
sumed undue proportions.

Then, again, the fact that she could hear very little
about Mr. Wendover from his cousins, stimulated her
curiosity about him, and intensified her interest in him.
Brian's merits were a subject which the Wendover
children always shirked, or passed over so lightly that
Ida was no wiser for her questioning; and maidenly
reserve forbade her too eager inquiry.

About Brian Walford, the son of Parson Wendover,
youngest of the three brothers, for seven years vicar of
a parish near Hereford, and for the last twelve years
at rest in the village church-yard, the young Wendovers
had plenty to say. He was good-looking, they assured
Ida. She would inevitably fall in love with him when
they met. He was the cleverest young man in England,
and was certain to finish his career as Lord Chancellor,
despite the humility of his present stage of being.

"He has no fortune, I suppose?" hazarded Ida, in
a conversation with Horatio.

She did not ask the question from any interest in the subject. Brian Walford was a being whose image never presented itself to her mind. She only made the remark for the sake of saying something.

"Not a denarius," said Horry, who liked occasionally to be classical. "But what of that? If I were as clever as Brian I shouldn't mind how poor I was. With his talents he is sure to get to the top of the tree."

"What can he do?" asked Ida.

"Ride a bicycle better than any man I know."

"What else?"

"Sing a first-rate comic song."

"What else?"

"Get longer breaks at billiards than any fellow I ever played with."

"What else?"

"Pick the winner out of a score of race-horses in the preliminary canter."

"Those are great gifts, I have no doubt," said Ida. "But do eminent lawyers, in a general way, win their advancement by riding bicycles and singing comic songs?"

"Don't sneer, Ida. When a fellow is clever in one thing he is clever in other things. Genius is many-sided, universal. Carlyle says as much. If Napoleon Bonaparte had not been a great general, he would have been a great writer like Voltaire—or a great lawyer like Thurlow."

From this time forward Ida had an image of Brian Walford in her mind. It was the picture of a vapid youth, fair-haired, with thin moustache elaborately trained, and thinner whiskers—a fribble that gave half its little mind to its collar, and the other half to its boots. Such images are photographed in a flash of lightning on the sensitive brain of youth, and are naturally more often false guesses than true ones.

There was delightful riot in the house of the Wendovers on the night before the picnic. The Colonel had developed a cold and cough within the last week, so he and his wife had jogged off to Bournemouth, in the T-cart, with one portmanteau and one servant, leaving Bessie mistress of all things. It was a grief to Mrs. Wendover to be separated from home and children at any time, and she was especially regretful at being absent on her eldest daughter's birthday; but the Colonel was paramount. If his cough could be cured by sea air, to the sea he must go, with his faithful wife in attendance upon him.

"Don't let the children turn the house quite out of windows, darling," said Mrs. Wendover, at the moment of parting.

"No, mother dear, we are all going to be goodness itself."

"I know, dears, you always are. And I hope you will all enjoy yourselves."

"We're sure to do that, mother," answered Reginald, with a cheerfulness that seemed almost heartless.

The departing parent would not have liked them to be unhappy, but a few natural tears would have been a pleasing tribute. Not a tear was shed. Even the little Eva skipped joyously on the doorstep as the phaeton drove away. The idea of the picnic was all absorbing.

The Colonel and his wife were to spend a week at Bournemouth. Ida would see them no more this year.

"You must come again next summer," Mrs. Wendover said heartily, as she kissed her daughter's friend.

"Of course she must," cried Horry. "She is coming every summer. She is one of the institutions of Kingthorpe. I only wonder how we ever managed to get on so long without her."

All that evening was devoted to the packing of hampers, and to general skirmishing. The picnic was to be held on the highest hill-top between Kingthorpe and Winchester, one of those little Lebanons, fair and green, on which the yew-trees flourished like the cedars of the East, but with a sturdy British air that was all their own.

The birthday dawned with the soft pearly gray and tender opal tints which presage a fair noontide. Before six o'clock the children had all besieged Bessie's door, with noisy tappings and louder congratulations. At seven, they were all seated at breakfast, the table strewn with birthday gifts, mostly of that useless and semi-idiotic character peculiar to such tributes—ormolu inkstands, holding a thimbleful of ink—penholders warranted to break before they have been used three times — purses with impossible snaps — photograph frames and pomatum-pots.

Bessie pretended to be enraptured with everything. The purse Horry gave her was "too lovely." Reginald's penholder was the very thing she had been wanting for an age. Dear little Eva's pomatum-pot was perfection. The point-lace handkerchief Ida had worked in secret was exquisite, Blanche's crochet slippers were so lovely that their not being big enough was hardly a fault. They were much too pretty to be worn. Urania

contributed a more costly gift, in the shape of a per-
fume cabinet, all cut-glass, walnut-wood, and ormolu.

"Urania's presents are always meant to crush one,"
said Blanche, disrespectfully; "they are like the shields
and bracelets those rude soldiers flung at poor Tar-
peia."

Urania was to be one of the picnic party. She
was to be the only stranger present. There had been
a disappointment about the two cousins. Neither Brian
had accepted the annual summons. One was supposed to be still in Norway, the other had neglected
to answer the letter which had been sent more than a
week ago to his address in Herefordshire.

"I'm afraid you'll find it dreadfully like our every-
day picnics," Bessie said to Ida, as they were starting.

"I shall be satisfied if it be half as pleasant."

"Ah, it would have been nice enough if the two
Brians had been with us. Brian Walford is so amusing."

"He would have sung comic songs, I suppose?"
said Ida, rather contemptuously.

"Oh, no; you must not suppose that he is always
singing comic songs. He is one of those versatile
people who can do anything."

"I don't want to be rude about your own flesh and
blood, Bess, but in a general way I detest versatile
people," said Ida.

"What a queer girl you are, Ida! I'm afraid you
have taken a dislike to Brian Walford," complained
Bessie.

"No," said Ida, deep in thought,—the two girls
were standing at the hall-door, waiting for the carriage,—"it is not that."

"You like the idea of the other Brian better?"

Ida's wild-rose bloom deepened to a rich carnation.

"Oh, Ida," cried Bessie; "do you remember what you said about marrying for money?"

"It was a revolting sentiment; but it was wrung from me by the infinite vexations of poverty."

"Wouldn't it be too lovely if Brian the Great were to fall in love with you, and ask you to be mistress of that dear old Abbey which you admire so much?"

"Don't be ecstatic, Bessie. I shall never be the mistress of the Abbey. I was not born under a propitious star. There must have been a very ugly concatenation of planets ruling the heavens at the hour of my birth. You see, Brian the Great does not even put himself in the way of falling captive to my charms."

This was said half in sport, half in bitterness—indeed, there was a bitter flavour in much of Ida Palliser's mirth. She was thinking of the stories she had read in which a woman had but to be young and lovely, and all creation bowed down to her. Yet her beauty had been for the most part a cause of vexation, and had made people hate her. She had been infinitely happy during the last six weeks; but embodied hatred had been close at hand in the presence of Miss Rylance; and if anyone had fallen in love with her during that time, it was the wrong person.

The young ladies were to go in the landau, leaving the exclusive enjoyment of Robin's variable humours to Horatio and the juveniles. There was a general idea that Robin, in conjunction with a hilly country, might be sooner or later fatal to the young Wendovers; but they went on driving him, nevertheless, as everybody knew that if he did ultimately prove disastrous

to them it would be with the best intentions and without loss of temper.

Bessie and Ida took their seats in the roomy carriage, Reginald mounted to the perch beside the coachman, and they drove triumphantly through the village
to the gate of Dr. Rylance's cottage, where Urania
stood waiting for them.

"I hope we haven't kept you long?" said Bessie.

"Not more than a quarter of an hour," answered
Urania, meekly; "but that seems rather long in a
broiling sun. You always have such insufferably hot
weather on your birthdays, Bessie."

"It will be cool enough on the hills by-and-by,"
said Bess, apologetically.

"I daresay there will be a cold wind," returned
Urania, who wore an unmistakable air of discontent.
"There generally is on these unnatural September days."

"One would think you bore a grudge against the
month of September because I was born in it," retorted
Bessie. And then, remembering her obligations, she
hastened to add, "How can I thank you sufficiently for
that exquisite scent-case? It is far too lovely."

"I am very glad you like it. One hardly knows
what to choose."

Miss Rylance had taken her seat in the landau by
this time, and they were bowling along the smooth
high road at that gentle jog-trot pace affected by a
country gentleman's coachman.

The day was heavenly; the wind due south; a day
on which life—mere sensual existence—is a delight.
The landscape still wore its richest summer beauty—
not a leaf had fallen. They were going upward, to
the hilly region between Kingthorpe and Winchester,

to a spot where there was a table-shaped edifice of stones, supposed to be of Druidic origin.

The young Wendovers were profoundly indifferent to the Druids, and to that hypothetical race who lived ages before the Druids, and have broken out all over the earth in stony excrescences, as yet vaguely classified. That three-legged granite table, whose origin was lost in the remoteness of past time, seemed to the young Wendovers a thing that had been created expressly for their amusement, to be climbed upon or crawled under as the fancy moved them. It was a capital rallying-point for a picnic or a gipsy tea-drinking.

"We are to have no grown-ups to-day," said Reginald, looking down from his place beside the coachman. "The pater and mater are away, and Aunt Betsy has a headache; so we can have things all our own way."

"You are mistaken, Reginald," said Urania; "my father is going to join us by-and-by. I hope he won't be considered an interloper. I told him that it was to be a young party, and that I was sure he would be in the way; but he wouldn't take my advice. He is going to ride over in the broiling sun. Very foolish, I think."

"I thought Dr. Rylance was in London?"

"He was till last night. He came down on purpose to be at your picnic."

"I am sure I feel honoured," said Bessie.

"Do you? I don't think *you* are the attraction," answered Urania, with a cantankerous glance at Miss Palliser.

Ida's dark eyes were looking far away across the hills. It seemed as if she neither heard Miss Rylance's speech nor saw the sneer which emphasized it.

Dr. Rylance's substantial hunter came plodding over the turfy ridge behind them five minutes afterwards, and presently he was riding at a measured trot beside the carriage door, congratulating Bessie on the beauty of the day, and saying civil things to every one.

"I could not resist the temptation to give myself a day's idleness in the Hampshire air," he said.

Reginald felt unutterably savage. What a trouble-feast the man was. They would have to adapt the proceedings of the day to his middle-aged good manners. There could be no wild revelry, no freedom. Dr. Rylance was an embodiment of propriety.

Half an hour after dinner they were all scattered upon the hills.

Reginald, who cherished a secret passion for Ida, which was considerably in advance of his years, and who had calculated upon being her guide, philosopher, and friend all through the day, found himself ousted by the West End physician, who took complete possession of Miss Palliser, under the pretence of explaining the history—altogether speculative—of the spot. He discoursed eloquently about the Druids, expatiated upon the City of Winchester, dozing in the sunshine yonder, among its fat water meadows. He talked of the Saxons and the Normans, of William of Wykeham, and his successors, until poor Ida felt sick and faint from very weariness. It was all very delightful talk, no doubt—the polished utterance of a man who read his *Saturday Review* and *Athenæum* diligently, saw an occasional number of *Fors Clavigera*, and even skimmed the more æsthetic papers in the *Architect;* but to Ida this expression of modern culture was all weariness. She would rather have been racing those wild young Wendovers down the slippery hill-side, on which they were perilling their necks; she would rather have been lying beside the lake in Kingthorpe Park, reading her well-thumbed Tennyson, or her shabby little Keats.

Her thoughts had wandered ever so far away when she was called back to the work-a-day world by finding that Dr. Rylance's conversation had suddenly slipped from archæology into a more personal tone.

"Are you really going away to-morrow?" he asked.

"Yes," answered Ida, sadly, looking at one of the last of the butterflies, whose brief summertide of existence was wearing to its close, like her own.

"You are going back to Mauleverer Manor?"

"Yes. I have another half-year of bondage. I am going back to drudgery and self-contempt, to be browbeaten by Miss Pew, and looked down upon by most of her pupils. The girls in my own class are very fond of me, but I'm afraid their fondness is half pity. The grown-up girls with happy homes and rich fathers despise me. I hardly wonder at it. Genteel poverty certainly is contemptible. There is nothing debasing in a smock-frock or a fustian jacket. The labourers I see about Kingthorpe have a glorious air of independence, and I daresay are as proud, in their way, as if they were dukes. But shabby finery—genteel gowns worn threadbare: there is a deep degradation in those."

"Not for you," answered Dr. Rylance, earnestly, with an admiring look in his blue-gray eyes. They were somewhat handsome eyes when they did not put on their cruel expression. "Not for you. Nothing could degrade, nothing could exalt you. You are superior to the accident of your surroundings."

"It's very kind of you to say that; but it's a fallacy, all the same," said Ida. "Do you think Napoleon at St. Helena, squabbling with Sir Hudson Lowe, is as dignified a figure as Napoleon at the Tuileries, in the zenith of his power? But I ought not to be grumbling at fate. I have been happy for six sunshiny weeks. If I were to live to be a century old, I could never forget how good people at Kingthorpe have been to me. I will go back to my old slavery, and live upon the memory of that happiness."

"Why should you go back to slavery?" asked Dr. Rylance, taking her hand in his and holding it with so strong a grasp that she could hardly have withdrawn it without violence. "There is a home at Kingthorpe ready to receive you. If you have been happy there in the last few weeks, why not try if you can be happy there always? There is a house in Cavendish Square whose master would be proud to make you its mistress. Ida, we have seen very little of each other, and I may be precipitate in hazarding this offer; but I am as fond of you as if I had known you half a lifetime, and I believe that I could make your life happy."

Ida Palliser's heart thrilled with a chill sense of horror and aversion. She had talked recklessly enough of her willingness to marry for money, and, lo! here was a prosperous man laying two handsomely furnished houses at her feet—a man of gentlemanlike bearing, good-looking, well-informed, well-spoken, with no signs of age in his well-preserved face and figure; a man whom any woman, friendless, portionless, a mere waif upon earth's surface, at the mercy of all the winds that blow, ought proudly and gladly to accept for her husband.

No, too bold had been her challenge to fate. She had said that she would marry any honest man who would lift her out of the quagmire of poverty: but she was not prepared to accept Dr. Rylance's offer, generous as it sounded. She would rather go back to the old treadmill, and her old fights with Miss Pew, than reign supreme over the dainty cottage at Kingthorpe and the house in Cavendish Square. Her time had not come.

Dr. Rylance had not risen to eloquence in making his offer; and Ida's reply was in plainest words.

"I am very sorry," she faltered. "I feel that it is very good of you to make such a proposal; but I cannot accept it."

"There is some one else," said the doctor. "Your heart is given away already."

"No," she answered sadly; "my heart is like an empty sepulchre."

"Then why should I not hope to win you? I have been hasty, no doubt: but I want if possible to prevent your return to that odious school. If you would but make me happy by saying yes, you could stay with your kind friends at The Knoll till the day that makes you mistress of my house. We might be married in time to spend November in Italy. It is the nicest month for Rome. You have never seen Italy, perhaps?"

"No. I have seen very little that is worth seeing."

"Ida, why will you not say yes? Do you doubt that I should try my uttermost to make you happy?"

"No," she answered gravely, "but I doubt my own capacity for that kind of happiness."

Dr. Rylance was deeply wounded. He had been petted and admired by women during the ten years of his widowhood, favoured and a favourite everywhere. He had made up his mind deliberately to marry this penniless girl. Looked at from a worldling's point of view, it would seem, at the first glance, an utterly disadvantageous alliance: but Dr. Rylance had an eye that could sweep over horizons other than are revealed to the average gaze, and he told himself that so lovely a woman as Ida Palliser must inevitably become the fashion in that particular society which Dr. Rylance most affected: and a wife famed for her beauty and elegance would assuredly be of more advantage to a fashionable physician than a common-place wife with a fortune. Dr. Rylance liked money; but he liked it only for what it could buy. He had no sons, and he was much too fond of himself to lead laborious days in order to leave a large fortune to his daughter. He had bought a lease of his London house, which would last his time; he had bought the freehold of the Kingthorpe cottage; and he was living up to his income. When he died there would be two houses of furniture, plate, pictures, horses and carriages, and the Kingthorpe cottage, to be realized for Urania. He estimated these roughly as worth between six and seven thousand pounds, and he considered seven thousand pounds an ample fortune for his only daughter. Urania was in happy ignorance of the modesty of his views. She imagined herself an heiress on a much larger scale.

To offer himself to a penniless girl, of whose belongings he knew absolutely nothing, and to be peremptorily refused! Dr. Rylance could hardly believe such a thing possible. The girl must be trifling with him, playing her fish, with the fixed intention of landing him presently. It was in the nature of girls to do that kind of thing. "Why do you reject me?" he asked seriously; "is it because I am old enough to be your father?"

"No, I would marry a man old enough to be my grandfather if I loved him," answered Ida, with cruel candour.

"And I am to understand that your refusal is irrevocable?" he urged.

"Quite irrevocable. But I hope you believe that I am grateful for the honour you have done me."

"That is the correct thing to say upon such occasions," answered Dr. Rylance, coldly; "I wonder the sentence is not written in your copybooks, among those moral aphorisms which are of so little use in after life."

"The phrase may seem conventional, but in my case it means much more than usual," said Ida; "a girl who has neither money nor friends has good reason to be grateful when a gentleman asks her to be his wife."

"I wish I could be grateful for your gratitude," said Dr. Rylance, "but I can't. I want your love, and nothing else. Is it on Urania's account that you reject me?" he urged. "If you think that she would be a hindrance to your happiness, pray dismiss the thought. If she did not accommodate herself pleasantly to my choice her life would have to be spent apart from us. I would brook no rebellion."

The cruel look had come into Dr. Rylance's eyes. He was desperately angry. He was surprised, humiliated, indignant. Never had the possibility of rejection occurred to him. It had been for him to decide whether he would or would not take this girl for his wife; and after due consideration of her merits and all surrounding circumstances, he had decided that he would take her.

"Is my daughter the stumbling-block?" he urged.

"No," she answered, "there is no stumbling-block. I would marry you to-morrow, if I felt that I could love you as a wife ought to love her husband. I said once—only a little while ago—that I would marry for money. I find that I am not so base as I thought myself."

"Perhaps the temptation is not large enough," said Dr. Rylance. "If I had been Brian Wendover, and the owner of Kingthorpe Abbey, you would hardly have rejected me so lightly."

Ida crimsoned to the roots of her hair. The shaft went home. It was as if Dr. Rylance had been inside her mind and knew all the foolish day-dreams she had dreamed in the idle summer afternoons, under the spreading cedar-branches, or beside the lake in the Abbey grounds. Before she had time to express her resentment a cluster of young Wendovers came sweeping down the greensward at her side, and in the next minute Blanche was hanging upon her bodily, like a lusty parasite strangling a slim young tree.

"Darling," cried Blanche gaspingly, "such news. Brian has come—cousin Brian—after all, though he thought he couldn't. But he made a great effort, and he has come all the way, as fast as he could tear, to be here on Bessie's birthday. Isn't it too jolly?"

"All the way from Norway?" asked Ida.

"Yes," said Urania, who had been carried down the hill with the torrent of Wendovers, "all the way from Norway. Isn't it nice of him?"

Blanche's frank face was brimming over with smiles. The boys were all laughing. How happy Brian's coming had made them!

Ida looked at them wonderingly.

"How pleased you all seem!" she said. "I did not know you were so fond of your cousin. I thought it was the other you liked."

"Oh, we like them both," cried Blanche, "and it is so nice of Brian to come on purpose for Bessie's birthday. Do come and see him. He is on the top of the hill, talking to Bess; and the kettle boils, and we are just going to have tea. We are all starving."

"After such a dinner!" exclaimed Ida.

"Such a dinner, indeed!—two or three legs of fowls and a plate or so of pie!" ejaculated Reginald, contemptuously. "I began to be hungry a quarter of an hour afterwards. Come and see Brian."

Ida looked round her wonderingly, feeling as if she was in a dream.

Dr. Rylance had disappeared. Urania was smiling at her sweetly, more sweetly than it was her wont to smile at Ida Palliser.

"One would think she knew that I had refused her father," mused Ida.

They all climbed the hill, the children talking perpetually, Ida unusually silent. The smoke of a gipsy fire was going up from a hollow near the Druid altar, and two figures were standing beside the altar; one, a young man, with his arm resting on the granite slab, and his head bent as he talked, with seeming earnestness, to Bessie Wendover. He turned as the crowd approached, and Bessie introduced him to Miss Palliser. "My cousin Brian—my dearest friend Ida," she said.

"She is desperately fond of the Abbey," said Blanche; "so I hope she will like you. "Love me, love my dog," says the proverb, so I suppose one might say, 'Love my house, love me.'"

Ida stood silent amidst her loquacious friends, looking at the stranger with a touch of wonder. No, this was not the image which she had pictured to herself. Mr. Wendover was very good-looking—interesting even; he had the kind of face which women call nice —a pale complexion, dreamy gray eyes, thin lips, a well-shaped nose, a fairly intellectual forehead. But the Brian of her fancies was a man of firmer mould, larger features, a more resolute air, an eye with more fire, a brow marked by stronger lines. For some unknown reason she had fancied the master of the Abbey like that Sir Tristram Wendover who had been so loyal a subject and so brave a soldier, and before whose portrait she had so often lingered in dreamy contemplation.

"And you have really come all the way from Norway to be at Bessie's picnic?" she faltered at last, feeling that she was expected to say something.

"I would have come a longer distance for the sake of such a pleasant meeting," he answered, smiling at her.

"Bessie," cried Blanche, who had been grovelling on her knees before the gipsy fire, "the kettle will go off the boil if you don't make tea instantly. If it were not your birthday I should make it myself."

"You may," said Bessie, "although it is my birthday."

She had walked a little way apart with Urania, and they two were talking somewhat earnestly.

"Those girls seem to be plotting something," said

Reginald; "a charade for to-night, perhaps. It's sure
to be stupid if Urania's in it."

"You mean that it will be too clever," said Horatio.

"Yes, that kind of cleverness which is the essence
of stupidity."

While Bessie and Miss Rylance conversed apart,
and all the younger Wendovers devoted their energies
to the preparation of a tremendous meal, Ida and Brian
Wendover stood face to face upon the breezy hill-top,
the girl sorely embarrassed, the young man gazing at
her as if he had never seen anything so lovely in his
life.

"I have heard so much about you from Bessie," he
said after a silence which seemed long to both. "Her
letters for the last twelve months have been a perpetual pæan—like one of the Homeric hymns with you
for the heroine. I had quite a dread of meeting you,
feeling that, after having my expectations strung up to
such a pitch, I must be disappointed. Nothing human
could justify Bessie's enthusiasm."

"Please don't talk about it. Bessie's one weak point
is her affection for me. I am very grateful. I love
her dearly, but she does her best to make me ridiculous."

"I am beginning to think Bessie a very sensible
girl," said Brian, longing to say much more; so deeply
was he impressed by this goddess in a holland gown,
with glorious eyes shining upon him under the shadow
of a coarse straw hat.

"Have you come back to Hampshire for good?"
asked Ida, as they strolled towards Bessie and Urania.

"For good? No, I never stay long."

"What a pity that lovely old Abbey should be deserted!"

"Yes, it is rather a shame, is it not? But then no one could expect a young man to live there except in the hunting season—or for the sake of the shooting."

"Could anyone ever grow tired of such a place?" asked Ida.

She was wondering at the young man's indifferent air, as if that solemn abbey, those romantic gardens, were of no account to him. She supposed that this was in the nature of things. A man born lord of such an elysium would set little value upon his paradise. Was it not Eve's weariness of Eden which inclined her ear to the serpent?

And now the banquet was spread upon the short smooth turf, and everybody was ordered to sit down. They made a merry circle, with the tea-kettle in the centre, piles of cake, and bread and butter, and jam-pots surrounding it. Blanche and Horatio were the chief officiators, and were tremendously busy ministering to the wants of others, while they satisfied their own hunger and thirst hurriedly between whiles. The damsel sat on the grass with a big crockery teapot in her lap, while her brother watched and managed the kettle, and ran to and fro with cups and saucers. Bessie, as the guest of honour, was commanded to sit still and look on.

"Dreadfully babyish, isn't it?" said Urania, smiling with her superior air at Brian, who had helped himself to a crust of home-made bread, and a liberal supply of gooseberry jam.

"Uncommonly jolly," he answered gaily. "I confess to a weakness for bread and jam. I wish people always gave it at afternoon teas."

"Has it not a slight flavour of the nursery?"

"Of course it has. But a nursery picnic is ever so much better than a swell garden-party, and bread and jam is a great deal more wholesome than salmon-mayonaise and Strasbourg pie. You may despise me as much as you like, Miss Rylance. I came here determined to enjoy myself."

"That is the right spirit for a picnic," said Ida. "People with grand ideas are not wanted."

"And I suppose in the evening you will join in the dumb charades, and play hide-and-seek in the garden, all among spiders and cockchafers."

"I will do anything I am told to do," answered Brian, cheerily. "But I think the season of the cockchafer is over."

"What has become of Dr. Rylance?" asked Bessie, looking about her as if she had only that moment missed him.

"I think he went back to the farm for his horse," said Urania. "I suppose he found our juvenile sports rather depressing."

"Well, he paid us a compliment in coming at all," answered Bessie, "so we must forgive him for getting tired of us."

The drive home was very merry, albeit Bessie and her friend were to part next morning—Ida to go back to slavery. They were both young enough to be able to enjoy the present hour, even on the edge of darkness.

Bessie clasped her friend's hand as they sat side by side in the landau.

"You must come to us at Christmas," she whispered: "I shall ask mother to invite you."

Brian was full of talk and gaiety as they drove

home through the dusk. He was very different from that ideal Brian of Ida's girlish fancy—the Brian who embodied all her favourite attributes, and had all the finest qualities of the hero of romance. But he was an agreeable, well-bred young man, bringing with him that knowledge of life and the active world, which made his talk seem new and enlightening after the strictly local and domestic intellects of the good people with whom she had been living.

With the family at The Knoll conversation had been bounded by Winchester on one side, and Romsey on the other. There was an agreeable freshness in the society of a young man who could talk of all that was newest in European art and literature, and who knew how the world was being governed.

But this fund of information was hinted at rather than expressed. To-night Mr. Wendover seemed most inclined to mere nonsense talk—the lively nothings that please children. Of himself and his Norwegian adventures he said hardly anything.

"I suppose when a man has travelled so much he gets to look upon strange countries as a matter of course," speculated Ida. "If I had just come from Norway, I should talk of nothing else."

The dumb-charades and hide-and-seek were played, but only by the lower orders, as Bessie called her younger brothers and sisters.

Ida strolled in the moonlit garden with Mr. Wendover, Bessia, Urania, and Mr. Ratcliffe, a very juvenile curate, who was Bessie's admirer and slave. Urania had no particular admirer. She felt that every one at King-thorpe must needs behold her with mute worship; but there was no one so audacious as to give expression to the feeling; no one of sufficient importance to be favoured with her smiles. She looked forward to her first season in London next year, and then she would be called upon to make her selection.

"She is worldly to the tips of her fingers," said Ida, as she and Bessie talked apart from the others for a few minutes: "I wonder she does not try to captivate your cousin."

"What, Brian? Oh, he is not at all in her line. He would not suit her a bit."

"But don't you think it would suit her to be mistress of the Abbey?"

Bessie gave a little start, as if the idea were new.

"I don't think she has ever thought of him in that light," she said.

"Don't you? If she hasn't, she is not the girl I think her."

"Oh, I know she is very worldly; but I don't think she's so bad as that."

"Not so bad as to be capable of marrying for money —no, I suppose not," said Ida, thoughtfully.

"I am sure you would not, darling," said Bessie. "You talked about it once, when you were feeling bitter; but I know that in your heart of hearts you never meant it. You are much too high-minded."

"I am not a bit high-minded. All my high-mindedness—if I ever had any—has been squeezed out of me by poverty. My only idea is to escape from subjection and humiliation—a degrading bondage to vulgar-minded people."

"But would the escape be worth having at the cost of your own degradation?" urged Bessie, who felt particularly heroic this evening, exalted by the moonlight, the loveliness of the garden, the thought of parting with her dearest friend. "Marry for love, dearest. Sacrifice everything in this world rather than be false to yourself."

"You dear little enthusiast, I may never be asked to make any such sacrifice. I have not much chance of suitors at Mauleverer, as you know—and as for falling in love——"

"Oh, you never know when the fatal moment may come. How do you like Brian?"

"He is very gentlemanlike; he seems very well informed."

"He is immensely clever," answered Bessie, almost offended at this languid praise; "he is a man who might succeed in any line he chose for himself. Do you think him handsome?"

"He is certainly nice looking."

"How cool you are! I had set my heart upon your liking him."

"What could come of my liking?" asked Ida, with a touch of bitterness. "Is there a portionless girl in all England who would not like the master of Wendover Abbey?"

"But for his own sake," urged Bessie, with a vexed air; "surely he is worthy of being liked for his own sake, without a thought of the Abbey."

"I cannot dissociate him from that lovely old house and gardens. Indeed, to my mind he rather belongs to the Abbey than the Abbey belongs to him. You see I knew the Abbey first."

Here they were interrupted by Brian and Urania, and presently Ida found herself walking in the moonlight in a broad avenue of standard roses, at the end

of the garden, with Mr. Wendover by her side, and
the voices of the other three sounding ever so far
away.   On the other side of a low quickset hedge
stretched a wide expanse of level meadow land, while
in the farther distance rose the Wiltshire hills, and
nearer the heathy highlands of the New Forest.   The
lamp-lit windows of Miss Wendover's cottage glimmered
a little way off, across gardens and meadows.

"And so you are really going to leave us to-morrow
morning?" said Brian regretfully.

"By the eight o'clock train from Winchester.   To-
morrow evening I shall be sitting on a form in a big
bare class-room, listening to the babble of a lot of
girls pretending to learn their lessons."

"Are you fond of teaching?"

"Just imagine to yourself the one occupation which
is most odious to you, and then you may know how
fond I am of teaching; and of school-girls; and of
school-life altogether."

"It is very hard that you should have to pursue
such an uncongenial career."

"It seems so to me; but, perhaps, that is my selfishness.   I suppose half the people in this world have to
live by work they hate."

"Allowing for the number of people to whom all
kind of work is hateful, I daresay you are right.   But
I think, in a general way, congenial work means successful work.   No man hates the profession that brings
him fame and money; but the doctor without patients,
the briefless barrister, can hardly love law or medicine."

He beguiled Ida into talking of her own life, with
all its bitterness.   There was something in his voice

and manner which tempted her to confide in him. He seemed thoroughly sympathetic.

"I keep forgetting what strangers we are," she said, apologizing for her unreserve.

"We are not strangers. I have heard of you from Bessie so much that I seem to have known you for years. I hope you will never think of me as a stranger."

"I don't think I ever can, after this conversation. I'm afraid you will think me horribly egotistical."

She had been talking of her father and step-mother, the little brother she loved so fondly, dwelling with delight upon his perfections.

"I think you all that is good and noble. How I wish this were not your last evening at The Knoll!"

"Do you think I do not wish it? Hark, there's Bessie calling us."

They went back to the house, and to the drawing-room, which wore quite a festive appearance, in honour of Bessie's birthday; ever so many extra candles dotted about, and a table laid with fruit and sandwiches, cake and claret-cup, the children evidently considering a superfluity of meals indispensable to a happy birth-day. Blanche and her juniors were sitting about the room, in the last stage of exhaustion after hide-and-seek.

"This has been a capital birthday," said Horatio, wiping the perspiration from his brow, and then filling for himself a bumper of claret-cup; "and now we are going to dance. Blanche, give us the Faust waltz, and go on playing till we tell you to leave off."

Blanche, considerably blown, and with her hair like a mop, sat down and began to touch the piano with resolute fingers and forcible rhythm. ONE, two, three,

ONE, two, three. The boys pushed the furniture into the corners. Brian offered himself to Ida; Bessie insisted upon surrendering the curate to Urania, and took one of her brothers for a partner; and the three couples went gliding round the pretty old room, the cool night breezes blowing in upon them from wide-open windows.

They danced and played, and sang and talked, till midnight chimed from the old eight-day clock in the hall,—a sound which struck almost as much consternation to Bessie's soul as if she had been Cinderella at the royal ball.

"TWELVE O'CLOCK! and the little ones all up!" she exclaimed, looking round the circle of towzled heads with remorseful eyes. "What would mother say? And she told me she relied on my discretion! Go to bed, every one of you, this instant!"

"Oh, come now," remonstrated Blanche, "there's no use in hustling us off like that, after letting us sit up hours after our proper time. I'm going to have another sandwich; and there's not a bit of good in leaving all those raspberry tarts. The servants won't thank us. *They* have as many jam tarts as they like."

"You greedy little wretches, you have been doing nothing but eat all day," said Ida. "When I am back at Mauleverer I shall remember you only as machines for the consumption of pudding and jam. Obey your grown-up sister, and go to bed directly."

"Grown-up, indeed! How long has she been grown-up, I should like to know?" exclaimed Blanche vindictively. "She's only an inch and a quarter taller than me, and she's a mere dumpling compared with Horry."

The lower orders were got rid off somehow—driven to their quarters, as it were, at the point of the bayonet; and then the grown-ups bade each other good night; the curate escorting Miss Rylance to her home, and Brian going up to the top floor to a bachelor's room.

"Who is going to drive Miss Palliser to the station?" he asked, as they stood, candlestick in hand, at the foot of the stairs.

"I am, of course," answered Reginald. "Robin will spin us over the hills in no time. I've ordered the car for seven sharp."

There was very little sleep for either Bessie or her guest that night. Both girls were excited by memories of the day that was past, and by thoughts of the day that was coming. Ida was brooding a little upon her disappointment in Brian Wendover. He had very pleasant manners, he seemed soft-hearted and sympathetic, he was very good-looking—but he was not the Brian of her dreams. That ideal personage had never existed outside her imagination. It was a shock to her girlish fancy. There was a sense of loss in her mind.

"I must be very silly," she told herself, "to make a fancy picture of a person, and to be vexed with him because he does not resemble my portrait."

She was disappointed, and yet she was interested in this new acquaintance. He was the first really interesting young man she had ever met, and he was evidently interested in her. And then she pictured him at the Abbey, in the splendid solitude of those fine old rooms, leading the calm studious life which Bessie had talked of—an altogether enviable life, Ida thought.

Mr. Wendover was in the dining-room at half-past six when the two girls went down to breakfast. All the others came trooping down a few minutes afterwards, Reginald got up to the last degree of four-in-handishness which the resources of his wardrobe allowed, and with a flower in his buttonhole. There was a loud cry for eggs and bacon, kippered herrings, marmalade, Yorkshire cakes; but neither Ida nor Bessie could eat.

"Do have a good breakfast," pleaded Blanche affectionately; "you will be having bread and scrape tomorrow. We have got a nice hamper for you, with a cake and a lot of jam puffs and things; but those will only last a short time."

"You dear child, I wouldn't mind the bread and scrape if there were only a little love to flavour it," answered Ida softly.

The jaunting-car came to the door as the clock struck seven. Ida's luggage was securely bestowed, then, after a perfect convulsion of kissing, she was handed to her place, Reginald jumped into his seat and took the reins, and Brian seated himself beside Ida.

"You are not going with them?" exclaimed Bessie.

"Yes, I am, to see that Miss Palliser is not spilt on the hills."

"What rot!" cried Reginald. "I should be rather sorry for myself if I were not able to manage Robin."

"This is a new development in you, who are generally the laziest of living creatures," said Bessie to Brian, and before he could reply, Robin was bounding cheerily through the village, making very little account of the jaunting-car and its occupants. Urania

was at her garden gate, fresh and elegant-looking in
pale blue cambric. She smiled at Ida, and waved
her a most gracious farewell.

"I don't think I ever saw Miss Rylance look so
amiable," said Ida. "She does not often favour me
with her smiles."

"Are you enemies?" asked Brian.

"Not open foes; we have always maintained an
armed neutrality. I don't like her, and she doesn't
like me, and we both know it. But perhaps I ought
not to be so candid. She may be a favourite of yours."

"She might be, but she is not. She is very elegant,
very lady-like—according to her own lights—very
viperish."

It was a lovely drive in the crisp clear air, across
the breezy hills. Ida could not help enjoying the
freshness of morning, the beauty of earth; albeit she
was going from comfort to discomfort, from love to
cold indifference or open enmity.

"How I delight in this landscape!" she exclaimed.
"Is it not ever so much better than Norway?" appeal-
ing to Brian.

"It is a milder, smaller kind of beauty," he answered. "Would you not like to see Norway?"

"I would like to see all that is lovely on earth;
yet I think I could be content to spend a lifetime
here. This must seem strange to you, who grow
weary of that beautiful Abbey."

"It is not of his house, but of himself, that a man
grows weary," answered Brian.

Robin was in a vivacious humour, and rattled the
car across the hills at a good pace. They had a
quarter of an hour to wait at the busy little station.

Brian and Ida walked up and down the platform talking, while Reginald looked after the pony and the luggage. They found so much to say to each other, that the train seemed to come too soon.

They bade each other good-bye with a tender look on Brian's part, a blush on Ida's. Reginald had to push his cousin away from the carriage window, in order to get a word with the departing guest.

"We shall all miss you awfully," he said; "but mind, you must come back at Christmas."

"I shall be only too glad, if Mrs. Wendover will have me. Good-bye."

The train moved slowly forward, and she was gone.

"Isn't she a stunner?" asked Reginald of his cousin, as they stood on the platform looking at each other blankly.

"She is the handsomest girl I ever saw, and out and away the nicest," answered Brian.

CHAPTER VII.

IN THE RIVER-MEADOW.

THE old hackneyed round of daily life at Mauleverer Manor seemed just a little worse to Ida Palliser after that happy break of six weeks' pure and perfect enjoyment. Miss Pew was no less exacting than of old. Miss Pillby, for whose orphaned and friendless existence there had been no such thing as a holiday, and who had spent the vacation at Mauleverer diligently employed in mending the house-linen, resented Ida's visit to The Knoll as if it were a personal injury, and vented her envy in sneers and innuendoes of the coarsest character.

"If *I* were to spoon upon one of the rich pupils, I dare say *I* could get invited out for the holidays," she said, *à propos* to nothing particular; "but I am thankful to say I am above such meanness."

"I never laid myself under an obligation I didn't feel myself able to return," said Miss Motley, the English governess, who had spent her holidays amidst the rank and fashion of Margate. "When I go to the sea-side with my sister and her family, I pay my own expenses, and I feel I've a right to be made comfortable."

Miss Pillby, who had flattered and toadied every well-to-do pupil, and laboured desperately to wind herself into the affections of Bessie Wendover, that warm-hearted young person seeming particularly accessible to flattery, felt herself absolutely injured by the kindness that had been lavished upon Ida. She drank in with greedy ears Miss Palliser's description of The Knoll and its occupants—the picnics, carpet-dances, afternoon teas; and the thought that all these enjoyments and festivities, the good things to eat and drink, the pleasant society, ought to have been hers instead of Ida's, was wormwood.

"When I think of my kindness to Bessie Wendover," she said to Miss Motley, in the confidence of that one quiet hour which belonged to the mistresses after the pupils' curfew-bell had rung youth and hope and gaiety into retirement, "when I think of the mustard poultices I have put upon her chest, and the bronchial troches I have given her when she had the slightest touch of cold or cough, I am positively appalled at the ingratitude of the human race."

"I don't think she likes bronchial troches," said

Miss Motley, a very matter-of-fact young person who saved money, wore thick boots, and was never unprovided with an umbrella; "I have seen her throw them away directly after you gave them to her."

"She ought to have liked them," exclaimed Miss Pillby, sternly. "They are very expensive."

"No doubt she appreciated your kindness," said Miss Motley, absently, being just then absorbed in an abstruse calculation as to how many yards of merino would be required for her winter gown.

"No, she did not," said Miss Pillby. "If she had been grateful she would have invited me to her home. I should not have gone, but the act would have given me a higher idea of her character."

"Well, she is gone, and we needn't trouble ourselves any more about her," retorted Miss Motley, who hated to be plagued about abstract questions, being a young woman of an essentially concrete nature, born to consume and digest three meals a day, and having no views that go beyond that function.

Miss Pillby sighed at finding herself in communion with so coarse a nature.

"I don't easily get over a blow of that sort," she said, "I am too tender-hearted."

"So you are," acquiesced Miss Motley. "It doesn't pay in a big boarding-school, however it may answer in private families."

Ida, having lost her chief friend and companion, Bessie Wendover, found life at Mauleverer Manor passing lonely. She even missed the excitement of her little skirmishes, her passages-at-arms, with Urania Rylance, in which she had generally got the best of the argument. There had been life and emotion in

these touch-and-go speeches, covert sneers, quick re-
torts, innuendoes met and flung back in the very face
of the sneerer. Now there was nothing but dull,
dead monotony. Many of the old pupils had departed, and many new pupils had come, daughters of
well-to-do parents, prosperous, well-dressed, talking
largely of the gaieties enjoyed by their elder sisters,
of the wonderful things done by their brothers at
Oxford or Cambridge, and of the grand things which
were to happen two or three years hence, when they
themselves should be "out." Ida took no interest in
their prattle. It was so apt to sting her with the re-
minder of her own poverty, the life of drudgery and
dependence that was to be her portion till the end of
her days. She did not, in the Mauleverer phraseology,
"take to" the new girls. She left them to be courted
by Miss Pillby, and petted by Miss Dulcibella. She
felt as lonely as one who has outlived her generation.

Happily the younger girls in the class which she
taught were fond of her, and when she wanted company she let these juveniles cluster round her in her
garden rambles; but in a general way she preferred
loneliness, and to work at the cracked old piano in
the room where she slept. Beethoven and Chopin,
Mozart and Mendelssohn were companions of whom
she never grew weary.

So the slow days wore on till nearly the end of
the month, and on one cool, misty, afternoon, when
the river flowed sluggishly under a dull gray sky she
walked alone along that allotted extent of the river-
side path which the mistresses and pupil-teachers were
allowed to promenade without *surveillance*. This river
walk skirted a meadow which was in Miss Pew's oc-

cupation, and ranked as a part of the Mauleverer
grounds, although it was divided by the high road
from the garden proper.

A green paling, and a little green gate, always
padlocked, secured this meadow from intrusion on the
road-side, but it was open to the river. To be en-
trusted with the key of this pastoral retreat was a privilege
only accorded to governesses and pupil-teachers.

It was supposed by Miss Pew that no young person
in her employment would be capable of walking quite
alone, where it was within the range of possibility
that her solitude might be intruded upon by an unknown member of the opposite sex. She trusted, as
she said afterwards, in the refined feeling of any person brought into association with her, and, until rudely
awakened by facts, she never would have stooped from
the lofty pinnacle of her own purity to suspect the
evil consequences which arose from the liberty too
generously accorded to her dependents.

Ida detested Miss Pillby and despised Miss Motley;
and the greatest relief she knew to the dismal monotony of her days was a lonely walk by the river, with
a shabby Wordsworth or a battered little volume of
Shelley's minor poems for her companions. She possessed so few books that it was only natural for
her to read those she had until love ripened with
familiarity.

On this autumnal afternoon she walked with slow
steps, while the river went murmuring by and now and
then a boat drifted lazily down the stream. The boating season was over for the most part—the season of
picnics and beanfeasts, and cockney holiday-making,
and noisy revelry, smart young women, young men in

white flannels, with bare arms and sunburnt noses. It was the dull blank time when everybody who could afford to wander far from this suburban paradise, was away upon his and her travels. Only parsons, doctors, schoolmistresses, and poverty stayed at home. Yet now and then a youth in boating costume glided by, his shoulders bending slowly to the lazy dip of his oars, his keel now and then making a rushing sound among long trailing weeds.

Such a youth presently came creeping along the bank, almost at Ida's feet, but passed her unseen. Her heavy lids were drooping, her eyes intent upon the familiar page. The young man looked up at her with keen gray eyes, recognised her, and pushed his boat in among the rushes by the bank, moored it to a pollard willow, and with light footstep leaped on shore.

He landed a few yards in the rear of Ida's slowly moving figure, followed softly, came close behind her, and read aloud across her shoulder.

> "'There was a Power in this sweet place,
> An Eve in this garden; a ruling grace
> Which to the flowers, did they waken or dream,
> Was as God is to the starry scheme.'"

Ida looked round, first indignant, then laughing.

"How you startled me!" she exclaimed; "I thought you were some horrid, impertinent stranger; and yet the voice had a familiar sound. How are they all at The Knoll? It is nearly a fortnight since Bessie wrote to me. If she only knew how I hunger for her letters."

"Very sweet of you," answered Mr. Wendover, holding the girl's hand with a lingering pressure, releasing it reluctantly when her rising colour told him it would be insolent to keep it longer.

How those large dark eyes beamed with pleasure at seeing him! Was it for his own sake, or for love of her friends at Kingthorpe? The smile was perhaps too frank to be flattering.

"Very sweet of you to care so much for Bessie's girlish epistles," he said lazily; "they are full of affection, but the style of composition always recalls our dear Mrs. Nickleby. 'Aunt Betsy was asking after you the other day: and that reminds me that the last litter of black Hampshires was sixteen—the largest number father ever remembers having. The vicar and his wife are coming to dinner on Tuesday, and do tell me if this new picture that everybody is talking about is really better than the Derby Day,' and that sort of thing. Not a very consecutive style, don't you know."

"Every word is interesting to me," said Ida, with a look that told him she was not one of those young ladies who enjoy a little good-natured ridicule of their nearest and dearest. "Is it long since you left Kingthorpe?"

"Not four-and-twenty hours. I promised Bessie that my very first occupation on coming to London should be to make my way down here to see you, in order that I may tell her faithfully and truly whether you are well and happy. She has a lurking conviction that you are unable to live without her, that you will incontinently go into a galloping consumption, and keep the fact concealed from all your friends until they receive a telegram summoning them to your death-bed. I know that is the picture Bessie's sentimental fancies have depicted."

"I did not think Bessie was so morbid," said Ida, laughing. "No, I am not one of those whom the gods

love. I am made of very tough material, or I should
hardly have lived till now. I see before me a per-
spective of lonely, loveless old age—finishing in a
governess's almshouse. I hope there are almshouses
for governesses."

"Nobody will pity your loneliness or lovelessness,"
retorted Brian, "for they will both be your own fault."

She blushed, looking dreamily across the dark-gray
river to the level shores beyond—the low meadows—
gentle hills in the back-ground—the wooded slopes of
Weybridge and Chertsey. If this speaker, whose voice
dropped to so tender a tone, had been like the Brian
of her imaginings—if he had looked at her with the
dark eyes of Sir Tristram's picture, how differently his
speech would have affected her! As it was, she
listened with airy indifference, only blushing girlishly
at his compliment, and wondering a little if he really
admired her—he the owner of that glorious old Abbey
—the wealthy head of the house of Wendover—the
golden fish for whom so many pretty fishers must have
angled in days gone by.

"Did you stay at The Knoll all the time," she inquired, her thoughts having flown back to Kingthorpe;
"or at the Abbey?"

"At The Knoll. It is ever so much livelier, and
my cousins like to have me with them."

"Naturally. But I wonder you did not prefer living in that lovely old house of yours. To occupy it
must seem like living in the middle ages."·

"Uncommonly. One is twelve miles from a station,
and four from post-office, butcher, and baker. Very
like the middle ages. There is no gas even in the
offices, and there are as many rats behind the wain-

scot as there were Israelites in Egypt. All the rooms are draughty and some are damp. No servant who has not been born and bred on the estate will stay more than six months. There is a deficient water supply in dry summers, and there are three distinct ghosts all the year round. Extremely like the middle ages."

"I would not mind ghosts, rats, anything, if it were my house," exclaimed Ida, enthusiastically. "The house is a poem."

"Perhaps; but it is not a house; in the modern sense of the word, that is to say, which implies comfort and convenience."

Ida sighed, deeply disgusted at this want of appreciation of the romantic spot where she had dreamed away more than one happy summer noontide, while the Wendover children played hide-and-seek in the overgrown old shrubberies.

No doubt life was always thus. The people to whom blind fortune gave such blessings were unable to appreciate them, and only the hungry outsiders could imagine the delight of possession.

"Are you living in London now?" she asked, as Mr. Wendover lingered at her side, and seemed to expect the conversation to be continued indefinitely.

His boat was safe enough, moving gently up and down among the rushes, with the gentle flow of the tide. Ida looked at it longingly, thinking how sweet it would be to step into it and let it carry her—— any whither, so long as it was away from Mauleverer Manor.

"Yes, I am in London for the present."

"But not for long, I suppose."

"I hardly know. I have no plans. I won't say with Romeo that I am fortune's fool—but I am fortune's shuttlecock; and I suppose that means pretty much the same."

"It was very kind of you to come to see me," said Ida.

"Kind to myself, for in coming I indulged the dearest wish of my soul," said the young man, looking at her with eyes whose meaning even her inexperience could not misread.

"Please don't pay me compliments," she said, hastily, "or I shall feel very sorry you came. And now I must hurry back to the house—the tea-bell will ring in a few minutes. Please tell Bessie I am very well, and only longing for one of her dear letters. Good-bye."

She made him a little curtsey, and would have gone without shaking hands, but he caught her hand and detained her in spite of herself.

"Don't be angry," he pleaded; "don't look at me with such cold, proud eyes. Is it an offence to admire, to love you too quickly? If it is, I have sinned deeply, and am past hope of pardon. Must one serve an apprenticeship to mere formal acquaintance first, then rise step by step to privileged friendship, before one dares to utter the sweet word love? Remember, at least, that I am your dearest friend's first cousin, and ought not to appear to you as a stranger."

"I can remember nothing when you talk so wildly," said Ida, crimson to the roots of her hair. Never before had a young lover talked to her of love. "Pray let me go. Miss Pew will be angry if I am not at tea."

"To think that such a creature as you should be under the control of any such harpy," exclaimed Brian. "Well, if I must go, at least tell me I am forgiven, and that I may exist upon the hope of seeing you again. I suppose if I were to come to the 'hall-door, and send in my card, I should not be allowed to see you?"

"Certainly not. Not if you were my own cousin instead of Bessie's. Good-bye."

"Then I shall happen to be going by in my boat every afternoon for the next month or so. There is a dear good soul at the lock who lets lodgings. I shall take up my abode there."

"Please never land on this pathway again," said Ida earnestly. "Miss Pew would be horribly angry if she heard I had spoken to you. And now I must go."

She withdrew her hand from his grasp, and ran off across the meadow, light-footed as Atalanta. Her heart was beating wildly, beating furiously, when she flew up to her room to take off her hat and jacket and smooth her disordered hair. Never before had any man, except middle-aged Dr. Rylance, talked to her of love: and that this man of all others, this man, sole master of the old mansion she so intensely admired, her friend's kinsman, owner of a good old Saxon name; this man, who could lift her in a moment from poverty to wealth, from obscurity to place and station; that this man should look at her with admiring eyes, and breathe impassioned words into her ear, was enough to set her heart beating tumultuously, to bring hot blushes to her cheeks. It was too wild a dream.

True, that for the man himself, considered apart from his belongings, his name and race, she cared not at all. But just now, in this tumult of excited feeling, she was disposed to confuse the man with his sur- roundings—to think of him, not as that young man with gray eyes and thin lips, who had walked with her at The Knoll, who had stood beside her just now by the river, but as the living embodiment of fortune, pride, delight.

Perhaps the vision really dominant in her mind was the thought of herself as mistress of the Abbey, herself as living for ever among the people she loved, amidst those breezy Hampshire hills, in the odour of pine-woods—rich, important, honoured, and beloved, doing good to all who came within the limit of her life. Yes, that was a glorious vision, and its reflected light shone upon Brian Wendover, and in somewise glorified him.

She went down to tea with such a triumphant light in her eyes that the smaller pupils who sat at her end of the table, so as to be under her *surveillance* during the meal, exclaimed at her beauty.

"What a colour you've got, Miss Palliser!" said Lucy Dobbs, "and how your eyes sparkle! You look as if you'd just had a hamper."

"I'm not quite so greedy as you, Lucy," retorted Ida; "I don't think a hamper would make my eyes sparkle, even if there were anybody to send me one."

"But there is somebody to send you one," argued Lucy, with her mouth full of bread and butter; "your father isn't dead?"

"No."

"Then he might send you a hamper."

"He might, if he lived within easy reach of Mauleverer Manor," replied Ida; "but as he lives in France——"

"He could send a post-office order to a confectioner in London, and the confectioner would send you a big box of cakes, and marmalade, and jam, and mixed biscuits, and preserved ginger," said Lucy, her cheeks glowing with the rapture of her theme. "That is what my mamma and papa did, when they were in Switzerland, on my birthday. I never had such a hamper as that one. I was ill for a week afterwards."

"And I suppose you were very glad your mother and father were away," said Ida, while the other children laughed in chorus.

"It was a splendid hamper," said Lucy, stolidly. "I shall never forget it. So you see your father might send you a hamper," she went on, for the sake of argument, "though he is in France."

"Certainly," said Ida, "if I were not too old to care about cakes and jam."

" *We* are not too old," persisted Lucy; "you might share them among us."

Ida's heart had not stilled its stormy vehemence yet. She talked lightly to her young companions, and tried to eat a little bread and butter, but that insipid fare almost choked her. Her mind was overcharged with thought and wonder.

Could he have meant all or half he said just now? —this young man with the delicate features, pale complexion, and thin lips. He had seemed intensely earnest. Those gray eyes of his, somewhat too pale of hue for absolute beauty, had glowed with a fire which even Ida's inexperience recognized as something above and beyond common feeling. His hand had trembled as it clasped hers. Could there be such a thing as love at first sight? and was she destined to be the object of that romantic passion? She had read of the triumphs of beauty, and she knew that she was handsome. She had been told the fact in too many ways—by praise sometimes, but much more often by envy—to remain unconscious of her charms. She was scornful of her beauty, inclined to undervalue the gift as compared with the blessings of other girls—a prosperous home, the world's respect, the means to gratify the natural yearnings of youth—but she knew that she was beautiful. And now it seemed to her all at once that beauty was a much more valuable gift than she had supposed hitherto—indeed, a kind of talisman or Aladdin's lamp, which could win for her all she wanted in this world—Wendover Abbey and the position of a country squire's wife. It was not a dazzling or giddy height to which to aspire; but to Ida just now it seemed the topmost pinnacle of social success.

"Oh, what a wretch I am!" she said to herself, presently; "what a despicable, mercenary creature! I don't care a straw for this man; and yet I am already thinking of myself as his wife."

And then, remembering how she had once openly declared her intention of marrying for money, she shrugged her shoulders disdainfully.

"Ought I to hesitate when the chance comes to me?" she thought. "I always meant to marry for money, if ever such wonderful fortune as a rich husband fell in my way."

And yet she had refused Dr. Rylance's offer, without a moment's hesitation. Was it really as he had said, in the bitterness of his wrath, because the offer was not good enough, the temptation not large enough? No; she told herself, she had rejected the smug physician, with his West End mansion and dainty Hampshire villa, his courtly manners, his perfect dress, because the man himself was obnoxious to her. Now, she did not dislike Brian Wendover—indeed, she was rather inclined to like him. She was only just a little disappointed that he was not the ideal Brian of her dreams, the dark-browed cavalier, with grave forehead and eagle eyes. She had a vague recollection of having once heard Blanche say that her cousin Brian of the Abbey was like Sir Tristram's portrait; but this must have been a misapprehension upon her part, since no two faces could have differed more than the pale, delicate-featured countenance of the living man and the dark rugged face in the picture.

She quieted the trouble of her thoughts as well as she could before tea was over and the evening task of preparation,—the gulfs and straits, the predicates and noun sentences, rule of three, common denominators, and all the dry-as-dust machinery was set in motion again.

Helping her pupils through their difficulties, battling with their stupidities, employed her too closely for any day-dreams of her own. But when prayers had been read, and the school had dispersed, and the butterfly-room was hushed into the silence of midnight, Ida Palliser lay broad awake, wondering at what Fate was doing for her.

"To think that perhaps I am going to be rich after all—honoured, looked up to, able to help those I love," she thought, thrilling at the splendour of her visions.

Ah! if this thing were verily to come to pass, how

kind, how good she would be to others! She would
have them all at the Abbey,—the shabby old half-pay
father, shabby no longer in those glorious days; the
vulgar little stepmother, improved into elegance; the
five-year old brother, that loveliest and dearest of
created beings. How lovely to see him rioting in the
luxuriance of those dear old gardens, rolling on that
velvet sward, racing his favourite dogs round and
round the grand old cedars! What a pony he should
ride! His daily raiment should be Genoa velvet and
old point lace. He should be the admiration and
delight of half the county. And Bessie—how kind
she could be to Bessie, repaying in some small measure
that which never could be fully repaid—the kindness
shown by the prosperous girl to the poor dependent.
And, above all,—vision sweeter even than the thought
of doing good,—how she would trample on Urania
Rylance—how the serpentine coils of that damsel's
malice and pride could be trodden under foot! Not a
ball, not a dinner, not a garden-party given at the
Abbey that would not be a thorn in Urania's side, a
nail in Urania's coffin.

So ran her fancies—in a very fever—all through
the troubled night; but when the first streak of the
autumn dawn glimmered coldly in the east, dismal
presage of the discordant dressing-bell, then she turned
upon her pillow with a weary sigh, and muttered to
herself:—

"After all I daresay Mr. Wendover is only fooling
me. Perhaps it is his habit to make love to every
decent-looking girl he meets."

The next day Ida walked on the same riverside
path, but this time not alone. Her natural modesty

shrank from the possibility of a second *tête-à-tête* with her admirer, and she stooped from her solitary state to ask Fräulein Wolf to accompany her in her afternoon walk.

Fräulein was delighted, honoured even, by the request. She was a wishy-washy person, sentimental, vapourish, altogether feeble, and she intensely admired Ida Palliser's vigorous young beauty.

The day was bright and sunny, the air deliciously mild, the river simply divine. The two young women paced the path slowly, talking of German poetry. The Fräulein knew her Schiller by heart, having expounded him daily for the last four years, and she fondly believed that after Shakespeare Schiller was the greatest poet who had ever trodden this globe.

"And if God had spared him for twenty more years, who knows if he would not have been greater than Shakespeare?" inquired the Fräulein, blandly.

She talked of Schiller's idea of friendship, as represented by the Marquis of Posa.

"Ah," sighed Ida, "I doubt if there is any such friendship as that out of a book."

"I could be like the marquis," said the Fräulein, smiling tenderly. "Oh, Ida, you don't know what I would do for anyone I loved—for a dear and valued friend, like you for instance, if you would only let me love you; but you have always held me at arm's length."

"I did not mean to do so," answered Ida, frankly; "but perhaps I am not particularly warm-hearted. It is not in my nature to have many friends. I was very fond of Bessie Wendover, but then she is such a dear clinging thing, like a chubby child that puts its fat arms round your neck—an irresistible creature. She made me love her in spite of myself."

"Why cannot I make you love me?" asked the fair Gertrude with a languishing look.

Ida could have alleged several reasons, but they would have been unflattering, so she only said feebly,—

"Oh, I really like you very much, and I enjoy talking about German literature with you. Tell me more about Schiller—you know his poetry so well— and Jean Paul. I never can quite understand the German idolatry of him. He is too much in the clouds for me."

"Too philosophic, you mean," said Fräulein. "I love philosophy."

"'Unless philosophy can make a Juliet it helps not, it avails not,'" said a manly voice from the river close by, and Brian Wendover shot his boat in against the bank and leapt up from among the rushes like a river-god.

Miss Palliser blushed crimson, but it hardly needed her blushes to convince Fräulein Wolf that this young stranger was a lover. Her sentimental soul thrilled at the idea of having plunged into the very midst of an intrigue.

Ida's heart throbbed heavily, not so much with emotion at beholding her admirer as at the recollection of her visions last night. She tried to look calm and indifferent.

"How do you do?" she said, shaking hands with him. "Mr. Wendover, Miss Wolf, our German mistress."

The Fräulein blushed, sniggered, and curtseyed.

"This gentleman is Bessie Wendover's first cousin, Fräulein," said Ida, with an explanatory air. "He was staying at The Knoll during the last part of my visit."

"Yes, and you saw much of each other, and you became heart-friends," gushed Miss Wolf, beaming benevolently at Brian with her pale green orbs.

Brian answered in very fair German, sinking his voice a little so as only to be heard by the Fräulein, who was in raptures with this young stranger. So good-looking, so elegant, and speaking Hanoverian German.

He told her that he had seen only too little of Ida at The Knoll, but enough to know that she was his "Schicksal;" and then he took the Fräulein's hand and pressed it gently.

"I know you are our friend," he said.

"Bis in den Tod," gasped Gertrude.

After this no one felt any more restraint. The Fräulein dropped into her place of confidante as easily as possible.

"What brings you here again this afternoon, Mr. Wendover?" asked Ida, trying to sustain the idea of being unconcerned in the matter.

"My lode-star; the same that drew me here yesterday, and will draw me here to-morrow."

"You had better not come here any more; you have no idea what a terrible person Miss Pew is. These riverside fields are her own particular property. Didn't you see the board, 'Trespassers will be prosecuted'?"

"Let her prosecute. If her wrath were deadly, I would risk it. You know what Romeo says—

> 'Wert thou as far
> As that vast shore wash'd with the farthest sea,
> I would adventure for such merchandize!'

And shall I be afraid of Miss Pew, when the path to my paradise lies so near?"

"Please don't talk such nonsense," pleaded Ida; "Fräulein will think you a very absurd person."

But Miss Wolf protested that she would think nothing of the sort. Sentiment of that kind was her idea of common sense.

"I am established at Penton Hook," said Brian. "I live on the water, and my only thought in life is to be near you. I shall know every stump of willow— every bulrush before I am a month older."

"But surely you are not going to stay at Penton Hook for a month!" exclaimed Ida, "buried alive in that little lock-house?"

"I shall have my daily resurrection when I see you."

"But you cannot imagine that I shall walk upon this path every afternoon, in order that you may land and talk nonsense?" protested Ida.

"I only imagine that this path is your daily walk, and that you would not be so heartless as to change your habits in order to deprive me of the sunshine of your presence," replied Brian, gazing at her tenderly, as if Miss Wolf counted for nothing, and they two were standing alone among the reeds and willows.

"You will simply make this walk impossible for me. It is quite out of the question that I should come here again so long as you are likely to be lying in wait for me. Is it not so, Fräulein? You know Miss Pew's way of thinking, and how she would regard such conduct."

Fräulein shook her head dolefully, and admitted that in Miss Pew's social code such a derogation from maiden dignity would be, in a manner, death—an offence beyond all hope of pardon.

"Hang Miss Pew!" exclaimed Brian. "If Miss Pew

were Minerva, with all the weight and influence of her father, the Thunderer, to back her up, I would defy her. Confess now, dear Fräulein—liebstes Fräulein"—how tender his accents sounded in German!—"*you* do not think it wrong for me to see the lady of my love for a few all-too-happy moments once a day?"

The Fräulein declared that it was the most natural thing in the world for them thus to meet, and that she for her part would be enchanted to play propriety, and to be her dearest Ida's companion on all such occasions, nor would thumbscrew or rack extort from her the secret of their loves.

"Nonsense!" exclaimed Ida, "in future I shall always walk in the kitchen-garden; the walls are ten feet high, and unless you had a horse that could fly, like Perseus, you would never be able to get at me."

"I will get a flying horse," answered Brian. "Don't defy me. Remember there are things that have been heard of before now in love-stories, called ladders."

After this their conversation became as light and airy as that dandelion seed which every breath of summer blows across the land. They were all three young, happy in health and hope despite of fortune. Ida began to think that Brian Wendover, if in nowise resembling her ideal, was a very agreeable young man. He was full of life and spirits; he spoke German admirably. He had the Fräulein's idolized Schiller on the tip of his tongue. He quoted Heine's tenderest love songs. Altogether his society was much more intellectual and more agreeable than any to be had at Mauleverer Manor. Miss Wolf parted from him reluctantly, and thought that Ida was unreasonably urgent when she insisted on leaving him at the end of half an hour's dawdling walk up and down the river path.

"Ach, how he is handsome! how he is clever! What for a man!" exclaimed Miss Wolf, as they went back to the Manor grounds across the dusty high-road, the mere passage over which had a faint flavour of excitement, as a momentary escape into the out-side world. "How proud you must be of his devotion to you!"

"Indeed I am not," answered Ida, frankly. "I only wonder at it. We have seen so little of each other; we have known each other so short a time."

"I don't think time counts for lovers," argued the romantic Gertrude. "One sees a face which is one's fate, and only wonders how one can have lived until that moment, since life must have been so empty with-out *him*."

"Have you done that sort of thing often?" asked Ida, with rather a cynical air. "You talk as if it were a common experience of yours."

Fräulein Wolf blushed and simpered.

"There was one," she murmured, "when I was very young. He was to me as a bright particular star. His father kept a shop, but, oh, his soul would have harmonized with the loftiest rank in the land. He was in the Landwehr. If you had seen him in his uniform—ach, Himmel. He went away to the Franco-Prussian war. I wept for him; I thought of him as Leonora of her Wilhelm.. He came back. Ach!"

"Was he a ghost? Did he carry you off to the churchyard?"

"Neither to churchyard nor church," sighed Gertrude. "He was false! He married his father's cook—a fat,

rosy-cheeked Swabian. All that was delicate and refined in his nature, every poetical yearning of his soul,
had been trampled out of him in that hellish war!"

"I daresay he was hungry after a prolonged existence upon wurst," said Ida, "and that instinct drew
him to the cook-maid."

After this there came many afternoons on which
the Fräulein and Ida walked in the meadow path by
the river, and walk there when they would, the light
wherry always came glancing along the tide, and shot
in among the reeds, and Miss Palliser's faithful swain
was in attendance upon her. On doubtful afternoons,
when Ida was inclined to stay indoors, the sentimental
Fräulein was always at her side to urge her to take
the accustomed walk. Not only was Mr. Wendover's
society agreeable to her poetic soul, but he occasionally
brought some tender offering in the shape of hot-house
grapes or Jersey pears, which were still more welcome
to the fair German.

The governesses, Miss Motley, Miss Pillby, and
Mademoiselle, were always on duty on fine afternoons,
in attendance upon the pupils' regulation walks, long
dusty perambulations of dull high roads; and thus it
happened that Ida and the Fräulein had the meadow
path to themselves.

Nothing occurred during the space of a fortnight
to disturb their sense of security. The river side
seemed a kind of Paradise, without the possibility of
a serpent. Ida's lover had not yet made her any
categorical and formal offer of marriage. Indeed, he
had never been one minute alone with her since their
first meeting; but he talked as if it was a settled thing

that they two were to be man and wife in the days to
come. He did not speak as if their marriage were an
event in the near future; and at this Ida wondered a
little, seeing that the owner of Wendover Abbey could
have no need to wait for a wife—to consider ways and
means—and to be prudently patient, as struggling
professional youth must be. This was curious; for
that he loved her passionately there could be little
doubt. Every look, every tone told her as much a
hundred times in an hour. Nor did she make any
protest when he spoke of her as one pledged to him,
though no formal covenant had been entered upon.
She allowed him to talk as he pleased about their
future; and her only wonder was, that in all his conversation he spoke so little of the house in which he
was born, and indeed of his belongings generally.

Once she expatiated to Fräulein Wolf in Brian's
presence upon the picturesque beauties of the Abbey.

"It is the dearest, noblest old house you can conceive," she said; "and the old, old gardens and park
are something too lovely: but I believe Mr. Wendover
does not care a straw about the place."

"You know what comes of familiarity," answered
Brian carelessly. "I have seen too much of the Abbey
to be moved to rapture by its Gothic charms, every
time I see it after the agony of separation."

"But you would like to live there?"

"I would infinitely prefer living anywhere else.
The place is too remote from civilization. A spot one
might enjoy, perhaps, on the downhill side of sixty;
but in youth or active middle age every sensible man
should shun seclusion. A man has to fight against an
inherent tendency to lapse into a vegetable."

"Fox did not become a vegetable," said Ida; "yet how he adored St. Ann's Hill!"

"Fox was a hard drinker and a fast liver," answered Brian. "If he had not let the clock run down now and then, the works would have worn out sooner than they did."

"But do you never feel the need of rest?" asked Ida. Brian stifled a yawn.

"No; I'm afraid I have never worked hard enough for that. The need will come, perhaps, later—when the work comes."

On more than one occasion when Ida talked of the Abbey, Mr. Wendover replied in the same tone. It was evident that he was indifferent to the family seat, or that he even disliked it. He had no pride in surroundings which might have inspired another man.

"One would think you had been frightened by the family ghost," Ida said laughingly, "you so studiously avoid talking about the Abbey."

"I have not been frightened by the ghost—I am too modern to believe in ghosts."

"Oh, but it is modern to believe in everything impossible—spirit-rapping, thought-reading."

"Perhaps; but I am not of that temper." And then, with a graver look than Ida had ever seen in his face, he said, "You are full of enthusiasm about that old place among the hills, Ida. I hope you do not care more for the Abbey than for me."

She crimsoned and looked down. The question touched her weakness too nearly.

"Oh, no," she faltered; "what are cedars and limestone as compared with humanity?"

"And if I were without the Abbey—if the Abbey and I were nothing to each other—should I be nobody in your sight?"

"It is difficult to dissociate a man from his surroundings," she answered; "but I suppose you would be just the same person?"

"I hope so," said Brian. "'The rank is but the guinea stamp, the man's a man for a' that.' But the guinea stamp is an uncommonly good thing in its way, I admit."

These afternoon promenades between four and five o'clock, while the rest of the school was out walking, had been going on for a fortnight, and no harm to Ida had come of her indiscretion. Perhaps she hardly considered how wrong a thing she was doing in violating Miss Pew's confidence by conduct so entirely averse from Miss Pew's ideas of good behaviour. The confidence had been so grudgingly given, Miss Pew had been so systematically unkind, that the girl may be forgiven for detesting her, nay, even for glorying in the notion of acting in a manner which would shock all Miss Pew's dearest prejudices. Her meeting with her lover could scarcely be called clandestine, for she took very little pains to conceal the fact. If the affair had gone on secretly for so long, it was because of no artifice on her part.

But that any act of any member of the Mauleverer household could remain long unknown was almost an impossibility. If there had been but one pair of eyes in the establishment, and those the eyes of Miss Pillby, the thing would have been discovered; for those pale unlovely orbs were as the eyes of Argus himself in their manifold power to spy out the proceedings of

other people—more especially of any person whom
their owner disliked.

Now Miss Pillby had never loved Ida Palliser, ob-
jecting to her on broad grounds as a person whose
beauty and talents were an indirect injury to mediocre
people. Since Ida's visit to The Knoll her angry feeling had intensified with every mention of the pleasures
and comforts of that abode. Miss Pillby, who never
opened a book for her own pleasure, who cared nothing for music, and whose highest notion of art was
all black-lead pencil and bread-crumbs, had plenty of
vacant space in her mind for other people's business.
She was a sharp observer of the fiddle-faddle of daily
life; she had a keen scent for evil motives underlying
simple actions. Thus when she perceived the inti-
macy which had newly arisen between the Fräulein
and Miss Palliser, she told herself that there must be
some occult reason for the fact. Why did those two
always walk together? What hidden charm had they
discovered in the river-meadow?

For this question, looked at from Miss Pillby's
point of view, there could be only one answer. The
attraction was masculine. One or other of the damsels
must have an admirer whom she contrived to see
somehow, or to correspond with somehow, during her
meadow walk. That the thing had gone so far as it
really had gone, that any young lady at Mauleverer
could dare to walk and talk with an unlicensed man
in the broad light of day, was more than Miss Pillby's
imagination could conceive. But she speculated upon
some transient glimpse of a man on the opposite bank,
or in the middle distance of the river—a handkerchief waved, a signal given, perhaps a love-letter

hidden in a hollow tree. This was about the culminating point to which any intrigue at Mauleverer had ever reached hitherto. Beyond this Miss Pillby's fancy ventured not.

It was on the second Sunday in October, when the Mauleverer pupils were beginning to look forward, almost hopefully, to the Christmas vacation, that a flood of light streamed suddenly upon Miss Pillby's troubled mind. The revelation happened in this wise. Evening service at a smart little newly-built church where the function was Anglican to the verge of Ritualism, was a privilege reserved for the elder and more favoured of the Mauleverer flock. All the girls liked this evening service at St. Dunstan's. It had a flavour of dissipation. The lamps, the music, the gaily decorated altar, the Saint's-day banners and processional hymn, were faintly suggestive of the opera. The change from the darkness of the country road to the glow and glitter of the tabernacle was thrilling. Evening service at St. Dunstan's was the most exciting event of the week. There was a curate who intoned exquisitely, with that melodious snuffle so dear to modern congregations, and whose voice had a dying fall when he gave out a hymn which almost moved girl-worshippers to tears. He was thought to be in a consumption— had a little dry hacking cough, actually caused by relaxed tonsils, but painfully recalling her of the camelias. The Mauleverer girls called him interesting, and hoped that he would never marry, but live and die like St. Francis de Sales. On this particular Sunday, Miss Pew—vulgarly Old Pew—happened to be unusually amiable. That morning's post had brought her the promise of three new pupils, daughters of a mighty sheep farmer lately returned from Australia, and supposed to be a millionaire. He was a widower, and wanted motherly care for his orphans. They were to be clothed as well as fed at Mauleverer; they were to have all those tender cares and indulgences which a loving mother could give them. This kind of trans-action was eminently profitable to the Miss Pews. Ma-ternal care meant a tremendous list of extra charges —treats, medical attendance, little comforts of all kinds, from old port to lambs-wool sleeping-socks. Orphans of this kind were the pigeons whose tender breasts furnished the down with which that experienced crow, Miss Pew, feathered her nest. She had read the Australian's letter over three times before evening service, and she was inclined to think kindly of the human race; so when Miss Palliser asked if she too— she, the Pariah, might go to St. Dunstan's—she, whose general duty of a Sunday evening was to hear the little ones their catechism, or keep them quiet by reading aloud to them "Pilgrim's Progress," or "Agathos," perhaps—Miss Pew said, loftily, "I do not see any ob-jection."

There was no kindness, no indulgence in her tone, but she said she saw no objection, and Ida flew off to put on her bonnet, that poor little black lace bonnet with yellow rosebuds which had done duty for so many services.

It was a relief to get away from school, and its dull monotony, even for a couple of hours; and then there was the music. Ida loved music too passionately to be indifferent to the harmony of village voices, carefully trained to sing her favourite hymns to the sound of a small but excellent organ.

The little church was somewhat poorly attended on this fine autumn evening, when the hunter's moon hung like a big golden shield above the river, glorifying the dipping willows, the narrow eyots, haunts of swan and cygnet, and the distant woodlands of Surrey. It was a night which tempted the free to wander in the cool shadowy river-side paths, rather than to worship in the warm little temple.

The Mauleverer girls made a solid block of humanity on one side of the nave, but on the other side the congregation was scattered thinly in the open oaken seats.

Miss Pillby, perusing those figures within her view, as she stood in the back row of the school seats, perceived a stranger—a stranger of elegant and pleasing appearance, who was evidently casting stolen glances at the lambs of the Mauleverer fold. Nor was Miss Pillby's keen eye slow to discover for which lamb those ardent looks were intended. The object of the stranger's admiration was evidently Ida Palliser.

"I thought as much," mused Miss Pillby, as she listened, or seemed to listen, to the trials and triumphs of the children of Israel, chanted by fresh young voices with a decidedly rural twang; "this explains everything."

When they left the church, Miss Pillby was perfectly aware of the stranger following the Mauleverer flock, evidently in the hope of getting speech with Miss Palliser. He hung on the pathway near them, he shot ahead of them, and then turned and strolled slowly back. All in vain. Ida was too closely hemmed in and guarded for him to get speech of her; and the maiden procession passed on without any violation of the proprieties.

"Did you see that underbred young man following us as we came home?" asked Miss Pillby, with a disgusted air, as she shared an invigorating repast of bread and butter and toast and water with the pupils who had been to church. "Some London shopman, no doubt, by his bad manners." She stole a look at Ida, who flushed ever so slightly, at hearing Brian Wendover thus maligned.

Fräulein Wolf slept in the room occupied by Miss Pillby and Miss Motley—three narrow iron bedsteads in a particularly inconvenient room, always devoted to governesses, and supposed to be a temple of learning.

While Miss Motley was saying her prayers, Miss Pillby wriggled up to the Fräulein, who was calmly brushing her flaxen tresses, and wispered impetuously, "I have seen him! I know all about it!"

"Ach Himmel," cried the Fräulein. "Thou wouldst not betray?"

"Nor for the world."

"Is he not handsome, godlike?" demanded the Fräulein, still in German.

"Yes, he is very nice-looking. Don't tell Palliser that I know anything about him. She mightn't like it."

The Fräulein shook her head, and put her finger to her lips, just as Miss Motley rose from her knees, remarking that it was impossible for anybody to pray in a proper business-like manner with such whispering and chattering going on.

Next day Miss Pillby contrived to get a walk in the garden before the early dinner. Here among the asparagus beds she had a brief conversation with a small boy employed in the kitchen-garden, a youth

whose mother washed for the school, and had frequent
encounters with Miss Pillby, that lady having charge of
the linen, and being, in the laundress's eye, a power
in the establishment. Miss Pillby had furthermore
been what she had called "kind" to the laundress's
hope. She had insisted upon his learning his catechism,
and attending church twice every Sunday, and she had
knitted him a comforter, the material being that harsh
and scrubby worsted which makes the word comforter
a sound of derision.

Strong in the sense of these favours, Miss Pillby
put it upon the boy as a duty which he owed to her
and to society to watch Ida Palliser's proceeding in the
river-meadow. She also promised him sixpence if he
found out anything bad.

The influence of the Church Catechism, learned by
rote, parrot fashion, had not awakened in the laundress's
boy any keen sense of honour. He had a dim feeling
that it was a shabby service which he was called upon
to perform; but then of course Miss Pillby, who taught
the young ladies, and who was no doubt a wise and
discreet personage, knew best; and a possible sixpence
was a great temptation.

"Them rushes and weeds down by the bank wants
cutting. Gar'ner told me about it last week," said the
astute youth. "I'll do 'em this very afternoon."

"Do, Sam. Be there between four and five. Keep
out of sight as much as you can, but be well within
hearing. I want you to tell me all that goes on."

"And when shall I see you agen, miss?"

"Let me see. That's rather difficult. I'm afraid it
can't be managed till to-morrow. You are in the house
at six every morning to clean the boots?"

10*

"Yes, miss."

"Then I'll come down to the boot-room at half-past six to-morrow morning and hear what you've got to tell me."

"Lor, miss, it's such a mucky place—all among the coal-cellars."

"I don't mind," said Miss Pillby; which was quite true. There was no amount of muckiness Miss Pillby would not have endured in order to injure a person she disliked.

"I have never shrunk from my duty, however painful it might be, Sam!" she said, and left the youth impressed by the idea of her virtues.

In the duskiness of the October dawn Miss Pillby stole stealthily down by back stairs and obscure passages to the boot-room, where she found Sam hard at work with brushes and blacking, by the light of a tallow candle, in an atmosphere flavoured with coals.

"Well, Sam?" asked the vestal, eagerly.

"Well, miss, I seed 'em and I heerd 'em," answered the boy; "such goin's on. Orful!"

"What kind of thing, Sam?"

"Love-makin' miss; keepin' company. The young ladies hadn't been there five minutes when a boat dashes up to the bank, and a young gent jumps ashore. My, how he went on! I was down among the rushes, right under his feet, as you may say, most of the time, and I heerd him beautiful. How he did talk; like a poetry book!"

"Did he kiss her?"

"Yes, miss, just one, as they parted company. She was very stand-offish with him, but he cotched hold of her just as she was wishing of him good-bye. He gave her a squeedge like, and took her unawares. It was only one kiss, yer know, miss, but he made it last as long as he could. The foreigner looked the other way."

"Shameful creatures, both of them!" exclaimed Miss Pillby. "There's your sixpence, Sam, and don't say a word to anybody about what you've seen, till I tell you. I may want you to repeat it all to Miss Pew. If I do, I'll give you another sixpence."

"Lawks, miss, that would be cheap at a shilling," said the boy. "It would freeze my blood to have to stand up to talk before Miss Pew."

"Nonsense, Sam, you will be only telling the truth, and there can be nothing to frighten you. However, I daresay she will be satisfied with my statement. She won't want confirmation from you."

"Confirmation from me," muttered Sam, as Miss Pillby left his den. "No, I should think not. Why, that's what the bishops do. Fancy old Pew being confirmed too—old Pew in a white frock and a weil. That is a good 'un," and Sam exploded over his blacking-brush at the preposterous idea.

It was Miss Pew's habit to take a cup of tea and a square of buttered toast every morning at seven, before she left her pillow; in order to fortify herself for the effort of getting up and dressing, so as to be in her place, at the head of the chief table in the school dining-room, when eight o'clock struck. Had Miss Pew consulted her own inclination she would have reposed until a much later hour; but the maintenance of discipline compelled that she should be the head and front of all virtuous movements at Mauleverer Manor. How could she inveigh with due force against the sin

of sloth if she were herself a slug-a-bed? Therefore
did Miss Pew vanquish the weakness of the flesh, and
rise at a quarter past seven, summer and winter. But
this struggle between duty and inclination made the
lady's temper somewhat critical in the morning hours.

Now it was the custom for one of the mistresses
to carry Miss Pew's tea-tray, and to attend at her bed-
side while she sipped her bohea and munched her
toast. It was a delicate attention, a recognition of
her dignity, which Miss Pew liked. It was the *lever du
roi* upon a small scale. And this afforded an opportunity for the mistress on duty to inform her principal
of any small fact in connection with the school or
household which it was well for Miss Pew to know.
Not for worlds would Sarah Pew have encouraged a
spy, according to her own view of her own character;
but she liked people with keen eyes, who could tell
her everything that was going on under her roof.

"Good morning, Pillby," said Miss Pew, sitting up
against a massive background of pillows, like a female
Jove upon a bank of clouds, an awful figure in frilled
white raiment, with an eye able to command, but
hardly to flatter; "what kind of a day is it?"

"Dull and 'eavy," answered Miss Pillby; "I shouldn't
wonder if there was a thunderstorm."

"Don't talk nonsense, child; it's too late in the
year for thunder. We shall have the equinoctial
gales soon, I dare say."

"No doubt," replied Miss Pillby, who had heard
about the equinox and its carryings on all her life
without having arrived at any clear idea of its nature
and properties, "we shall have it very equinoctial before the end of the month, I've no doubt."

"Well, is there anything going on? Any of the girls bilious? One of my black draughts wanted anywhere?"

Miss Pew was not highly intellectual, but she was a great hand at finance, household economies, and domestic medicine. She compounded most of the doses taken at Mauleverer with her own fair hands, and her black draughts were a feature in the school. The pupils never forgot them. However faint became the memory of youthful joys in after years, the flavour of Miss Pew's jalap and senna was never obliterated.

"No; there's nobody ill this morning," answered Miss Pillby, with a faint groan.

"Ah, you may well sigh," retorted her principal; "the way those girls ate veal and ham yesterday was enough to have turned the school into a hospital—and with raspberry jam tart after, too."

Veal with ham was the Sunday dinner at Mauleverer, a banquet upon which Miss Pew prided herself, as an instance of luxurious living rarely to be met with in boarding-schools. If the girls were ill after it, that was their look out.

"There's something wrong, I can see by your face," said Miss Pew, after she had sipped half her tea and enjoyed the whole of her toast; "is it the servants or the pupils?"

Strange to say, Miss Pew did not look grateful to the bearer of evil tidings. This was one of her idiosyncrasies. She insisted upon being kept informed of all that went wrong in her establishment, but she was apt to be out of temper with the informant.

"Neither," answered Miss Pillby, with an awful

shake of her sandy locks; "I don't believe there is a servant in this house who would so far forget herself. And as to the pupils——"

"We know what they are," snapped Miss Pew; "I never heard of anything bad enough to be beyond their reach. Who is it?"

"Your clever pupil teacher, Ida Palliser."

"Ah," grunted Miss Pew, setting down her cup; "I can believe anything of her. That girl was born to be troublesome. What has she done now?"

Miss Pillby related the circumstances of Miss Palliser's crime, setting forth her own cleverness in the course of her narrative—how her misgivings had been excited by the unwonted familiarity between Ida and the Fräulein — a young person always open to suspicion as a stranger in the land—how her fears had been confirmed by the conduct of an unknown man in the church; and how, urged by her keen sense of duty, she had employed Mrs. Jones's boy to watch the delinquents.

"I'll make an example of her," said Miss Pew, flinging back the bed-clothes with a tragic air as she rose from her couch. "That will do, Pillby. I want no further details. I'll wring the rest out of that bold-faced minx in the face of all the school. You can go."

And without any word of praise or thanks from her principal, Miss Pillby retired; yet she knew in her heart that for this piece of ill news Miss Pew was not ungrateful.

Never had Sarah Pew looked more awful than she appeared that morning at the breakfast table, clad in sombre robes of olive-green merino, and a cap bristling with olive-green berries and brambly twigs—a cap which to the more advanced of the pupils suggested the head-gear of Medusa.

Miss Dulcibella, gentle, limp, sea-greeny, looked at her stronger-minded sister, and was so disturbed by the gloom upon that imperial brow as to be unable to eat her customary rasher. Not a word did Miss Pew speak to sister or mistresses during that brief but awful meal; but when the delf breakfast cups were empty, and the stacks of thick bread and butter had diminished to nothingness, and the girls were about to rise and disperse for their morning studies, Miss Pew's voice arose suddenly amidst them like the sound of thunder.

"Keep your seats, if you please, young ladies. I am about to make an example; and I hope what I have to say and do may be for the general good. Miss Palliser, stand up."

Ida rose in her place, at that end of the table where she was supposed to exercise a corrective influence upon the younger pupils. She stood up where all the rest were seated, a tall and perfect figure, a beautiful statuesque head, supported by a neck like a marble column. She stood up among all those other girls, the handsomest of them all, pale, with flashing eyes, feeling very sure that she was going to be ill treated.

"Pray, Miss Palliser, who is the person whom it is your daily habit to meet and converse with in my grounds? Who is the man who has dared to trespass on my meadow at your invitation?"

"Not at my invitation," answered Ida, as calm as marble. "The gentleman came of his own accord. His name is Brian Wendover, and he and I are engaged to be married."

Miss Pew laughed a loud ironical laugh, a laugh which froze the blood of all the seventeen-year-old pupils who were not without fear or reproach upon the subject of clandestine glances, little notes, or girlish carryings-on in the flirtation line.

"Engaged?" she exclaimed, in her stentorian voice. "That is really too good a joke. Engaged? Pray, which Mr. Brian Wendover is it?"

"Mr. Wendover of the Abbey."

"Mr. Wendover of the Abbey, the head of the Wendover family?" cried Miss Pew. "And you would wish us to believe that Mr. Wendover, of Wendover Abbey—a gentleman with an estate worth something like seven thousand a year, young ladies—has engaged himself to the youngest of my pupil-teachers, whose acquaintance he has cultivated while trespassing on my meadow? Miss Palliser, when a gentleman of Mr. Wendover's means and social status wishes to marry a young person in your position—a concatenation which occurs very rarely in the history of the human race—he comes to the hall door. Mr. Wendover no more means to marry you than he means to marry the moon. His views are of quite a different kind, and you know it."

Ida cast a withering look at her tyrant, and moved quickly from her place.

"You are a wretch to say such a thing to me," she cried passionately; "I will not stay another hour under your roof to be so insulted."

"No, you will not stay under my roof, Miss Palliser," retorted Miss Pew. "My mind was made up more than an hour ago on that point. You will not be allowed to stay in this house one minute longer than is needed for the packing up of your clothes, and that, I take it," added the schoolmistress, with an insolent laugh, "will not be a lengthy operation. You are expelled, Miss Palliser—expelled from this establishment for grossly improper conduct; and I am only sorry for your poor father's sake that you will have to begin your career as a governess with disgrace attached to your name."

"There is no disgrace, except in your own foul mind," said Ida. "I can imagine that as nobody ever admired you or made love to you when you were young, you may have mistaken ideas as to the nature of lovers and love-making,"—despite the universal awe, this provoked a faint, irrepressible titter—"but it is hard that you should revenge your ignorance upon me. Mr. Wendover has never said a word to me which a gentleman should not say. Fräulein Wolf, who has heard his every word, knows that this is true."

"Fräulein will leave this house to-morrow, if she is not careful," said Miss Pew, who had, however, no intention of parting with so useful and cheap a teacher.

She could afford to revenge herself upon Ida, whose period of tutelage was nearly over.

"Fräulein knows that Mr. Wendover speaks of our future as the future of man and wife."

"Ja wohl," murmured the Fräulein, "that is true; ganz und gar."

"I will not hear another word!" cried Miss Pew, swelling with rage, while every thorn and berry on her autumnal cap quivered. "Ungrateful, impudent young woman! Leave my house instantly. I will not have these innocent girls perverted by your vile ex-

ample. In speech and in conduct you are alike detestable."

"Good-bye, girls," cried Ida, lightly; "you all know
how much harm my speech and my example have done
you. Good-bye, Fräulein; don't you be afraid of dis-
missal,—you are too well worth your salt."

Polly Cobb, the brewer's daughter, sat near the
door by which Ida had to make her exit. She was
quite the richest, and perhaps the best-natured girl in
the school. She caught hold of Ida's gown and thrust
a little Russia-leather purse into her hand, with a
tender squeeze.

"Take it, dear," she whispered; "I don't want it;
I can get plenty more. Yes, yes, you must; you shall.
I'll make a row, and get myself into disgrace, if you
refuse. You can't go to France without money."

"God bless you, dear. I'll send it back," answered Ida.

"Don't; I shall hate you if you do."

"Is that young woman gone?" demanded Miss Pew's
awful voice.

"Going, going, gone!" cried Miss Cobb, forgetting
herself in her excitement, as the door closed behind Ida.

"Who was that?" roared Miss Pew.

Half a dozen informants pronounced Miss Cobb's
name.

Now Miss Cobb's people were wealthy, and Miss
Cobb had younger sisters, all coming on under a
homely governess to that critical stage in which they
would require the polishing processes of Mauleverer
Manor: so Sarah Pew bridled her wrath, and said
quietly—

"Kindly reserve your jocosity for a more appropriate

season, Miss Cobb. Young ladies, you may proceed
with your matutinal duties."

CHAPTER VIII.
AT THE LOCK-HOUSE.

Miss Pew had argued rightly that the process of
packing would not be a long one with Ida Palliser.
The girl had come to Mauleverer with the smallest
number of garments compatible with decency; and her
stock had been but tardily and scantily replenished
during her residence in that manorial abode. It was
to her credit that she had contrived still to be clean,
still to be neat, under such adverse conditions; it was
Nature's royal gift that she had looked grandly beautiful in the shabbiest gowns and mantles even seen at
Mauleverer.

She huddled her poor possessions into her solitary
trunk—a battered hair trunk which had done duty
ever since she came as a child from India. She put
a few necessaries into a convenient morocco bag, which
the girls in her class had clubbed their pocket-money
to present to her on her last birthday; and then she
washed the traces of angry tears from her face, put
on her hat and jacket, and went downstairs, carrying
her bag and umbrella.

One of the housemaids met her in the hall, a
buxom, good-natured country girl.

"Is it true that you are going to leave us, miss?"
she asked.

"What, you all know it already?" exclaimed Ida.

"Everybody is talking about it, miss. The young

ladies are all on your side; but they dared not speak up before Miss Pew."

"I suppose not. Yes, it is quite true; I am expelled, Eliza; sent out into the world without a character, because I allowed Mr. Wendover to walk and talk with the Fräulein and me for half an'hour or so in the river meadow! Mr. Wendover, my best, my only friend's first cousin. Rather hard, isn't it?"

"Hard? it's shameful," cried the girl. "I should like to see old Pew turning me off for keeping company with my young man. But she daren't do it. Good servants are hard to get nowadays; or any servants, indeed, for the paltry wages she gives."

"And governesses are a drug in the market," said Ida, bitterly. "Good-bye, Eliza."

"Where are you going, miss? Home?"

"Yes; I suppose so."

The reckless tone, the careless words, alarmed the good-hearted housemaid.

"Oh, miss, pray go home, straight home—wherever your home is. You are too handsome to be going about alone among strangers. It's a wicked world, miss—wickeder than you know of, perhaps. Have you got money enough to get you home comfortable?"

"I'll see," answered Ida, taking out Miss Cobb's fat little purse and looking into it.

There were two sovereigns and a good deal of silver—a tremendous fortune for a schoolgirl; but then it was said that Cobb Brothers coined money by the useful art of brewing.

"Yes; I have plenty of money for my journey," said Ida.

"Are you certain sure, now, miss?" pleaded the

housemaid; "for if you ain't, I've got a pound laid by in my drawer ready to put in the Post Office Savings Bank, and you're as welcome to it as flowers in May, if you'll take it off me."

"God bless you, Eliza. If I were in any want of money, I'd gladly borrow your sovereign; but Miss Cobb has lent me more than I want. Good-bye."

Ida held out her hand, which the housemaid after wiping her own paw upon her apron, clasped affectionately.

"God bless you, Miss Palliser," she said, fervently; "I shall miss the sight of your handsome face when I waits at table."

A minute more and Ida stood in the broad carriage sweep, with her back to the stately old mansion which had sheltered her so long, and in which, despite her dependency and her poverty, she had known some light-hearted hours. Now, where was she to go? and what was she to do with her life? She stood with the autumn wind blowing about her—the fallen chestnut leaves drifting to her feet—pondering that question.

Was she or was she not Brian Wendover's affianced wife? How far was she to trust in him, to lean upon him, in this crucial hour of her life? There had been so much playfulness in their love-making, his tone had been for the most part so light and sportive, that now, when she stood, as it were, face to face with destiny, she hardly knew how to think of him, whether as a rock that she might lean upon, or as a reed that would give way at her touch. Rock or reed, womanly instinct told her that it was not to this fervent admirer she must apply for aid or counsel yet awhile. Her duty was to go home at once—to get across the Channel, if possible, as quickly as Miss Pew's letter to her father.

Intent on doing this, she walked along the dusty high road by the river, in the direction of the railway station. This station was more than two miles distant, a long, straight walk by the river, and then a mile or so across fields and by narrow lanes to an arid spot, where some newly-built houses were arising round a hopeless-looking little loop-line station, in a desert of agricultural land.

She had walked about three-quarters of a mile, when she heard the rapid dip of oars, as if in pursuit of her, and a familiar voice calling to her.

It was Brian, who almost lived in his boat, and who had caught sight of her in the distance, and followed at racing speed.

"What are you doing?" he asked, coming up close to the bank, and standing up in his boat. "Where are you going at such a pace? I don't think I ever saw a woman walk so fast."

"Was I walking fast?" she asked, unconscious of the impetus which excitement had given to her movements.

She knew in her heart of hearts that she did not love him—that love—the passion which she had read of in prose and poetry, was still a stranger to her soul: but just at this moment, galled and stung by Miss Pew's unkindness, heart-sick at her own absolute desolation, the sound of his voice was sweet in her ears, the look of the tall slim figure, the friendly face turned towards her, was pleasant to her eyes. No, he was not a reed, he was a rock. She felt protected and comforted by his presence.

"Were you walking fast? Galloping like a three-year-old—*quæ velut latis equa trima campis*, quoted Brian. "Are you running away from Mauleverer Manor?"

"I am going away," she answered calmly. "I have been expelled."

"Ex——what?" roared Brian.

"I have been expelled—sent away at a minute's notice—for the impropriety of my conduct in allowing you to talk to me in the river-meadow."

Brian had been fastening his boat to a pollard willow as he talked. He leapt on to the bank and came close to Ida's side.

"My darling, my dearest love, what a burning shame! What a villainous old hag that Pew woman must be! Bessie told me she was a Tartar, but this beats everything. Expelled! Your conduct impeached because you let me talk to you——I, Bessie's cousin, a man who at the worst has some claim to be considered a gentleman, while you have the highest claim to be considered a lady. It is beyond all measure infamous."

"It was rather hard, was it not?" said Ida quietly.

"Abominable, insufferable! I—well. I'll call upon the lady this afternoon, and make her acquainted with my sentiments upon the subject. The wicked old harridan."

"Please don't," urged Ida, smiling at his wrath; "it doesn't give me any consolation to hear you call her horrid names."

"Did you tell her that I had asked you to be my wife?"

"I said something to that effect—in self-defence—not from any wish to commit you: and she told me that a man in your position, who intended to marry a girl in my position, would act in a very different manner from the way in which you have acted."

"Did she? She is a wise judge of human nature —and of a lover's nature, above all. Well, Ida, dearest, we have only one course open to us, and that is to give her the lie at once—by our conduct. Deeds, not words, shall be our argument. You do care for me— just a little—don't you, pet? just well enough to marry me? All the rest will come after?"

"Whom else have I to care for?" faltered Ida, with downcast eyes and passionately throbbing heart. "Who else has ever cared for me?"

"I am answered. So long as I am the only one I will confide all the rest to Fate. We will be married to-morrow."

"To-morrow! No, no, no."

"Yes, yes, yes. What is there to hinder our immediate marriage? And what can be such a crushing answer to that old Jezebel? We will be married at the little church where I saw you last Sunday night, looking like St. Cecilia when you joined in the Psalms. We have been both living in the same parish for the last fortnight. I will run up to Doctors' Commons this afternoon, bring back the licence, interview the parson, and have everything arranged for our being married at ten o'clock to-morrow morning."

"No, no, not for the world."

For some time the girl was firm in her refusal of such a hasty union. She would not marry her lover except in the face of the world, with the full consent of his friends and her own. Her duty was to go by the first train and boat that would convey her to Dieppe, and to place herself in her father's care.

"Do you think your father would object to our marriage?" asked Brian.

"No, I am sure he would not object," she answered, smiling within herself at the question.

As if Captain Palliser, living upon his half-pay, and the occasional benefactions of a rich kinsman, could by any possibility object to a match that would make his daughter mistress of Wendover Abbey!

"Then why delay our marriage, in order to formally obtain a consent which you are sure of beforehand? As for my friends, Bessie's people are the nearest and dearest, and you know what their feelings are on your behalf."

"Bessie likes me as her friend. I don't know how she might like me as her cousin's wife," said Ida.

"Then I will settle your doubts by telling you a little secret. Bessie sent me here to try and win you for my wife. It was her desire as well as mine."

More arguments followed, and against the lover's ardent pleading there was only a vague idea of duty in the girl's mind, somewhat weakened by an instinctive notion that her father would think her an arrant fool for delaying so grand a triumph as her marriage with a man of fortune and position. Had he not often spoken to her wistfully of her beauty, and the dim hope that her handsome face might some day win her a rich husband?

"It's a poor chance at the best," he told her. "The days of the Miss Gunnings have gone by. The world has grown commercial. Nowadays money marries money."

And this chance, which her father had speculated upon despondently as a remote contingency, was now at her feet. Was she to spurn it, and then go back to the shabby little villa near Dieppe, and expect to be praised for her filial duty?

While she wavered, Brian urged every argument which a lover could bring to aid his suit. To-morrow they might be married, and in the meanwhile Ida could be safely and comfortably housed with the good woman at the Lock-house. Brian would give up his lodgings to her, and would stay at the hotel at Chertsey. Ida listened, and hesitated: before her lay the dry, dusty road, the solitary journey by land and sea, the doubtful welcome at home. And here by her side stood the wealthy lover, the very embodiment of protecting power—is not every girl's first lover in her eyes as Olympian Jove?—eager to take upon himself the burden of her life, to make her footsteps easy.

"Step into the boat, dearest," he said; "I know your heart has decided for me. You are not afraid to trust me, Ida?"

"Afraid? no," she answered, frankly, looking at him with heavenly confidence in her large dark eyes; "I am only afraid of doing wrong."

"You can do no wrong with me by your side, your husband to-morrow, responsible for all the rest of your existence."

"True; after to-morrow I shall be accountable to no one but you," she said, thoughtfully. "How strange it seems!"

"At the worst, I hope you will find me better than old Pew," answered Brian lightly.

"You are too good—too generous," she said; "but I am afraid you are acting too much from impulse. Have you considered what you are going to do? have you thought what it is to marry a penniless girl, who can give you none of the things which the world cares for in exchange for your devotion?"

"I have thought what it is to marry the woman I fondly love, the loveliest girl these eyes ever looked upon. Step into my boat, Ida; I must row you up to the lock, and then start for London by the first train I can catch. I don't know how early the licence-shop closes."

She obeyed him, and sank into a seat in the stern of the cockle-shell craft, exhausted, mentally and physically, by the agitation of the last two hours. She felt an unspeakable relief in sitting quietly in the boat, the water rippling gently past, like a lullaby, the rushes and willows waving in the mild western breeze. Henceforth she had little to do in life but to be cared for and cherished by an all-powerful lord and master. Wealth to her mind meant power; and this devoted lover was rich. Fate had been infinitely kind to her.

It was a lovely October morning, warm and bright as August. The river banks still seemed to wear their summer green, the blue bright water reflected the cloudless blue above. The bells were ringing for a saint's-day service as Brian's boat shot past the waterside village, with its old square-towered church. All the world had a happy look, as if it smiled at Ida and her choice.

They moved with an easy motion past the pastoral banks, here and there a villa garden, here and there a rustic inn, and so beneath Chertsey's wooded heights to the level fields beyond, and to a spot where the Thames and the Abbey River made a loop round a verdant little marshy island; and here was the silvery weir, brawling noisily in its ceaseless fall, and the lock-house, where Mr. Wendover had lodgings.

The proprietress of that neat abode had just been letting a boat through the lock, and stood leaning lazily against the wood-work, tasting the morning air. She was a comfortable, well-to-do person, who rented a paddock or two by the towing-path, and owned cows. Her little garden was gay with late geraniums and many-coloured asters.

"Mrs. Topman, I have brought you a young lady to take care of for the next twenty-four hours," said Brian, coolly, as he handed Ida out of the boat. "Miss Palliser and I are going to be married to-morrow morning; and, as her friends all live abroad, I want you to take care of her, in a nice, motherly way, till she and I are one. You can give her my rooms, and I can put up at the inn."

Mrs. Topman curtsied, and gazed admiringly at Ida.

"I shall be proud to wait upon such a sweet young lady," she said. "But isn't it rather sudden? You told me there was a young lady in the case, but I never knowed you was going to be married off-hand like this."

"I never knew it myself till an hour ago, Mrs. Topman," answered Brian, gaily. "I knew that I was to be one of the happiest of men some day; but I did not know bliss was so near me. And now I am off to catch the next train from Chertsey. Be sure you give Miss Palliser some breakfast; I don't think she has had a very comfortable one."

He dashed into the cottage and came out again five minutes afterwards, having changed his boating clothes for a costume more appropriate to the streets of London. He clasped Ida's hand, murmured a loving good-bye, and then ran with light footsteps along the towing-path, while Ida stood leaning against the lock door looking dreamily down at the water.

How light-hearted he was! and how easily he took life! This marriage, which was to her an awful thing, signifying fate and the unknown future, seemed to him as a mere whim of the hour, a caprice, a fancy. And yet there could be no doubt of his affection for her. Even if his nature was somewhat shallow, as she feared it must be, he was at least capable of a warm and generous attachment. To her in her poverty and her disgrace he had proved himself nobly loyal.

"I ought to be very grateful to him," she said to herself; and then in her schoolgirl phrase she added, "and he is very nice."

Mrs. Topman was in the house, tidying and smartening that rustic sitting-room, which had not been kept too neatly during Mr. Wendover's occupation. Presently came the clinking of cups and saucers, and anon Mrs. Topman appeared on the doorstep, and announced that breakfast was ready.

What a luxurious breakfast it seemed to the schoolgirl, after a month of the Mauleverer bread and scrape! Frizzled bacon, new laid eggs, cream, marmalade, and a dainty little cottage loaf, all served with exquisite cleanliness. Ida was too highly strung to do justice to the excellent fare, but she enjoyed a cup of strong tea, and ate one of the eggs, to oblige Mrs. Topman, who waited upon her assiduously, palpably panting with friendly curiosity.

"Do take off your hat, miss," she urged; "you must be very tired after your journey—a long journey,

I daresay. Perhaps you would like me to send a boy
with a barrow for your luggage directly after breakfast. I suppose your trunks are at the station?"

"No; Mr. Wendover will arrange about my trunk
by-and-by," faltered Ida; and then looking down at
her well-worn gray cashmere gown, she thought that it
was hardly a costume in which to be married. Yet
how was she to get her box from Mauleverer Manor
without provoking dangerous inquiries? and even if
she had the box its contents would hardly solve the
question of a wedding gown. Her one white gown
would be too cold for the season; her best gown was
black. Would Brian feel very much ashamed of her,
she wondered, if she must needs be married in that
shabby gray cashmere?

And then it occurred to her that possibly Brian,
while procuring the licence, might have a happy thought
about a wedding gown, and buy her one ready made
at a London draper's. He, to whom money was no
object, could so easily get an appropriate costume. It
would be only for him to go into a shop and say, "I
want a neat, pretty travelling dress for a tall slim
young lady," and the thing would be packed in a box
and put into his cab in a trice. Everything in life is
made so easy for people with ample means.

It was some time before Mrs. Topman would consent to leave her new lodger. She was so anxious to
be of use to the sweet young lady, and threw out as
many feelers as an octopus in the way of artfully-devised
conjectures and suppositions calculated to extract information. But Miss Palliser was not communicative.

"You *must* be tired after your journey. Those
railways are so hot and so dusty," said Mrs. Topman,

with a despairing effort to discover whence her unexpected guest had come that morning.

"I am rather tired," admitted Ida; "I think, if you don't mind, I'll take a book and lie down on that comfortable sofa for an hour or two."

"Do, miss. You'll find some books of Mr. Wendover's on the cheffonier. But perhaps you'll be glad to take a little nap. Shall I draw down the blind and darken the room for you?"

"No, thanks, I like the sunshine."

Mrs. Topman unwillingly withdrew, and Ida was alone in the sitting-room which her lover had occupied for the last fortnight.

Much individuality can hardly be expected in a temporary lodging—a mere caravansary in life's journey; and yet, even in the brief space of a fortnight, a room takes some colour from the habits and ideas of the being who has lived in it.

Ida looked round curiously, wondering whether she would discover any indications of her lover's character in Mrs. Topman's parlour. The room, despite its open casements, smelt strongly of tobacco. That was a small thing, for Ida knew that her lover smoked. She had seen him several times throw away the end of his cigar as he sprang from his boat by the river meadow. But that array of various pipes and cigar-holders— that cedar cigar box—that brass tobacco jar on the mantelpiece, hinted at an ardent devotion to the nymph Nicotina such as is rarely pleasing to woman.

"I am sorry he is so wedded to his pipes," thought Ida with a faint sigh.

And then she turned to the cheffonier, to inspect her lover's stock of literature.

A man who loves his books never travels without
a few old favourites—Horace or Montaigne, Elia, an
odd volume of De Quincey, a battered Don Juan, a worn-
out Faust, a shabby Shelley, or a ponderous Burton in
his threadbare cloth raiment. But there was not one
such book among Mr. Wendover's possessions. His
supply of mental food consisted of half a dozen shilling
magazines, the two last numbers of *Punch*, and three
or four sporting papers. Ida turned from them with
bitter disappointment. She seemed to take the measure
of Brian Wendover's mind in that frivolous collection,
and she was deeply pained at the idea of his shallowness.

"What has he done with himself in the long evenings?" she asked herself. "Has he done nothing but
smoke and read those magazines?"

She took up the *Cornhill*, and found its graver
essays uncut. It was the same with the other magazines.
Only the most frivolous articles had been looked at.
Mr. Wendover was evidently anything but a reading
man.

"No wonder he does not like the Abbey," she
thought. "The country must always seem dull to a
man who does not care for books."

And then she reminded herself remorsefully of his
generous affection, his single-minded devotion to her,
and how much gratitude she owed him.

She read all that was worth reading in the magazines, she laughed at all that was laughable in *Punch*,
and the long, slow day wore on somehow. Mrs. Topman brought her lunch, and consulted her about
dinner.

"You will not dine until Mr. Wendover comes

back, I suppose, miss? You and he can have a nice
little dinner together at seven."

Ida blushed at the mere notion of hobnobbing
alone with a gentleman in that water-side lodging.

"No, thanks, this will be my dinner," she answered
quietly. "Please don't get anything more for me. No
doubt Mr. Wendover will dine at the hotel, if he has
not dined in London. I shall want nothing more except a cup of tea."

After luncheon Ida went out and strolled by the
river, that river of which no one ever seems to grow
weary. She wandered about the level meadows, where
the last of the wild-flowers were blooming, or she sat
on the bank, watching the ripple of the water, the
slow smooth passage of pleasure-boat or barge, and
the day was long but not dreary. It was so new to
her to be idle, to be able to fold her hands and watch
the stream, and not to fear reproof because she had
ceased from toil. At Mauleverer, at this tranquil afternoon hour, while those rooks were sailing so calmly
high above her head—yonder belated butterfly fluttering so happily over the feathery grasses—all nature so
full of rest—they were grinding away in the hot schoolroom, grinding at the weekly geography lesson, addling
their brains with feeble efforts to repeat by rote dry-
as-dust explanations about the equator and the torrid
zone, latitude, longitude, winds and tides, the height
of mountains, the population of towns, manufactures,
creeds; not trying in the least to understand, or caring
to remember; only intent on getting over to-day's
trouble and preparing in some wise to meet the debts
of to-morrow.

"Oh, thank God, to have got away from that tread-

mill," said Ida, looking up at the blue, bright sky;
"can I ever be sufficiently grateful to Providence, and
to the man whose love has rescued me?"

Her deliverer came strolling across the fields in
quest of her, presently, tired and dusty, but delighted
to be with her again.

He sat down by her side, and put his arm round
her waist for the first time in his life.

"Don't," he said, as she instinctively recoiled from
him; "you are almost my own now. I have got the
licence, I have seen the parson, and he is quite charmed
at the idea of marrying us to-morrow morning. He
had heard of your little escapade, it seems, and he
thinks we are doing quite the wisest thing possible."

"He had heard—already!" exclaimed Ida, deeply
mortified. "Has Miss Pew been calling out my delin-
quencies from the house-top? Oh, no, I understand.
Tuesday is Mr. Daly's afternoon for Bible class, and
he has been at the school."

"Exactly; and Miss Pew unburdened her mind to
him."

"Did he think me a dreadful creature?"

"He thinks you charming, but that I ought to have
gone to the hall-door when I courted you; as I should
have done, dearest, only I wanted to be sure of you
first. He was all kindness, and will marry us quietly
at nine o'clock to-morrow, just after Matins, when there
will be nobody about to stare at us; and he has promised to say nothing about our marriage until we give
him leave to make the fact public."

"I am glad of that," said Ida, looking at her shabby
gown. "Do you think it will matter much, will you

be very much ashamed of me, if I am married in this thread-bare old cashmere?"

She had a faint hope that he would exclaim, "My love, I have brought you a wedding dress from Regent Street, come and see it." But he only smiled at her tenderly, and said—

"The gown does not matter a jot; you are lovelier in your shabby frock than any other bride in satin and pearls. And some of these days you shall have smart frocks."

He said it hopefully, but as if it were a remote contingency.

He spoke very much as her impecunious father might have spoken. He, the master of Wendover Abbey, to whom the possession of things that money could buy must needs be a dead certainty. But it was evidently a part of his character to make light of his wealth; assuredly a pleasant idiosyncrasy.

They dawdled about on the bank for half an hour or so, talking somewhat listlessly, for Ida was depressed and frightened by the idea of that fateful event, giving a new colour to all her life to come, which was so soon to happen. Brian was very kind, very good to her; she wished with all her heart that she had loved him better; yet it seemed to her that she did love him—a little. Surely this feeling was love, this keen sense of obligation, this warm admiration for his generous and loyal conduct. Yes, this must be love. And why, loving him, should she feel this profound melancholy at the idea of a marriage which satisfied her loftiest ambition?

Perhaps the cause of her depression lay in the strangeness of this sudden union, its semi-clandestine

character, her loneliness at a crisis in life when most
girls are surrounded by friends. Often in her reckless
talk with Bessie Wendover she had imagined her marriage. She would marry for money. Yes, the soap-
boiler, the candlestick maker—anybody. It should be
a splendid wedding—a dozen of the prettiest girls at
Mauleverer for her bridesmaids, bells ringing, flowers
strewn upon her pathway, carriage and four, postillions
in blue jackets and white favours, all the world and his
wife looking on and wondering at her high fortune.
This is how fancy had painted the picture when Ida
discoursed of her future in the butterfly-room at Mauleverer; Miss Rylance listening and making sarcastic
comments; Bessie in fits of smothered laughter at all
the comic touches in the description; for did not true-
hearted Bessie know that the thing was a joke, and
that her noble Ida would never so degrade herself as
to marry for money? And now Ida was going to do
this thing, scarcely knowing why she did it, not at all
secure in her own mind of future happiness; not with
unalloyed pride in her conquest, but yielding to her
lover because he was the first who had ever asked
her; because he was warm and true when all else in
life seemed cold and false; and because the alternative
—return to the poor home—was so dreary.

The conversation flagged as the lovers walked in
the twilight. The sun was sinking behind the low
hedge of yonder level meadow. Far away in mountain-
ous regions the same orb was setting in rocky amphi-
theatres, distant, unapproachable. Here in this level
land he seemed to be going down into a grave behind
that furthest hedge.

It was a lovely evening—orange and rosy lights

reflected on the glassy river, willows stirred with a murmurous movement by faintest zephyrs—a wind no louder than a sigh. Brian proposed that they should go on the river; his boat was there ready, it was only to step into the light skiff, and drift lazily with the stream.

They got into the Abbey river, among water-lilies whose flowers had all died long ago, face downwards. The season of golden flowers, buttercup, marsh-mallow, was over. The fields were grayish-green, with ruddy tinges here and there. The year was fading.

Ida sat in dead silence watching the declining light, one listless hand dipping in the river.

Brian was thoughtful, more thoughtful than she had known him in any period of their acquaintance.

"Where shall we go for our honeymoon?" he asked abruptly, jingling some loose coins in his pocket.

"Oh, that is for you to decide. I—I know what I should like best," faltered Ida.

"What is that?"

"I should like you to take me to Dieppe, where we could see my father, and explain everything to him."

"Did you write to him to-day?"

"No; I thought I would tell him nothing till after our marriage. You might change your mind at the last."

"Cautious young party," said Brian, laughing. "There is no fear of that. I am too far gone in love for that. For good or ill I am your faithful slave. Yes, we will go to Dieppe if you like. It is late in the year for a place of that kind; but what do we care for seasons? Do you think your father and I will be able to get on?"

"My father is the soul of good nature. He would get on with anyone who is a gentleman, and I am sure he will like you very much. My stepmother is—well, she is rather vulgar. But I hope you won't mind that. She is very warm-hearted."

"Vulgarians generally are, I believe," answered Brian lightly. "At least, one is always told as much. It is hard that the educated classes should monopolize all the cold hearts. Vulgar but warm-hearted—misplaces her aspirates—but affectionate! That is the kind of thing one is told when Achilles marries a housemaid. Never mind, Ida dearest, I feel sure I shall like your father; and for his sake I will try to make myself agreeable to his wife. And your little brother is perfection. I have heard enough about him from those dear lips of yours."

"He is a darling little fellow, and I long to see him again. How I wish they could all be with me to-morrow!"

"It would make our wedding more domestic, but don't you think it would vulgarize it a little?" said Brian. "There is something so sweet to me in the idea of you and me alone in that little church, with no witnesses but the clerk and the pew-opener."

"And God!" said Ida, looking upward.

"Did you ever read the discourses of Colonel Bob Ingersoll?" asked Brian, smiling at her.

"No; what has that to do with it?"

"He has curious ideas of omnipotence; and I fancy he would say that the Infinite Being who made every shining star is hardly likely to be on the look-out for our wedding."

"He cares for the lilies, and the sparrows."

"That's a gospel notion. Colonel Bob is not exactly a gospel teacher."

"Then don't you learn of him, Brian," said Ida,
earnestly.

CHAPTER IX.

A SOLEMN LEAGUE AND COVENANT.

THE sun shone upon Ida's wedding morning. She
was dressed and down before seven—her shabby cashmere gown carefully brushed, her splendid hair neatly
arranged, her linen collar and cuffs spotlessly clean.
This was all she could do in the way of costume in
honour of this solemn day. She had not even a new
pair of gloves. Mrs. Topman, who was to go to church
with her in a fly from Chertsey, was gorgeous in purple
silk and a summer bonnet—a grand institution, worn
only on Sundays. Breakfast was ready in the neat
little parlour, but Ida would only take a cup of tea.
She wandered out to the river-side, and looked at the
weir and the little green island round which the shining blue water twined itself like a caress. All things
looked lovely in the pure freshness of morning.

"What a sweet spot it is!" said Ida to Mrs. Topman, who stood at her gate, watching for the fly, which
was not due for half an hour; "I should almost like to
spend my life here."

"Almost, but not quite," answered the matron.
"Young folks like you wants change. But I hope you
and Mr. Wendover will come here sometimes in the
boating season, in memory of old times."

"We'll come often," said Ida; "I hope I shall always remember how kind you have been to me."

A distant church clock struck the half hour.

"Only half-past seven," exclaimed Mrs. Topman, "and Simmons's fly is not to be here till eight. Well, we *are* early."

Ida strolled a little way along the bank, glad to be alone. It was an awful business, this marriage, when she came to the very threshold of Hymen's temple. Yesterday it had seemed to her that she and Brian Wendover were familiar friends; to-day she thought of him almost as a stranger.

"How little we know of each other, and yet we are going to take the most solemn vow that ever was vowed," she thought, as she read the marriage service in a Prayer-book which Mrs. Topman had lent her for that purpose.

"It's as well to read it over and understand what you're going to bind yourself to," said the matron; "I did before I married Topman. It made me feel more comfortable in my mind to know what I was doing. But I must say it's high time there was a change made in the service. It never can have been intended by Providence for all the obedience to be on the wife's side, or God Almighty wouldn't have made husbands such fools. If Topman hadn't obeyed me he'd have died in a workhouse; and if I'd obeyed him I shouldn't have a stick of furniture belonging to me."

Ida was not deeply interested in the late Mr. Topman's idiosyncrasies, but she was interested in the marriage bond, which seemed to her a very solemn league and covenant, as she read the service beside the quietly flowing river.

"For better for worse, for richer or poorer, in sick-

ness and in health, to love and to cherish, till death
us do part."

Yes, those were awful words—words to be pronounced by her presently, binding her for the rest of
her life. She who was marrying a rich man for the
sake of his wealth was to swear to be true to him in
poverty. She who was marrying youth and good
spirits was to swear to be true to sickness and feeble
age. A terrible covenant! And of this man for whom
she was to undertake so much she knew so little.

The fly drove along the towing-path, and drew up
in front of Mr. Topman's garden gate as the Chertsey
clocks struck the hour, and Mrs. Topman and her
charge took their places in that vehicle, and were jolted
off at a jog-trot pace towards the town, and then on by
a dusty high road towards that new church in the
fields at which the Mauleverer girls deemed it such a
privilege to worship.

It was about forty minutes' drive from the lock to
the church, and Matins were only just over when the
fly drew up at the Gothic door.

The incumbent was hovering near in his surplice,
and the pew-opener was all in a fluster at the idea of
a runaway marriage. Brian came out of the dusky
background—the daylight being tempered by small
painted windows in heavy stone mullions—as Ida
entered the church. Everything was ready. Before
she knew how it came to pass, she was standing before the altar, and the fatal words were being spoken.

"Brian Walford, wilt thou have this woman to be
thy wedded wife?"

"Brian Walford!" she heard the words as in a
dream.

12*

Surely Walford was the second name of Bessie's other cousin, the poor cousin! Ida had heard Bessie so distinguish him from the master of the Abbey. But no doubt Walford was some old family name borne by both cousins.

Brian Walford. She had not much time to think about this,· when the same solemn question was asked of her.

And then in a low and quiet voice the priest read the rest of the time-hallowed ceremonial, and Brian and Ida, glorified by a broad ray of morning sunshine, streaming through an open window, stood up side by side man and wife.

Then came the signing of the register in the snug little vestry, Mrs. Topman figuring largely as witness.

"I did not know your name was Walford," said Ida, looking over her husband's shoulder as he wrote.

"Didn't you? Second names are of so little use to a man, unless he has the misfortune to be Smith or Jones, and wants to borrow dignity from a prefix. Wendover is good enough for me."

The young couple bade Mrs. Topman good-bye at the church-door. The fly was to take them straight to the station, on the first stage of their honeymoon trip.

"You know where to send my luggage," Brian said to his landlady at parting.

"Yes, sir, I've got the address all right," and the fly drove along another dusty high road, still within sight of the river, till it turned at right angles into a bye road leading to the station.

At that uncongenial place they had to wait a quarter of an hour, walking up and down the windy platform, where the porter abandoned himself to the contemplation of occasional rooks, and was sometimes surprised by the arrival of a train for which he had waited so long as to have become sceptical as to the existence of such things as trains in the scheme of the universe. The station was a terminus, and the line was a loop, for which very few people appeared to have any necessity.

"Would you mind telling me where we are going, Brian?" Ida asked her husband presently, when they had discussed the characteristics of the station, and Brian had been mildly facetious about the porter.

She had grown curiously shy since the ceremonial. Her lover seemed to her transformed into another person by those fateful words. He was now the custodian of her life, the master of her destiny.

"Would I mind telling you, my dearest? What a question! You proposed Dieppe for our honeymoon and we are going to Dieppe."

"Does this train go to Newhaven?"

"Not exactly. Nothing in this life is so convenient as that. This train will deposit us at Waterloo Station. The train for Newhaven leaves London Bridge at seven, in time for the midnight boat. We will go to my chambers and have some lunch."

"Chambers!" exclaimed Ida, wonderingly. "Have you really chambers in London?"

"Yes."

"What a strange man you are!"

"That hardly indicates strangeness. But here at last is our train."

A train had come slowly in and deposited its handful of passengers about ten minutes ago, and the same train was now ready to start in the opposite direction.

Ida and her husband got into an empty first class compartment, and the train moved slowly off. And now that they were alone, as it were within four walls, she summoned up courage to say something that had been on her mind for the last quarter of an hour—a very hard thing for a bride of an hour old to say, yet which must be said somehow.

"Would you mind giving me a little money, while we are in London, to buy some clothes?" she began hesitatingly. "It is a dreadful thing to have to ask you, when, if I were not like the beggar girl in the ballad, I should have a trousseau. But I don't know when I may get my box from Mauleverer, and when I do most of the things in it are too shabby for your wife; and in the meantime I have nothing, and I should not like to disgrace you, to make you feel ashamed of me while we are on our honeymoon tour."

She sat with downcast eyes and flaming cheeks, deeply humiliated by her position, hating her poverty more than she had ever hated it in her life before. She felt that this rich husband of hers had not been altogether kind to her—that he might by a little fore-thought have spared her this shame. He must have known that she had neither clothes nor money. He who had such large means had done nothing to sweeten her poverty. On this her wedding morning he had brought her no gift save the ring which the law prescribed. He had not brought her so much as a flower by way of greeting; yet she knew by the gossip of her schoolfellows that it was the custom for a lover to ratify his engagement by some splendid ring, which was ever afterwards his betrothed's choicest jewel. The girls had talked of their sisters' engagement-rings: how one had diamonds, another rubies, another catseyes, more distinguished and artistic than either.

And now she sat with drooping eyelids, expecting her lover-husband to break into an outburst of self reproach, then pour a shower of gold into her lap. But he did neither. He rattled some loose coins in his pocket, just as he had done yesterday when he talked of the honeymoon; and he answered hesitatingly, with evident embarrassment.

"Yes, you'll want some new clothes, I daresay. All girls do when they marry, don't they? It's a kind of unwritten law—new husband, new gowns. But I'm sure you can't look better than you do in that gray gown, and it looks to me just the right thing for travelling. And for any other little things you may want for the moment, if a couple of sovereigns will do"—producing those coins—"you can get anything you like as we drive to my chambers. We could stop at a draper's on our way."

Ida was stricken dumb by this reply. Her cheeks changed from crimson to pale. Her wealthy husband —the man whose fortune was to give her all those good things she had ever pictured to herself in the airy visions of a splendid future—offered her, with a half-reluctant air, as if offering his life's blood, two sovereigns with which to purchase a travelling outfit. What could she buy for two sovereigns? Not all the economy of her girlhood could screw half the things she wanted out of that pitiful sum.

She thought of all those descriptions of weddings which were so eagerly devoured at Mauleverer, whenever a fashionable newspaper fell in the way of those

eager neophytes. She recalled the wonderful gifts
which the bridegroom and the bridegroom's friends
showered on the bride—the glorious gown and bonnet
in which the bride departed on her honeymoon journey.
And she was offered two sovereigns, wherewith to
supply herself with all things needful for comfort
and respectability.

Pride gave her strength to refuse the sordid boon.
She had the contents of her small travelling bag, and
she was going to her father's house, where her step-
mother would, perhaps, contrive to provide what was
absolutely necessary. Anything was better than to be
under an obligation to this rich husband who so little
understood her needs.

Could she have married that most detestable of all
monsters, a miser? No, she could hardly believe that.
It was not in a Wendover to be mean. And all that
she had observed hitherto of Brian's way of acting and
thinking rather indicated a recklessness about money,
than an undue care of pounds, shillings, and pence.

"If you don't object to this gown and hat, I can
manage very well till we get to my father's house," she
said quietly.

"I adore you in that hat and gown," replied Brian,
eagerly, dropping the sovereigns back into his pocket;
and so the question was settled.

An elderly lady came into the carriage at the next
station, and there was no renewal of confidences between bride and bridegroom till they came to Waterloo,
nor even then, for there is not much opportunity for
confidential utterances in a hansom, and it was that
convenient vehicle which carried Brian and his bride
to Gray's Inn Lane.

"What a horrid part of London!" exclaimed Ida, with a shudder, for that Holborn end of Gray's Inn is not lovely, least of all so to eyes accustomed to green fields and the gracious curves and reaches of a silvery stream. "Surely you do not live here?"

"Yes, I do, when I am in town," answered Brian, "and it's not half a bad place to live in, as you'll see presently."

They alighted at a door in Verulam Buildings, a very dull and dingy row of houses on this side, but pleasant enough facing the famous garden where Bacon mused and philosophized in the golden age of learning. Brian led his wife up the uncarpeted stair to the second floor, where he ushered her into a room with two old-fashioned windows looking out upon grass, and trees, and old-fashioned buildings, all grave and gray, and having an air of sober peacefulness, as of a collegiate or monastic seclusion.

"What a nice old place!" said Ida, looking down at the garden. "How quiet, how grave, how learned looking! I don't wonder you like this *pied-à-terre* in London, as a change from your grand old Abbey."

Brian gave a little nervous cough, as if something were choking him. He came to the window, and put his arm round his wife's waist.

"Ida," he began, somewhat huskily, "I am going to tell you a secret."

"What is that?" she asked, turning and looking at him.

"The Abbey does not belong to me!"

"What?" she cried, with wide-open eyes.

"You have been rather fond of talking about the Abbey; but I hope your heart is not too much set upon it. You told me the other day, you know, that you did not value me upon account of the Abbey or my position as its owner. I hope that was the truth, Ida; for Wendover Abbey belongs to my cousin. You have married the poor Brian, and not the rich one!"

"What?" she cried. "You have lied to me all this time—you have fooled and deluded me!"

She turned and faced him with eyes that flamed indignant fire, with lips that quivered with unrestrained passion.

"It was not my doing," he faltered, shrinking before her like the veriest craven; "it was the girls —Urania and Bessie—who started the notion as a practical joke, just to see what you would think of me, believing me to be my cousin. And when you seemed to like me—a little—Bessie, who is fond of me and who adores you, urged me to follow up my advantage."

"But not to cheat me into a marriage. No; it is not in Bessie to suggest such falsehood."

"She hardly contemplated an immediate marriage. I was to win your heart, and when I was sure of that——"

"You were to tell me the truth," said Ida, looking him straight in the eyes.

His head drooped upon his breast.

"And you did not tell me. You knew that I saw in you Brian Wendover, the head of the family, the owner of a great estate; that I was proud of being loved and sought by a man who stooped from such a high position to love me, who renounced the chance of a brilliant marriage to marry me, a penniless nobody! You knew that it was in that character I admired you and respected you, and was grateful to you! Not as the briefless barrister—the man without means or position!"

"You harped a good deal upon the Abbey. But I had some right to suppose you liked me for my own sake, and that you would forgive me for a stratagem which was prompted by my love for you. How could I know that you looked upon marriage as a matter of exchange and barter?"

"No," said Ida, bitterly. "You are right. You could not know how mean I am. I did not know it myself till now. And now," she pursued, with flashing eyes, with a look in her splendid face that seemed to blight and wither him, with all her beauty, all her womanhood up in arms against him, "and now to punish you for having kept the truth from me, I will tell *you* the truth—plainly. I have never cared one straw for you. I thought I did while I still believed you Brian Wendover of the Abbey. I was dazzled by your position; I was grateful in advance for all the good things that your wealth was to bring me. I tried to delude myself into the belief that I really loved you; but the voice of my conscience told me that it was not so, that I was, in sober truth, the basest of creatures— a woman who marries for money. And now, standing here before you, I know what a wretch I seem—what a wretch I am."

"You are my wife," said Brian, trying to take her hand; "and we must both make the best of a bad bargain."

"Your wife?" she echoed, in a mocking voice.

"Yes, my very wife, Ida. The knot that was tied to-day can only be loosened by death—or dishonour."

"You have married me under a false name."

"No, I have not. You married Brian Walford
Wendover. There is no other man of that name."

"You have cheated me into a miserable marriage.
I will never forgive that cheat. I will never acknowledge you as my husband. I will never bear your
name, or be anything to you but a stranger, except
that I shall hate you all the days of my life. That
will be the only bond between us," she added, with a
bitter laugh.

"Come, Ida," said Brian, soothingly, feeling himself
quite able to face the situation now the first shock was
over, "I was prepared for you to be disappointed—to
be angry, even; but you are carrying matters a little
too far. Even your natural disappointment can hardly
excuse such language as this. I am the same man I
was yesterday morning when I asked you to marry me."

"No, you are not. I saw you in a false light—
glorified by attributes that never belonged to you."

"In plain words, you thought me the owner of a
big house and a fine income. I am neither; but I am
the same Brian Wendover, for all that—a briefless
barrister, but with some talent; not without friends;
and with as fair a chance of success as most young
men of my rank."

"You are an idler—I have heard that from your
uncle—self-indulgent, fond of trivial pleasures. Such
men never succeed in life. But if you were certain to
be Lord Chancellor—if you could this moment prove
yourself possessed of a splendid fortune—my feelings
would be unchanged. You have lied to me as no
gentleman would have lied. I will own no husband
who is not a gentleman."

"You carry things with a high hand," said Brian,

with sullen wrath; and then love prevailed over anger, and he flung himself on his knees at her feet, clasping her reluctant hands, urging every impassioned argument which young lips could frame; but to all such prayers she was marble. "You are my wife," he pleaded; "you are my snared bird; your wings are netted, darling. Do you think I will let you go? Yes, I was false, but it was love made me deceive you. I loved you so well that I dared not risk losing you."

"You have lost me for ever," she cried, breaking from him and moving towards the door; "perhaps, had you been loyal and true, you might have taught me to love you for your own sake. Women are easier won by truth than falsehood."

"It seems to me they are easier won by houses and lands," answered Brian, with a sneer.

And then he followed her to the door, caught her in his arms, and held her against his passionately beating heart, covering her angry face with kisses.

"Let me go!" she cried, tearing herself from his arms, with a shriek of horror; "your kisses are poison to me. I hate you—I hate you!"

He recoiled a few paces, and stood looking at her with a countenance in which the passionate love of a moment ago gave place to gloomy anger.

"So be it," he said; "if we cannot be friends we must be enemies. You reveal your character with an admirable candour. You did not mind marrying a man who was absolutely repulsive to you—whose kisses are poison—so long as you thought he was rich. But directly you are told he is poor you inform him of your real sentiments with a delightful frankness. Suppose this confession of mine were a hoax, and that I really were the wealthy Brian after all—playing off a practical joke to test your feelings—what a sorry figure you would cut!"

"Despicable," said Ida, with her hand on the handle of the door. "Yes, I know that. I despise and loathe myself as much as I despise and loathe you. I have drained the cup of poverty to the dregs, and I languished for the elixir of wealth. When you asked me to marry you, I thought Fate had thrown prosperity in my way—that it would be to lose the golden chance of a lifetime if I refused you."

"Not much gold about it," said Brian, lightly.

He had one of those shallow natures to which the tragedy of life is impossible. He was disappointed— angry at the turn which affairs had taken; but he was not reduced to despair. To take things easily had been his complete code of morals and philosophy from earliest boyhood. He was not going to break his heart for any woman, were she the loveliest, the cleverest, the noblest that ever the gods endowed with their choicest gifts. She might be ever so fair, but if she were not fair for him she was, in a manner, non-existent. Life, in his philosophy, was too short to be wasted in following phantoms.

"You must have thought me a mean cad this morning, when I offered you a couple of sovereigns," he said; "yet they constituted a third of my worldly possessions, and I was sorely puzzled how we were to get to Dieppe on less than four pounds. I have been living from hand to mouth ever since I left the university, picking up a few pounds now and then by literature, writing criticisms for a theatrical journal, and so on— by no means a brilliant living. Perhaps, after all, it is

as well you take things so severely," he added, with a
sneer. "If we had been well disposed towards each
other, we must have starved."

"I could have lived upon a crust with a husband
whom I loved and respected; but not with a man who
could act a lie, as you did," said Ida.

She took her bag from the chair where Brian had
thrown it as they entered the room, and went out on
the landing.

"Good-bye, Mrs. Wendover," he called after her;
"let me know if I can ever be of any use to you."

She was going downstairs by this time, and he was
looking down at her across the heavy old banister rail.

"I suppose you are going straight to your father's?"

"Yes."

"Hadn't you better stop and have some lunch?
The train doesn't go for hours."

"No, thanks."

The gray gown fluttered against the sombre brown
panelling as his wife turned the corner of the lower
landing and disappeared from his view—perhaps for
ever.

Brian went back to his room, and stood in the
middle of it, looking round him with a contemplative
air. It was a pleasant room, arranged with rather a
dandified air—pipes, walking-sticks, old engravings,
bric-à-brac—the relics of his college life.

"Well, if she had been more agreeable I should
have had to get new rooms, and that would have been
a bore," he said to himself; and then he sank into a
chair, gave a laugh that was half a sob, and wiped a
mist of tears from his eyes.

"What fools we have both been!" he muttered to

himself. "I knew she was in love with the Abbey; but
I don't believe a word she says about hating me!"

And yet—and yet—she had seemed very much in
earnest when she tore herself from his arms with that
agonised shriek.

CHAPTER X.

A BAD PENNY.

IDA hurried along the shabby, squalid looking
street towards Holborn, hardly knowing where she was
going or what she was going to do. The airy castle
which she had built for herself had fallen about her
ears, and she was left standing amidst the ruins.
Wendover Abbey, wealth, position, independence, the
world's respect were all as far from her as they had
been a month ago. Her sense of disappointment was
keen, but not so keen as the sense of her self-abasement. Her own character stood revealed to herself in
all its meanness—its sordid longing for worldly wealth
—its willingness to stoop to falsehood in the pursuit
of a woman's lowest aim, a good establishment. Seen
in the light of abject failure, the scheme of her life
seemed utterly detestable. Success would have gilded
everything. As the wife of the rich Brian she would
have done her duty in all wifely meekness and obedience, and would have gone down to the grave under
the comforting delusion that she had in no wise forfeited honour or self-respect. Cheated, duped, degraded,
she now felt all the infamy implied in her willingness
to marry a man for whom she cared not a straw.

"Oh, it was cruel, iniquitous," she said to herself,
as she hurried along the dusty pavement, impelled by

agitated thoughts, "to trade upon my weakness—my misery—to see me steeped to the lips in odious poverty, and to tempt me with the glitter of wealth. I never pretended to love him—never—thank God for that! I let him tell me that he loved me, and I consented to be his wife; but I pretended no love on my side. Thank God for that! He cannot say that I lied to him."

She stood in broad, busy Holborn, with all the traffic hastening by her, staring helplessly at the cabs and omnibuses, wagons, carriages streaming east and west under the murky London sky, vaguely wondering what she was to do next.

He—her husband—had asked her if she were going back to her father, and she had said "Yes." Indeed it was the only course open to her. She must go home and face the situation, and accept any paternal reproof that might be offered her. She had lost a day. No doubt Miss Pew's indictment would have arrived before her; and she would have to explain her conduct to father and step-mother. But the little white-walled house near Dieppe was the only shelter the universe held for her, and she must go there.

"Wendover Abbey!" she repeated to herself. "I the mistress of Wendover Abbey! That was too good a joke. Why did I not see the folly of such a dream? But it was just like other dreams. When one dreams one is a queen, or that one can fly, there is no consciousness of the absurdity of the thing."

She stood staring at the omnibuses till the conductor of one that was nearly empty murmured invitingly in her ear, "London Bridge?"

It was the place to which she wanted to go. She nodded to the man, who opened his door and let her in.

She was at the station at a quarter to four, and the train for Newhaven did not leave till seven—a long dismal stretch of empty time to be lived through. But she could not improve her situation by going anywhere else. The station, with its dingy waiting-rooms and garish refreshment room, was as good an hotel for her as any other. She was faint for want of food, having taken nothing since her apology for breakfast at seven o'clock.

"Can one get a cup of tea here?" she asked of the dry-as-dust matron in charge of the waiting-room; whereupon the matron good-naturedly offered to fetch her some tea.

"If you would be so kind," she faltered, too exhausted to speak above a whisper; "I don't like going into that crowded refreshment room."

"No, to be sure—not much used to travelling alone, I daresay. You will be better when you've had a cup of tea."

The tea, with a roll and butter, revived exhausted nature. Ida paid for this temperate refreshment, went to the booking-office, made some inquiries about her ticket, and bought herself a book at the stall, wherewith to beguile the time and to distract her mind from brooding on its own miseries.

She felt it was a frightful extravagance as she paid away two of Miss Cobb's shillings for Bulwer's "Caxtons;" but she felt also that to live through those three tedious hours without such aid would be a step on the road to a lunatic asylum.

Armed with her book, she went back to the waiting-room, settled herself in a corner of the sofa, and remained there absorbed, immovable; while travellers

came and went, all alike fussy, flurried, and full of
their own concerns—not one of them stopping to notice the pale tired-looking girl reading in the remotest
corner of the spacious room.

A somewhat stormy passage brought the boat which
carried Ida and her fortunes to straggling, stony, smelly
Dieppe, now abandoned to its native population, and
deprived of that flavour of fashion which pervades its
beach in the brighter months of August and September.
The town looked gray, cold, and forbidding in the
bleak October morning, when Ida found herself alone
amidst its stoniness, the native population only just
beginning to bestir itself in the street above the quay,
and making believe, by an inordinate splashing and a
frantic vehemence in the use of birch-brooms, to be
the cleanest population under the sun; an assertion of
superiority somewhat belied by an all-pervading odour
of decomposed vegetable matter, a small heap of which
refuse, including egg-shells and fishy offal—which the
town in the matutinal cleansing process offered up to
the sun-god as incense upon an altar—lay before
every door, to be collected by the local scavenger at
his leisure, or to be blown about and disseminated by
the winds of heaven.

Alone upon the stony quay, in the freshness and
chilliness of early morning, Ida took temporary refuge
in the humblest *café* she could find, where a feeble
old woman was feebly brooming the floor, and where
there was no appearance of any masculine element.
Here she expended another of Miss Cobb's shillings
upon a cup of coffee and a roll. She had spent five
and twenty shillings for her second-class ticket. The
debt to Miss Cobb now amounted to a sovereign and

a half; and Ida Palliser thought of it with an aching
sense of her own helplessness to refund so large a sum.
Yesterday morning, believing herself about to become
the wife of a rich man, she had thought what fun it
would be to send "Cobby" a five-pound note in the
prettiest of ivory purses from one of those shops in
the street yonder.

She drank her coffee slowly, not anxious to hasten
the hour of a home-coming which could not be altogether pleasant. She was as fond of her father as adverse circumstances had allowed her to be; she adored
her half-brother, and was not unkindly disposed towards her step-mother. But to go back to them penniless, threadbare, disgraced—to go back to be a burden
upon their genteel poverty. That was bitter.

She had made up her mind to walk to Les Fontaines rather than make any further inroad upon Miss
Cobb's purse for coach-hire. What was she that she
should be idle or luxurious, or spare the labour of her
young limbs? She went along the narrow stony street
where the shops were only now being opened, past the
wide market where the women were setting out their
stalls in front of the fine old church, and where
Duguesclin, heroic and gigantic, defied the stormy
winds that had ruffled his sculptured hair.

Two years and a half ago it had been a treat to
her to walk in that market-place, hanging on her
father's arm, to stand in the sombre stillness of that
solemn cathedral, while the organ rolled its magnificent
music along the dusky aisles. They two had chaffered
for fruit at those stalls, laughing gaily with the good-
tempered countrywomen. They had strolled on the
beach and amused themselves economically, from the

outside, with the diversions of the *établissement*. An afternoon in Dieppe had meant fun and holiday-making. Now she looked at the town with weary eyes, and thought how dull and shabby it had grown.

The walk to Les Fontaines, along a white dusty road, seemed interminable. If she had not been told again and again that it was only four miles from the town to the village, she would have taken the distance for eight—so long, so weary seemed the way. There were hills in the background, hills right and left of her, orchards, glimpses of woodland—here and there a peep of sea—a pretty enough road to be whirled along in a comfortable carriage with a fast horse, but passing flat, stale, and unprofitable to the heavy-hearted pedestrian.

At last the little straggling village, the half-dozen new houses—square white boxes, which seemed to have been dropped accidentally in square enclosures of ragged garden—white-walled penitentiaries on a small scale, deriving an air of forced liveliness from emerald-green shutters, here a tree, and there a patch of rough grass, but never a flower—for the scarlet geraniums in the plaster vases on the wall of the grandest of the mansions had done blooming, and beyond scarlet geraniums on the wall the horticultural taste of Les Fontaines had never risen. The old cottages, with heavy thatched roofs and curious attic windows, with fruit trees sprawling over the walls, and orchards in the rear, were better than the new villas; but even these lacked the neatness and picturesque beauty of an English cottage in a pastoral landscape. There was a shabby dustiness, a barren, comfortless look about everything; and the height of ugliness was attained in the new church, a plastered barn, with a gaudily painted figure of our Blessed Lady in a niche above the door, all red and blue and gold, against the white-washed wall.

Ida thought of Kingthorpe,—the rustic inn with its queer old gables, shining lattices, quaint dovecots, the green, the pond, with its willowy island, the lovely old Gothic church — solid, and grave, and gray — calm amidst the shade of immemorial yews. The country about Les Fontaines was almost as pretty as that hilly region between Winchester and Romsey; but the English village was like a gem set in the English landscape, while the French village was a wart on the face of a smiling land.

"Why call it Les Fontaines?" Ida wondered, in her parched and dusty weariness. "It is the dryest village I ever saw; and I don't believe there is anything like a fountain within a mile."

Her father's house was one of the white boxes with green shutters. It enjoyed a dignified seclusion behind a plaster wall, which looked as if anyone might knock it down in very wantonness. The baby-boy had varied the monotony of his solitary sports by picking little bits out of it. There was a green door opening into this walled forecourt or garden, but the door was not fastened, so Ida pushed it open and went in. The baby-boy, now a sturdy vagabond of five years old, was digging an empty flower-bed. He caught sight of his sister, and galloped off into the house before she could take him in her arms, shouting "Maman, une dame—une dame! lady, lady, lady!" exercising his lungs upon both those languages which were familiar to his dawning intelligence.

His mother came out at his summons, a pretty, blue-eyed woman with an untidy gown and towzley hair, aged and faded a little since Ida had seen her.

"Oh, Ida," she said, kissing her step-daughter heartily enough, despite her reproachful tone, "how could you go on so? We have had such a letter from Miss Pew. Your father is awfully cut up. And we were expecting you all yesterday. He went to Dieppe to meet the afternoon boat. Where have you been since Tuesday?"

"I slept at the lock-house with a nice civil woman, who gave me a night's lodging," said Ida, somewhat embarrassed by this question.

"But why not have come home at once, dear?" asked the stepmother mildly. She always felt herself a poor creature before her Juno-like daughter.

"I was flurried and worried—hardly knew what I was doing for the first few hours after I left Mauleverer; and I let the time slip by till it was too late to think of travelling yesterday," answered Ida. "Old Pew is a demon."

"She seems to be a nasty unkind old thing," said Mrs. Palliser; "for, after all, the worst she can bring against you is flirting with your friend's cousin. I hope you are engaged to him, dear; for that will silence everybody."

"No, I am not engaged to him—he is nothing to me," answered Ida, crimsoning; "I never saw him, except in Fräulein's company. Neither you nor my father would like me to marry man without sixpence."

"But in Miss Pew's letter she said you declared you were engaged to Mr. Wendover of the Abbey, a gentleman of wealth and position. She was wicked enough to say she did not believe a word you said; but still, Ida, I do hope you were not telling falsehoods."

"I hardly knew what I said," replied Ida, feeling the difficulties of her position rising up on every side and hemming her in. She had never contemplated this kind of thing when she repudiated her marriage and turned her face homewards. "She maddened me by her shameful attack, talking to me as if I were dirt, degrading me before the whole school. If you had been treated as I was you would have been beside yourself."

"I might have gone into hysterics," said Mrs. Palliser, "but I don't think I should have told deliberate falsehoods: and to say that you were engaged to a rich man when you were not engaged, and the man hasn't a sixpence, was going a little too far. But don't fret, dear," added the stepmother, soothingly, as the tears of shame and anger—anger against fate, life, all things—welled into Ida's lovely eyes. "Never mind. We'll say no more about it. Come upstairs to your own room—it's Vernie's day-nursery now, but you won't mind that, I know—and take off your hat. Poor thing, how tired and ill you look!"

"I feel as if I was going to be ill and die, and I hope I am," said Ida, petulantly.

"Don't dear, it's wicked to say such a thing as that. You needn't be afraid of your poor pa, he takes everything easily."

"Yes, he is always good. Where is he?"

"Not up yet. He comes down in time for his little *déjeûner à la fourchette*. Poor fellow, he had to get up so early in India."

Captain Palliser had for the last seven years been

trying to recover those arrears of sleep incurred during his Eastern career. He had been active enough under a tropical sky, when his mind was kept alive by a modicum of hard work and a very wide margin of sport—pig-sticking, peacock-shooting, paper-chases, all the delights of an Indian life. But now, vegetating on a slender pittance in the semi-slumberous idleness of Les Fontaines, he had nothing to do and nothing to think about; and he was glad to shorten his days by dozing away the fresher hours of the morning, while his wife toiled at the preparation of that elaborate meal which he loved to talk about as tiffin.

Poor little Mrs. Palliser made strenuous efforts to keep the sparsely furnished dusty house as clean and trim as it could be kept; but her life was a perpetual conflict with other people's untidiness.

The house was let furnished, and everything was in the third-rate French style—inferior mahogany and cheap gilding, bare floors with gaudy little rugs lying about here and there, tables with flaming tapestry covers, chairs cushioned with red velvet of the commonest kind, sham tortoiseshell clock and candelabra on the dining-room chimney-piece, alabaster clock and candelabra in the drawing-room. There was nothing homelike or comfortable in the house to atone for the smallness of the rooms, which seemed mere cells to Ida after the spaciousness of Mauleverer Manor and The Knoll. She wondered how her father and mother could breathe in such rooms.

That bed-chamber to which Mrs. Palliser introduced her step-daughter was even a shade shabbier than the rest of the house. The boy had run riot here, had built his bricks in one corner, had stabled a headless

wooden horse and cart in another, and had scattered
traces of his existence everywhere. There were his
little Windsor chair, the nurse-girl's rocking chair, a
battered old table, a heap of old illustrated newspapers,
and torn toy-books.

"You won't mind Vernon's using the room in the
day, dear, will you?" said Mrs. Palliser, apologetically.
"It shall be tidied for you at night."

This meant that in the daytime Ida would have no
place for retreat, no nook or corner of the house which
she might call her own. She submitted meekly even
to this deprivation, feeling that she was an intruder
who had no right to be there.

"I should like to see my father soon," she said,
with a trembling lip, stooping down to caress Vernon,
who had followed them upstairs.

He was a lovely fair-haired boy, with big candid
blue eyes, a lovable, confiding child, full of life and
spirits and friendly feeling towards all mankind and the
whole animal creation, down to its very lowest forms.

"You shall have your breakfast with him," said
Mrs. Palliser, feeling that she was conferring a great
favour, for the Captain's breakfast was a meal apart.
"I don't say but what he'll be a little cross to you at
first; but you must put up with that. He'll come
round afterwards."

"He has not seen me for two years and a half,"
said Ida, thinking that fatherly affection ought to count
for something under such circumstances.

"Yes, it's only two years and a half," sighed Mrs.
Palliser, "and you were to have stayed at Mauleverer
Manor three years. Miss Pew is a wicked old woman
to cheat your father out of six months' board and

tuition. He paid her fifty pounds in one lump when he articled you—fifty pounds—a heap of money for people in our position; and here you are, come back to us like a bad penny."

"I am very sorry," faltered Ida, reddening at that unflattering comparison. "But I worked very hard at Mauleverer, and am tolerably experienced in tuition. I must try to get a governess's situation directly, and then I shall be paid a salary, and shall be able to give you back the fifty pounds by degrees."

"Ah, that's the dreadful part of it all," sighed Mrs. Palliser, who was very seldom in the open air, and had that despondent view of life common to people who live within four narrow walls. "Goodness knows how you are ever to get a situation without references. Miss Pew says you are not to refer to her; and who else is there who knows anything of you or your capacity?"

"Yes, there is some one else. Bessie Wendover and her family."

"The people you went to visit in Hampshire. Ah! there went another five pounds in a lump. You have been a heavy expense to us, Ida. I don't know whether anyone wanting to employ you as a governess would take such a reference as that. People are so particular. But we must hope for the best, and in the meantime you can make yourself useful at home in taking care of Vernon and teaching him his letters. He is dreadfully backward."

"He is an angel," said Ida, lifting the cherub in her arms, and letting the fair, curly head nestle upon her shoulder. "I will wait upon him like a slave. You do love me, don't you, pet?"

"Ess, I love 'oo, but I don't know who 'oo is. *Con-nais pas*," said Vernon, shaking his head vehemently.

"I am your sister, darling, your only sister."

"My half-sister," said Vernon. "Maman said I had a half-sister, and she was naughty. *Dites donc*, would a whole sister be twice as big as you?"

Thus in his baby language, which may be easier imagined than described, gravely questioned the boy.

"I am your sister, dearest, heart and soul. There is no such thing as half-love or half-sisterhood between us. You should not have talked to him like that, mother," said Ida, turning her reproachful gaze upon her step-mother, who was melted to tears.

"Your father was so upset by Miss Pew's letter," she murmured apologetically. "To pay fifty pounds for you, and for it to end in such humiliation as that. You must own that it was hard for us."

"It was harder for me," said Ida; "I had to stand up and face that wicked woman, who knew that I had done no wrong, and who wreaked her malignity upon me because I am cleverer and better-looking than ever she was in her life."

"I must go and make your father's omelette," said the step-mother, "while you tidy yourself for breakfast. I think there's some water on the washstand, and Vernon shall bring you a clean towel."

The little fellow trotted out after his mother, and trotted back presently with the towel—one towel, which was about in proportion to the water-jug and basin. Ida shuddered, remembering the plentitude of water and towels at The Knoll. She made her toilet as well as she could, with the scantiest materials, as she might have done on board ship; shook and brushed the shabby gray cashmere—her wedding gown, she thought, with a bitter smile—before she put it on again, and then went down the bare narrow deal stair case, superb in all the freshness of her youth and beauty, which neither care nor poverty could spoil.

Captain Palliser was pacing up and down his little dining parlour, looking flurried and anxious. He turned suddenly as Ida entered, and stood staring at her.

"By Jove, how handsome you have grown!" he said, and then he took her in his arms and kissed her. "But you know, my dear, this is really too bad," he went on in a fretful tone, "to come back upon us like a bad penny."

"That is what my step-mother said just now."

"My dear, how can one help saying it, when it's the truth? After my paying fifty pounds, don't you know, and thinking that you were comfortably disposed of for the next three years, and that at the expiry of the term Miss Pew would place you in a gentleman's family, where you would receive from sixty to a hundred per annum, according to your acquirements—those were her very words—to have you sent back to us like this, in disgrace, and to be told that you had been carrying on in an absurd way with a young man on the bank of a river. It is most humiliating. And now my wife tells me the young man has not a sixpence, which makes the whole thing so very culpable."

"Please let me tell you the extent of my iniquity, father, and then you can judge what right Miss Pew had to expel me."

Whereupon Ida quietly described her afternoon promenades upon the river-path, with the Fräulein always in her company, and how her friend's cousin had been permitted to walk up and down with them.

"Nobody supposes there was any actual harm," replied Captain Palliser, "but you must have been perfectly aware that you were acting foolishly—that this kind of thing was a violation of the school etiquette. Come, now, you knew Miss Pew would disapprove of such goings on, did you not?"

"Well, yes, no doubt I knew old Pew would be horrified. Perhaps it was the idea of that which gave a zest to the thing."

"Precisely! and you never thought of my fifty pounds, and you ran this risk for the sake of a young man without a penny, who never could be your husband."

Ida grew scarlet and then deadly pale.

"There, don't look so distressed, child. I must try to forget my fifty pounds, and to think of your future career. It is a deuced awkward business—here comes the omelette and the coffee—an escapade of this kind is always cropping up against a girl in after life—sit down and make yourself comfortable—capital dish of kidneys—the world is so small; and of course every pupil at Mauleverer Manor will gabble about this business. No mushrooms—what is the little woman thinking about?"

Captain Palliser seated himself, and arranged his napkin under his chin, French fashion. His features were of that aquiline type which seems to have been invented on purpose for army men. His eyes were light blue, like his boy's—Ida's dark eyes were a maternal inheritance—his hair was auburn, sprinkled with gray, his moustache straw-colour, and with a carefully trained cavalry droop. His clothes and boots were perfect of their kind, albeit they had seen good wear. He had been heard to declare that he had rather wear feathers and war-paint, like a red Indian, than a coat made by a third-rate tailor. He was tall and inclining to stoutness, broad-shouldered, and with an easy carriage and a nonchalant air, which were not without their charm. He had what most people called a patrician look—that is to say, the air of never having done anything useful in the whole course of his existence—not such a patrician as a Palmerston, a Russell, a Derby, or a Salisbury, but the ideal lotus-eating aristocrat, who dresses, drives, and dines, and gossips through a languid existence.

The Captain's career in the East had not been particularly brilliant. His lines had not lain in great battles or stirring campaigns. Except during the awful episode of the Mutiny, when he was still a young man, he had seen little active service. His life, since his return from India, had been a blank.

His mind never vigorous, had rusted slowly in the slow monotony of his days. He had come to accept the rhythmical ebb and flow of life's river as all sufficient for content. Breakfast and dinner were the chief events of his life—if it was well with these it was well with him.

There was a rustic tavern where in summer a good many people came to dine, either in the house or the garden, and in a room adjoining the kitchen there was a small French billiard-table with very big balls. Here the Captain played of an evening with the *habitués* of the place, and was much looked up to for his superior skill. An occasional drive into Dieppe on the *banquette* of the diligence, and a saunter by the sea, was his only other amusement.

His daughter poured out his coffee, and ministered
to his various wants as he breakfasted, eating with but
little appetite herself, albeit the fare was excellent.

Captain Palliser talked in a desultory way as he
ate, not often looking up from his plate, but meandering on. Happily for Ida, who had been reduced to
the lowest stage of self-abasement by her welcome, he
said no more about Miss Pew or his daughter's gloomy
prospects. It was not without a considerable mental
effort that he was able to bring his thoughts to bear
upon other people's business. He had strained his
mind a good deal during the last twenty-four hours,
and he was very glad to relax the tension of the bow.

"Rather a dull kind of life for a man who has
been used to society—eh, Ida?" he murmured, as he
ate his omelette; "but we contrive to rub on somehow.
Your step-mother likes it, and the boy likes it—wonderful healthy air, don't you know—no smoke—no
fogs—only three miles from the sea, as the crow flies.
It suits them, and it's cheap—a paramount consideration with a poor devil on half-pay; and in the season
there are some of the best people in Europe to be
seen at the *établissement*."

"I suppose you go to Dieppe often in the season,
father?" said Ida, pleased to find he had dropped
Miss Pew and the governess question.

"Well, yes; I wander in almost every fine day."

"You don't walk?" exclaimed Ida, surprised at
such activity in a man of his languid temper.

"Oh, no; I never walk. I just wander in—on the
diligence—or in a return fly. I wander in and look
about me a little, and perhaps take a cup of coffee
with a friend at the Hotel des Bains. There is generally

some one I know at the Bains or the Royal. Ah, by-the-bye whom do you think I saw there a fortnight ago?"

"I haven't the least idea," answered Ida; "I know so few of your friends."

"No, of course not. You never saw Sir Vernon Palliser, but you've heard me talk about him."

"Your rich brother, the wicked old baronet in Sussex, who never did you a kindness in his life?"

"My dear, old Sir Vernon has been dead two years."

"I never heard of his death."

"No, by-the-bye. It wasn't worth while worrying you about it, especially as we could not afford to go into mourning. Your stepmother fretted about that dreadfully, poor little woman; as if it could matter to her, when she had never seen the man in her life. She said if one had a baronet in one's family one ought to go into mourning for him. I can't understand the passion some women have for mourning. They are eager to smother themselves in crape at the slightest provocation, and for a mean old beggar like Vernon, who never gave me a sixpence. But as I was saying, these two young fellows turned up the other day in front of the Hôtel des Bains."

"Which two young fellows, my dear father? I haven't the faintest idea of whom you are talking," protested Ida, who found her father's conversation very difficult to follow.

"Why, Sir Vernon, of course—the present Sir Vernon and his brother Peter: ugly name, isn't it, Ida? but there has always been a Peter in the family; and as a rule," added Captain Palliser, growing slower and dreamier of speech as he fell into reminiscences of the past—"as a rule the Peter Pallisers have gone to the dogs. There was Major Palliser—fought in the Peninsula—knew George the Fourth—married a very pretty woman and beat her—died in the Bench."

"Tell me about the present Sir Vernon," asked Ida, more interested in the moving, breathing life of to-day than in memories of the unknown dead. "Is he nice?"

"He is a fine broad-shouldered young fellow— seven or eight and twenty. No, not handsome—my brother Vernon was never distinguished for beauty, though he had all the markings of race. There is nothing like race, Ida; you see it in a man's walk; you hear it in every tone of a man's voice."

"Dear father, I was asking about this particular Sir Vernon," urged Ida, with a touch of impatience, unaccustomed to this slow meandering talk.

"And I was telling you about him," answered the Captain, slightly offended. His little low-born wife never hurried and hustled his thoughts in this way. She was content to sit at his feet, and let him meander on for hours. True that she did not often listen, but she was always respectful. "I was remarking that Sir Vernon is a fine young fellow, and likely to live to see himself a. great grandfather. His brother, too, is nearly as big and healthy—healthy to a degree. The break-fast I saw those two young men devour at the hotel would have made your hair stand on end. But, thank heaven, I have never been the kind of man to wait for dead men's shoes."

"I see," said Ida. "If these boys had been sickly and had died young, you would have succeeded to the baronetcy."

"To the baronetcy and to the estate in Sussex, which is a very fine estate, worth eight thousand a year."

"Then, of course, they are strong, and likely to live to the age of Methuselah!" exclaimed Ida, with a laugh of passing bitterness. "Who ever heard of luck coming our way? It is not in our race to be fortunate."

The shame and agony of her own failure to win fortune was still strong upon her.

"Who knows what might happen?" said the Captain, with amiable listlessness. "I have never allowed my thoughts to dwell upon the possibilities of the future; yet it is a fact that, so long as those young men remain unmarried, there are only two lives between me and wealth. They feel the position themselves; for, when Sir Vernon came over here to lunch, he patted my boy on the head and said, in his joking way, "If Peter and I had fallen down a crevasse the other day in the Oberland, this little chap would have been heir to Wimperfield.""

"No doubt Sir Vernon and his brother will marry and set up nurseries of their own within the next two or three years," said Ida, carelessly. Eager as she had been to be rich during those two and a half bitter years in which she had so keenly felt the sting of poverty, she was not capable of seeing her way to fortune through the dark gate of death.

"Yes, I daresay they will both marry," replied Captain Palliser, gravely, folding his napkin and whisking an accidental crumb off his waistcoat. "Young men always get drifted into matrimony. If they are rich all the women are after them. If they are poor —well, there is generally some woman weak enough

14*

to prefer dual starvation to bread and cheese and solitude. Vernon told me he had no idea of marriage. He and his brother are both rovers—fond of mountain-climbing, yachting, every open-air amusement."

"Did you see much of them while they were at Dieppe?"

"They only stayed three days. They walked over here to lunch, put the poor little woman in a fluster —although they were very pleasant and easy about everything—invited me to dinner, tipped the boy muni-ficently, and went off by the night-boat, bound straight for Wimperfield and the partridges. Very fine partridge shooting at Wimperfield! Vernon asked me to go across with him and stay at the old place for a week or two; but my sporting days are over. I can't get up early; and I can't walk in shooting-boots. Besides, the little woman would have fretted if I had left her alone so long."

"But the change would have done you good, father."

"No, my dear; any change of habits would worry me. I have dropped into my groove and I must stay in it. What a pity you were not here when your cousins called! Who knows what might have hap-pened? Vernon might have fallen over head and ears in love with you."

"Don't, father!" cried Ida, with absolute pain in her voice. "Don't talk about marrying for money. There is nothing in life so revolting, so degrading. Be sure, it is a sin which always brings its own punishment."

"My dear," said the Captain, gravely, "there are so many love-matches which bring their own punish-ment, that I am inclined to believe that marrying for money is a virtue which ought to ensure its own

reward. You may depend, if we could get statistics
upon the subject, one would find that after ten years'
marriage the couples who were drawn together by
prudential motives are just as fond of each other as
those more romantic pairs who wedded for love. A
decade of matrimony rounds a good many sharp angles,
and dispels a good many illusions."

CHAPTER XI.

ACCOMPLISHMENT AT A DISCOUNT.

Now began for Ida a life of supreme dullness—an
empty, almost hopeless life, waiting upon fortune. Her
father was kind to her in his easy-going lymphatic
way, liking well enough to have her about him, pleased
with her affection for his boy, proud of her beauty
and her talents, but with no earnest care for her wel-
fare in the present or the future. What was to become of wife, son, and daughter when he was dead
and gone, was a question which Captain Palliser dared
not ask himself. For the widow there would be a
pittance, for son and daughter nothing. It was therefore vital that Ida should either marry well or become
a money-earning personage. Of marriage at Les
Fontaines there seemed not the faintest probability,
since the experiences of the past afford so few in-
stances of wandering swains caught and won by a face
at a window, or the casual appearance of a beautiful
girl on a country road.

Of friends or acquaintance, in his present abode,
Captain Palliser had none. The only people he had
ever cared for were the men and women he had known
in India; and he had lost sight of those since his mar-

riage. They were scattered; and he was too proud to
expose his fallen fortunes to those who had known
him in his happier days, those days when the careless
expenditure of his modest capital had given him a
false air of easy circumstances.

His life at Les Fontaines suited him well enough,
individually. It was a kind of hibernation. He slept
a good deal, and ate a good deal, and smoked in-
cessantly, and took very little exercise. For all that
is best and noblest in life, Captain Palliser might just
as well have been dead. He had outlived hope and
ambition, thought, invention. He exercised no influence
upon the lives of others, except upon the little homely
wife, who was a slave to him. He was no possible
good in the world. Yet his daughter was fond of him,
and pleased to bear him company when he would
have her; and under her influence his sluggish intellect
brightened a little.

For the first few weeks of her residence at Les
Fontaines, Ida was tortured by a continually recurring
fear of Brian Wendover's pursuit. He had let her go
coolly enough; but what if he were to change his mind
and follow and claim her? She belonged to him. She
was his goods, his chattels—to have and to hold till
death did them part. Her life was no longer her own
to dispose of as she pleased. Would he let her alone?
he who had held her in his arms with passionate force,
who had entreated her to stay with him, and had sur-
rendered her reluctantly in sullen anger.

What if anger, which had been stronger with him
than love at that last moment, should urge him to
denounce her—to tell the world how base a thing she
was—a woman who had been eager to marry a rich

man, and had been trapped by a pauper! She glanced with a sickening dread at every letter which her father received, lest it should be from Brian, telling her shameful story. She counted the days as they went by, saying to herself, "A fortnight since we were married; surely if he had meant to claim me he would have come before now." "Three weeks! now I must be safe!" And then came the dull November morning which completed the calendar month since her wedding-day, and her husband had made no sign. She began to feel easier, to believe that he repented his marriage as deeply as she did, and that he was very glad to be free from its bondage.

And now she was able to think more seriously of her future. She had answered a great many advertisements in the *Times*, wherein paragons were demanded for the tuition of youth or the companionship of age; but as she saw the papers only on the day after their publication, other paragons, on the spot, were beforehand with her. She did not receive a single answer to those carefully written letters, setting forth her qualifications and her willingness to work hard.

"I shall waste a small fortune in postage-stamps, father," she said at last, "and shall be no nearer the mark. My only chance is to advertise. Will you give me the money for an advertisement? I am sorry to ask you, but——"

"My dear, you are always asking me for money," replied Captain Palliser, peevishly; which was hardly fair, as she had asked him nothing since her return, except the sum of thirty shillings, being the exact amount of which she stood indebted to kind-hearted Miss Cobb. "However, I suppose you must have it."

He produced a half sovereign from his meagrely-furnished purse. "It is only right you should do something; indeed, anything is better than wasting your life in such a hole as this. But what if you do get any answers to your advertisement? Who is to give you a character, since that old witch at Mauleverer Manor has chosen to put up her back against you?"

"That must be managed somehow," answered Ida moodily. "Will it not be enough for the people to know who you are, and that I have never been in a situation before? Why should they apply to the schoolmistress who finished my education?"

"People are so suspicious," said the Captain, "and the handsomer a girl is the more questions they ask. They seem to think she has no right to be so handsome. However, you must risk it."

Ida wrote her advertisement, an unvarnished statement of her qualifications as a teacher, and of her willingness to be useful; not a word about references. The advertisement appeared a few days later, and the little family at Les Fontaines anxiously awaited the result, even little Vernon eagerly expressing himself on the subject, his youthful ears being open to every topic discussed in his presence, and his youthful mind quick to form opinions.

"You shan't go away," he exclaimed. "Ma, she shan't go, shall she? lady shan't have her; I want her always; you musn't go, sissie," all in baby language, with a curious perversion of consonants. He had climbed on her knee, and had his arms round her neck—energetic young arms which almost throttled her. She had been his chief companion and playfellow for the last five weeks, had read him all his favourite fairy-tales over and over again, had sat with him of an evening till he fell asleep, an invincible defence against bogies and vague fears of darkness. She had taken him for long rural rambles, over breezy downs towards the sea, had dug and delved with him on the lonely beach below the great white lighthouse, warmly coated and shawled, and working hard in the November wind; and now, just when he had grown fonder of her than anyone else in the world, she was going to leave him. He lifted up his head and howled, and refused all comfort from mother or father. Ida cried with him. "My pet, I can't bear to leave you, but I must; my darling, I shall come back," she protested, clasping him to her breast, kissing his fair, tearful face, soft round cheeks, lovely blue eyes swimming in tears.

"To-morrow?" inquired Vernon, with a strangled sob.

"No, darling, not to-morrow; there would be no use in my going just for one day; but I am not going yet—I don't know when I am going—Vernon must not cry. See how unhappy he is making poor mamma."

Mrs. Palliser put her hands before her face, and made a bohooing noise to keep up the illusion; whereupon the affectionate little fellow slipped off his sister's knee, and ran to his mother to administer comfort.

"I am not going away yet, Vernon; indeed, I hardly know whether I am ever going at all. I have come back like a bad penny, and I seem likely to be as difficult to get rid of as other bad pennies," said Ida, despondingly, for three posts had gone by since the insertion of her advertisement, and had brought her nothing. The market was evidently overstocked with young ladies knowing French and German, able to play and sing, and willing to be useful.

After this Vernon would hardly let his sister out of his sight. He had a suspicion that she would leave him unawares—slip out of the door some day, and be gone without a moment's warning. That is how joy flees.

"My pet, be reasonable," said Ida; "I can't go away without my trunk."

This comforted him a little, and he made a point of sitting upon one of Ida's trunks, when they two were alone in that barely furnished chamber which served for her bed-room and his day-nursery.

She contrived to tell him fairy-tales, and to keep him amused; albeit she was now busy at carefully overhauling, patching, and repairing her scanty wardrobe—trying to make neat mending do duty for new clothes, and getting ready against any sudden summons. She could not bring herself to ask her father for money, sadly as she wanted new garments. He had given her five pounds in August, and two sovereigns since her return, and the way he had doled out those sums indicated the low state of his funds. No, the gown that had been new at The Knoll must still be her best gown. Last winter's jacket, albeit threadbare in places, must do duty for this winter. Before the next summer she might be in the receipt of a salary and able to clothe herself decently, and to send presents to this beloved boy, who was not much better clad than herself.

But the days wore on, and brought no answer to her advertisement.

"I shouldn't wonder if it were the foreign address," said Captain Palliser, when they were all speculating upon the cause of this dismal silence. "People are suspicious of anyone living abroad. If you had been able to advertise from a rectory in Lincolnshire, or even an obscure street at the westend of London—they'd have thought better of you. But Boulogne, Calais, Dieppe, they all hint at impecuniosity and enforced exile. It's very unlucky."

The postman stopped at the little green gate next morning, and Ida flew to receive his packet. It was a letter for her—a bulky letter—in a hand she knew well, and her heart seemed to stop beating as she looked at the address.

The hand was Bessie Wendover's. Who could tell what new trouble the letter might announce? Brian might have told his family the whole history of his marriage and her unworthy conduct. Oh, what shame, what agony, if this were so! and how was she to face her father when he asked her the contents of the letter? She ran out into the garden—the little bare, joyless garden—to read her letter alone, and to gain time.

This is how the dreaded epistle ran:—

"My dear darling, ill-used, cruel thing,—

"However could you treat me so badly? What is friendship worth, if you set no higher value upon it than this? I don't believe you know what friendship means, or you never could act so. How miserable you have made me! how wretched you must have been yourself! you proud, noble-minded darling—under the sting of such vile treatment.

"I wrote to you three times last month, and could not imagine why my letters were unanswered. Brian had told me that you were perfectly well, and looking splendid when he saw you in October, so I did not

think it could be illness that kept you silent; and at
last I began to feel angry, and to fancy you had forgotten me, and were ungrateful. No, I don't mean
that, dearest. What reason had you for gratitude?
The obligation was all on my side.

"Towards the end of October I wrote to Brian,
telling him of your silence, and asking if he could
find out if you were well. He answered with one of
his short, unsatisfactory scrawls that he had reason to
know you were quite well. After this I felt *really*
offended; for I thought you must have deceived me all
along, and that you had never cared a straw about
me; so I coiled myself up in my dignity, and although
I felt very unhappy, I resolved never to write you
another line till you wrote to me. I was very miserable,
but still I felt that I owed a duty to my own self-
respect, don't you know; and just at this time we all
went to Bournemouth, where we were very gay. Father
and mother knew no end of people there, and I began
to feel what it really is to be out, which no girl ever
could at Kingthorpe, where there are about three
parties in a twelvemonth.

"Well, darling, so I went on leading a frivolous
life among people I did not care twopence for, and
hardening my heart against my dearest friend, when,
on the day we came home, I happened to take up the
Times in the railway carriage. I hate newspapers in
a common way, but one reads such things when one
is travelling, and out of mere idleness I amused myself
skimming the advertisements, which I found ever so
much more interesting than the leading articles. What
should my eye light upon but an advertisement from a
young lady wanting to go out as a governess—address

I. P., Le Rosier, Les Fontaines, near Dieppe—and the
whole murder was out. You must have left old Pew's,
and be living with your father. I was horribly indignant with you—as, indeed, I am still—for not having told me anything about it; but directly I got home
I telegraphed to Polly Cobb, as the best-natured girl I
knew at Mauleverer, asking where you were, and why
you had left. I had such a letter from her next day
—spelling bad, but full of kind feeling—giving me a
full account of the row, and old Pew's detestable conduct. She told me that Fräulein vouched for your
having behaved with the most perfect propriety, and
never having seen Brian out of her presence; but
Brian's meanness in not having told me about the
trouble he had brought upon you is more than I can
understand.

"Well, darling, I went off to Aunt Betsy, who is
always my *confidante* in all delicate matters, because
she's ever so much cleverer than dear warm-hearted
mother, who never could keep a secret in her life,
sweet soul, and is no better than a speaking-tube for
conveying information to the Colonel. I told Aunt
Betsy everything—how it was all Brian's fault, and
how I adore you, and how miserable I felt about you,
and how you were trying to get a situation as governess, in spite of that malignant old Pew—she must be
a lineal descendant of the wicked fairy—having said
she would give you no certificate of character or ability.

"Now, what do you think that sweetest and best
of aunties said? 'Let her come to me,' she said; 'I
am getting old and dull, and I want something bright
and clever about me, to cheer me and rouse me when
I feel depressed. Let her come to me as a companion

and amanuensis, help me to look after my cottagers, who are getting too much for me, and play to me of an evening. I like that girl, and I should like to have her in my house.'

"I was enchanted at the thought of your being always near us, and I fancied you wouldn't altogether dislike it; although Kingthorpe certainly is the dullest, sleepiest old hole in the universe. So I begged Aunt Betsy to write to you *instanter;* said I knew you would be charmed to accept such a situation, and that she would secure a treasure; and, in all probability, you'll have a letter from her to-morrow.

"And now, dear, I must repeat that you have treated me shamefully. Why did you not write to me directly you left Mauleverer? Could you think that I could believe you had really done wrong—that I could possibly be influenced by the judgment of that old monster, Pew? If you could think so, you are not worthy to be loved as I love you. However, come to us, sweetest, directly you get auntie's letter, and all shall be forgiven and forgotten, as the advertisements say."

Ida kissed the loving letter. So far, therefore, Brian had not betrayed her; and, having kept her secret so long, it might be supposed he would keep it for all time.

Poor little warm-hearted Bessie! Was not she by her foolish falsification—a piece of mild jocosity, no doubt—the prime author of all the evil that had followed? And yet Ida could not feel angry with her, any more than she could have been angry with Vernon for some piece of sportive mischief.

"Thank God, he has kept our wretched secret," she thought, as she folded Bessie's long letter, and went back to the house. "I am grateful to him for that."

She went in radiant, gladdened at the thought of being able to relieve her father and stepmother of the burden of her maintenance; for the fact that she was a burden had not been hidden from her. They had been kind; they had given her to eat and to drink of their best, and had admired her talents and accomplishments; but they had let her know at the same time that she was a failure, and that her future was a dark problem still far from solution—a problem which troubled them in the silent watches of the night. Nor did they forget to remind her from time to time that by her imprudence—pardonable although that imprudence might be—she had forfeited six months' board and lodging, together with those educational advantages the Captain's fifty pounds had been intended to purchase for her. These facts had been reiterated, not altogether unkindly, but in a manner that made life intolerable; and she felt that were she to continue at Les Fontaines for the natural term of her existence, the same theme would still furnish the subject for parental harpings.

"Father," she said, going behind Captain Palliser's chair, as he smoked his after-breakfast cigar, and read yesterday's *Times*, "I want you to read this letter. It is a foolish schoolgirl letter, perhaps; but it will show you that my friends are not going to discard me on account of Miss Pew."

The Captain laid down his paper, and slowly made his way through Bessie's lengthy epistle, which, although prettily written, with a good deal of grace in the slopes and curves of the penmanship, gave him considerable trouble to decipher. It was only when he had discovered that all the B's looked like H's, and that all the G's were K's, and all the L's S's, and had, as it were, made a system for himself, that he was able to get on comfortably.

"Bless my soul," he murmured, "why cannot girls write legibly?"

"It is the real Mauleverer hand, papa, and is generally thought very pretty," said Ida.

"Pretty, yes; you might have a zigzag pattern over the paper that would be just as pretty. One wants to be able to read a letter. This is almost as bad as Arabic. However, the girl seems a good warm-hearted creature, and very fond of you; and I should think you could not do better than accept her aunt's offer. It will be a beginning."

"It is Hobson's choice, papa; but I am sure I shall be happy with Miss Wendover," said Ida; and then she gave a faint sigh, and her heart sank at the thought of that Damoclesian sword always hanging over her head—the possibility of her husband claiming her.

Mrs. Palliser was much more rapturous when she heard the contents of the letter—much more interested in all details about Ida's future home. She wanted to know what Miss Wendover was like—how many servants she kept—whether carriage or no carriage—what kind of a house she lived in, and how it was furnished.

"You will be quite a grand lady," she said, with a touch of envy, when Ida had described the cosy red-brick cottage, the verandahed drawing-room and conservatory added by Miss Wendover, the pair of cobs which that lady drove, the large well-kept gardens; "you will look down upon us with our poor ways, and this house, in which all the rooms smell of whitewash."

"No, indeed, mamma, I shall always think of you with affection; for you have been very kind to me, although I know I have been a burden."

"Everything is a burden when one is poor," sighed her stepmother; "even one extra in the washing-bills makes a difference; and we shall feel it awfully when Vernon grows up. Boys are so extravagant; and one cannot talk to them as one can to girls."

"But I hope you will be better off then, mamma."

"My dear, you might as well hope we should be dukes and duchesses. What chance is there of any improvement? Your poor papa has no idea of earning money. I'm sure I have said to him, often and often, 'Reginald, do *something*. Write for the magazines! Surely you can do *that*. Other men in your position do it.' 'Yes,' he growled, 'and that's why the magazines are so stupid.' No, Ida, your father's circumstances will never improve; and when the time comes for giving Vernon a proper education we shall be paupers."

"Poor papa!" sighed Ida; "I am afraid he is not strong enough to make any great effort."

"He has given way, my dear, that is the root of it all. We shall never be better off, unless those two healthy, broad-shouldered young men were to go and get themselves swallowed up by an earthquake; and that is rather too much for anyone to expect."

"What young men?" asked Ida, absently.

"Your two cousins."

"Oh, Sir Vernon and his brother. No, I don't suppose they will die to oblige us poor creatures."

"They went up the what's-its-name Horn, in

Switzerland," said Mrs. Palliser, plaintively. "It made my blood run cold to hear them talk about it. 'By Jove, Peter, I thought it was all over with you,' said Sir Vernon, when he told us how foolhardy his brother had been. But you see they got to the bottom all safe and sound, though ever so many people have been killed on that very mountain."

"I'm glad they did, mamma. We may want their money very badly, but we are not murderers, even in thought."

"God forbid," sighed the little woman. "They are fine grown gentlemanly young men, too. Sir Vernon gave my Vernie a sovereign, and promised him a pony next year; but, good gracious, how could we afford to keep a pony, even if we had a stable? 'You had better make it the other kind of pony,' says your father, and then they all burst out laughing."

"So little makes a man laugh," said Ida, somewhat contemptuously. That picture of her father making sport of his poverty irritated her. "Well, dear mamma," she said presently, moved by one of those generous impulses which were a part of her frank unwise nature, "if ever I can earn a hundred a year—and there are many governesses who get as much—you shall have fifty to help pay Vernon's schooling."

"You are a dear generous 'arted girl," exclaimed the stepmother, and the two women kissed again with tears, an operation which they usually performed in the hour of domestic trouble.

Miss Wendover's letter came next day, a hearty, frank, affectionate letter, offering a home that was really meant to be like home, and a salary of forty pounds a year, "just to buy your gowns," Miss Wendover said. "I know it is not sufficient remuneration for such accomplishments as yours, but I want *you* rather than your accomplishments, and I am not rich enough to give as much as you are worth. But you will, at least, stave off the drudgery of a governess's life till you are older, and better able to cope with domineering mothers and insolent pupils."

Such a salary was a long way off that hundred per annum which Ida had set before her eyes as the golden goal to be gained by laborious pianoforte athletics and patient struggles with the profundities of German grammar; but, as Captain Palliser said, it was a beginning; and Ida was very glad so to begin. She wrote to Miss Wendover gratefully accepting her offer, and in a very humble spirit.

"I fear it is pity that prompts your kind offer," she wrote, "and that you take me because you know I left Mauleverer Manor in disgrace, and that nobody else would have me. I am a bad penny. That is what my father called me when I came home to him. And now I am to go back to Kingthorpe as a bad penny. But, please God, I will try to prove to you that I am not altogether worthless; and, whatever may happen, I shall love you and be grateful to you till the end of my life.

"As you are so kind as to say I may come as soon as I like, I shall be with you on the day after you receive this letter."

Ida's preparations for departure were not elaborate. Her scanty wardrobe had been put in the neatest possible order. A few hours sufficed for packing trunk and bonnet-box. On the last afternoon Mrs. Palliser came to her highly elated, and proposed a walk to Dieppe, and a drive home in the diligence which left the Market-Place at five o'clock.

15*

"I am going to give you a new hat," she said, triumphantly. "You must have a new hat."

"But, dear mamma, I know you can't afford it."

"I *will* afford it, Ida. You will have to go to church at Kingthorpe"—Mrs. Palliser regarded church-going as an oppressive condition of prosperous respectability. One of the few privileges of being hard up and quite out of society was that one need not go to church—"and I should like you to appear like a lady. You owe it to your pa and I. A hat you must 'ave. I can pay for it out of the housekeeping money, and your pa will never know the difference."

"No, mamma, but you and Vernon will have to pinch for it," said Ida, knowing that there was positively no margin to that household's narrow means of existence.

"A little pinching won't hurt us. Vernie is as bilious as he can be; he eats too many compots and little fours. I shall keep him to plain bread and butter for a bit, and it will do him a world of good. There's no use talking, Ida, I mean you to 'ave a 'at; and if you won't come and choose it I must choose it myself," concluded the little woman, dropping more aspirates as she grew more excited.

So mother and daughter walked to Dieppe in the dull November afternoon, Vernon trudging sturdily by his sister's side. They bought the hat, a gray felt with partridge plumage, which became Ida's rich dark bloom to perfection; and then they went to the Cathedral, and knelt in the dusky aisle, and heard the solemn melody of the organ, and the subdued voices of the choir, in the plaintive music of Vesper Psalms, monotonous somewhat, but with a sweet soothing influence, music that inspired gentle thoughts.

Then they went back to the Market-Place, and

were in time to get good places on the *banquette* of
the diligence, before the big white Norman horses
trotted and ambled noisily along the street.

Ida left Dieppe late on the following evening, by
the same steamer that had brought her from Newhaven.   The British stewardess recognized her.

"Why, you was only across the other day, miss,"
she said; "what a gad-about you must be."

She arrived in London by ten o'clock next morning, and left Waterloo at a quarter-past eleven, reaching Winchester early in the day.   How different were
her feelings this time, as the train wound slowly over
those chalky hills! how full of care was her soul! And
yet she was no longer a visitor going among strangers
—this time she went to an assured home, she was to
be received among friends.   But the knowledge that
her liberty was forfeited for ever, that she was a free-
agent only on sufferance, made her grave and depressed.   Never again could she feel as glad and frank
a creature as she had been in the golden prime of the
summer that was gone, when she and Bessie and
Urania Rylance came by this same railway, over those
green English hill-sides, to the city that was once the
chief seat of England's power and splendour.

A young man in a plain gray livery and irreproachable top-boots stood contemplatively regarding the
train as it came into the station.   He touched his hat
at sight of Miss Palliser, and she remembered him as
Miss Wendover's groom.

"Any luggage, ma'am?" he asked, as she alighted; as
if it were as likely as not that she had come without any.

"There is one box, Needham.   That is all besides
these things."

Her bonnet-box—frail ark of woman's pride—was

in the carriage, with a wrap and an umbrella, and her dressing bag.

"All right, ma'am. If you'll show me which it is I'll tell the porter to bring it. I've got the cobs outside."

"Oh, I am so sorry,—how good of Miss Wendover!"

"They wanted exercise, 'um. 'They was a bit above themselves, and the drive has done 'em good."

Miss Wendover's cherished brown cobs, animals which in the eyes of Kingthorpe were almost as sacred as that Egyptian beast whose profane slaughter was more deeply felt than the nation's ruin—to think that these exalted brutes should have been sent to fetch that debased creature, a salaried companion. But then Aunt Betsy was never like anyone else.

Needham took the cobs across the hills at a pace which he would have highly disapproved in any other driver. Had Miss Wendover so driven them, he would have declared she was running them off their legs. But in his own hands, Brimstone and Treacle—so called to mark their difference of disposition—could come to no harm. "They wanted it," he told Miss Palliser, when she remarked upon their magnificent pace, "they never got half work enough."

The hills looked lovely, even in this wintry season —yew trees and grass gave no token of November's gloom. The sky was bright and blue, a faint mist hung like a veil over the city in the valley, the low Norman tower of the cathedral, the winding river, and flat fertile meadows—a vision very soon left far in the rear of Brimstone and Treacle.

"How handsome they look!" said Ida, admiring their strong bold crests, like war-horses in a Ninevite picture, their shining black-brown coats. "Is Brimstone such a very vicious horse?"

"Vicious, mum? no, not a bit of vice about him," answered Needham promptly, "but he's a rare difficult horse to groom. There ain't none but me as dares touch him. I let the boy try it once, and I found the poor lad half an hour afterwards standing in the middle of the big loose box like a statter, while Brimstone raced round him as hard as he could go, just like one of them circus horses. The boy dursn't stir. If he'd moved a limb Brimstone 'ud have 'molished him."

"What an awful horse! But isn't that viciousness?"

"Lor', no mum. That ain't vice," answered the groom, smiling amusedly at the lady's ignorance. "Vice is crib-biting, or jibbing, or boring, or summat o' that kind. Brimstone is a game hoss, and he's got a bit of a temper, but he ain't got no vice."

Here was Kingthorpe, looking almost as pretty as it had looked when she gazed upon it with tearful eyes in her sad farewell at the close of summer. The big forest trees were bare, but there were flowers in all the cottage gardens, even late lingering roses on southern walls, and the clipped yew-tree abominations —dumb-waiters, peacocks, and other monstrosities— were in their pride of winter beauty. The ducks were swimming gaily in the village pond, and the village inn was still glorious with red geraniums, in redder pots. The Knoll stood out grandly above all other dwellings—the beds full of chrysanthemums, and a bank of big scarlet geraniums on each side of the hall door.

It seemed strange to be driven swiftly past the familiar carriage-drive, and round into the lane leading to Miss Wendover's cottage. It was only an accommodation lane—or a back-out lane, as the boys called it, since no two carriages could pass each other in that narrow channel—and in bad weather the approach

to the Homestead was far from agreeable. A carriage
and horses had been known to stick there, with wheels
hopelessly embedded in the clay, while Miss Wendover's guests picked their footsteps through the mud.

But the Homestead, when attained, was such a delightful house, that one forgot all impediments in the
way thither. The red brick front—old red brick, be
it noted, which has a brightness and purity of colour
never retained for above a twelve-month by the red
brick of to-day—glowing, athwart its surrounding
greenery, like the warm welcome of a friend; the exquisite neatness of the garden, where every flower that
could be coaxed into growing in the open air bloomed
in perfection; the spick-and-span brightness of the windows; the elegant order that prevailed within, from
cellar to garret; the old, carefully-chosen furniture,
which had for the most part been collected from other
old-world homesteads; the artistic colouring of draperies
and carpets—all combined to make Miss Wendover's
house delightful.

"My house had need be orderly," she said, when
her friends waxed rapturous; "I have so little else to
think about."

Yet the sick and poor, within a radius of ten
miles, might have testified that Miss Wendover had
thought and care for all who needed them, and that
she devoted the larger half of her life to other people's
interests.

It was a clear balmy day, one of those lovely
autumn days which hang upon the edge of winter, and
Miss Wendover was pacing her garden walks bare-
headed, armed with gardening scissors and formidable
brown leather gauntlets, nipping a leaf here, or a
withered rose-bud there; with eyes whose eagle glance

not so much as an aphis could escape. From the slope of her lawn Aunt Betsy saw the cobs turn into the lane, and she was standing at the gate to welcome the traveller when the carriage drew up.

There was no carriage-drive on this side of the house, only a lawn with a world of flower-beds. Those visitors who wanted to enter in a ceremonious manner had to drive round by shrubbery and orchard to the back, where there were an old oak door and an entrance-hall. On this garden front there were only glass doors and long French windows, verandahs, and sunny parlours, opening one out of another.

"How do you do, my dear?" said the spinster heartily, as Ida alighted; "I am very glad to see you. Why, how bright and blooming you look—not a bit like a sea-sick traveller."

"Dear Miss Wendover, I ought to look bright when I am so glad to come to you; and as to the other thing, I am never sea-sick."

"What a splendid girl! That unhappy little Bessie can't cross to the Wight without being a martyr. But, Ida, I am not going to be called Miss Wendover. Only bishops and county magnates, and people of that kind call me by that name. To you I am to be Aunt Betsy, as I am to the children at The Knoll."

"Is not that putting me too much on a level——"

"With my own flesh and blood? Nonsense! I mean you to be as my own flesh and blood. I could not bear to have any one about me who was not."

"You are too good," faltered Ida. "How can I ever repay you?"

"You have only to be happy. It is your nature to be frank and truthful, so I will say nothing about that."

Ida blushed deepest scarlet. Frank and truthful—

she—whose very name was a lie! And yet there could be no wrong done to Miss Wendover, she told herself, by her suppression of the truth. It was a suppression that concerned only Brian Walford and herself. No one else could have any interest in the matter.

Betsy Wendover herself led the way to the bed-chamber that had been prepared for the new inmate. It was a dear old room, not spacious, but provided with two most capacious closets, in each of which a small gang of burglars could have hidden—dear old closets, with odd little corner cupboards inside them, and a most elaborate system of shelves. One closet had a little swing window at the top for ventilation, and this, Miss Wendover told Ida, was generally taken for a haunted corner, as the ventilating window gave utterance to unearthly noises in the dead watches of the night, and sometimes gave entrance to a stray cat from adjacent tiles. A cat less agile than the rest of his species had been known to entangle himself in the little swing window, and to hang there all the night, sending forth unearthly caterwaulings, to the unspeakable terror of Miss Wendover's guest, unfamiliar with the mechanism of the room, and wondering what breed of Hampshire demon or afrit was thus making night hideous.

There was a painted wooden dado halfway up the wall, and a florid rose and butterfly paper above it. There was a neat little brass bedstead on one side of the room, a tall Chippendale chest of drawers, with writing-table and pigeon-holes on the other side; the dearest, oldest dressing-table and shield-shaped glass in front of the broad latticed window; while in another window there was a cushioned seat, such as Mariana of the Moated Grange sat upon when she looked across

the fens and bewailed her dead-and-gone joys.   There
were old cups and saucers on the high, narrow chimney-
piece, below which a cosy fire burned in a little old
basket grate.   Altogether the room was the picture of
homely comfort.

"Oh, what a lovely room!" cried Ida, inwardly
contrasting this cheery chamber with that whitewashed
den at Les Fontaines, with its tawdry mahogany and
brass fittings, its florid six feet of carpet on a deal
floor stained brown, its alabaster clock and tin candelabra—a cheap caricature of Parisian elegance.

"I'm glad you like it, my dear," answered Miss
Wendover.   "Bessie said it would suit you; and all I
ask you is to keep it tidy.   I hope I am not a tyrant;
but I am an old maid.   Of course, I shall never pry
into your room; but I warn you that I have an eye
which takes in everything at a flash; and if I happen
to go past when your door is open, and see a bonnet
and shawl on your bed, or a gown sprawling on your sofa,
my teeth will be set on edge for the next half hour."

"Dear Miss Wen——, dear Aunt Betsy," said Ida,
corrected by a frown, "I hope you will come into my
room every day, and give me a good scolding, if it is
not exactly as you like.   Everything in this house
looks lovely.   I want to learn your nice neat ways."

"Well, my love, you might learn something worse,"
replied Miss Wendover, with innocent pride.   "And
now come down to luncheon, I kept it back on purpose
for you, and I am sure you must be starving."

The luncheon was excellent, served with a tranquil
perfection only to be attained by careful training; and
yet Miss Wendover's youthful butler three years ago
had been a bird boy; while her rosy-cheeked parlour-
maid was only eighteen, and had escaped but two

years from the primitive habits of cottage life. Aunt Betsy had a genius for training young servants.

"You had better unpack your boxes directly after luncheon," said Miss Wendover, when Ida had eaten with very good appetite, "and arrange your things in your drawers. That will take you an hour or so, I suppose—say till five o'clock, when Bessie is coming over to afternoon tea."

"Oh, I am so glad. I am longing to see Bessie. Is she as lovable and pretty as ever?"

"Well, yes," replied Aunt Betsy, with a critical air; "I think she has rather improved. She is plump enough still, in all conscience, but not quite so stumpy as she was last summer. Her figure is a little less like a barrel."

"I hope she was very much admired at Bournemouth."

"Yes, strange to say, she had a good many admirers," answered Miss Wendover coolly. She made a point of never being enthusiastic about her relations. "She had always partners at the dances, I am told, even when there was a paucity of dancing men; and she was considered rather remarkable at lawn tennis. No doubt she will tell you all about it this afternoon. I have some work to do in the village, and I shall leave you two girls together."

This was a delicacy which touched Ida. She was very anxious to see Bessie, and to talk to her as they could only talk when they were alone. She wanted to know her faithful friend's motive for that cruel deception about Brian Walford. That the frank, tender-hearted Bessie could have so deceived her from any unworthy motive was impossible.

Five o'clock struck, and Ida was sitting alone in the drawing-room, waiting to receive her friend, just as if she were the daughter of the house, instead of a salaried dependent. The pretty carved Indian tea-table—a gem in Bombay blackwood—was wheeled in front of the fire-place, which was old, as regarded the high wooden mantel-piece and capacious breadth of the hearth, but essentially new in its glittering tiles and dainty brass fire-irons.

The clock had hardly finished striking when Bessie bounced into the room, rosy and smiling, in sealskin jacket and toque.

"Oh, you darling! isn't this lovely?" she exclaimed, hugging Ida. "You are to live here for ever and ever, and never, never, never to leave us again, and never to marry, unless you marry one of the Brians. Don't shudder like that, pet, they are both nice! And I'm sure you like Brian Walford, though, perhaps, not quite so much as he liked you. You do like him now, don't you, darling?" urged Bess.

Ida had withdrawn from her embrace, and was seated before the low Bombay table, occupied with the tea-pot. There was no light but the fire and one shaded lamp on a distant table. The curtains were not yet drawn, and white mists were rising in the garden outside, like a sea.

"Bessie," Ida began, gravely, as her old school-fellow sat on a low stool in front of the fire, "how could you deceive me like that? What could put such a thing in your head—*you*, so frank, so open?"

"I am sure I hardly know," answered Bess, innocently. "It was my birthday, don't you know, and we were all wild. Perhaps the champagne had something to do with it, though I didn't take any. But that sort of excitement communicates itself; and running up and down hill gets into one's head. We all thought it would be such fun to pass off penniless B. W. for his wealthy cousin—and just to see how you liked him, with that extra advantage. But there was no harm in it, was there, dear? Of course, he told you afterwards, when you saw him at Mauleverer?

"Yes, he told me—afterwards."

"Naturally; and having begun to like him as the rich Brian, you didn't leave off liking him because of his poverty—did you, darling? The man himself was the same."

Ida was silent, remembering how, with the revelation of the fraud that had been practised upon her, the very man himself had seemed to undergo a transformation—as if a disguise, altering his every characteristic, had been suddenly flung aside.

She did not answer Bessie's question, but, looking down at her with grave, searching eyes, she said,—

"Dear Bessie, it was a very foolish jest. I know it is not in your nature to mean unkindly to anyone, least of all to me, to whom you have been an angel of light; but all practical jokes of that kind are liable to inflict pain and humiliation upon the victim—however innocently meant. Whose idea was it, Bess? Not yours, I think?"

"No; it was Urania who proposed it. She said it would be such fun."

"Miss Rylance is not usually so—funny."

"No; but she was particularly jolly that day, don't you remember? in positively boisterous spirits—for her."

"And the outcome of her amiability was this suggestion?"

"Yes, darling. She had noticed that you had a kind of romantic fancy about Brian of the Abbey— that you had idealised his image, as it were—and set him up as a kind of demi-god. Not because of his wealth, darling—don't suppose that we supposed that —but on account of that dear old Abbey and its romantic associations, which gave a charm to the owner. And so she said what fun it would be to pass off Brian Walford as his cousin, and see if you fell in love with him. "I know she is ready to lay her heart at the feet of the owner of the Abbey," Urania said; and I thought it would be too delicious if you were to fall in love with Brian Walford, who could not help falling in love with you, for of course it would end in your marrying him, and his getting on splendidly at the bar; for, with his talents, he must do well. He only wants a motive for industry. And then you would be our very own cousin! I hope it wasn't a very wicked idea, Ida, and that you will find it in your heart to forgive me," pleaded Bess, kneeling by her friend's chair, with clasped hands upon Ida's knees, and sweet, half-tearful face looking up.

"My darling, I have never been angry with you," answered Ida, clasping the girl to her heart, with a stifled sob. "But I don't think Miss Rylance meant so kindly. Her idea sprang from a malevolent heart. She wanted to humiliate me—to drag my most sordid characteristics into the light of day—to make me more abject than poverty had made me already. That was the motive of her joke."

"Never mind her motive, dear. All I am interested in is your opinion of Brian. I hope he behaved nicely at Mauleverer."

"Very nicely."

"Cobb says that Fräulein positively raves about him—declares he is quite the most gentlemanly young man she ever saw—a godly young man she çalled him, in her funny English. And, she says, that he was madly in love with you. Of course he made you an offer?"

"How could he do that when I was always with the Fräulein?"

"Oh, nonsense. Brian is not the kind of young man to be kept at bay by a mild nonentity like the Fräulein. He told me before he left that he was desperately in love with you, and that he meant to win you for his wife. I asked him how he intended to keep a wife, and he said he should write for the magazines, and do theatrical criticisms for the newspapers, till briefs began to drop in. He was determined to win you if you were to be won. So I feel sure that he made you an offer, unless, indeed, that horrid old Pew spoiled all by her venomous conduct."

"That is it, dear. Miss Pew brought matters to an abrupt close."

"And you are not engaged to Brian?" said Bess, dolefully.

"No."

"And he didn't follow you to Dieppe?"

"No."

"Then he is not half so fine a fellow as I thought him."

"Suppose, Bessie, that after a little mild flirtation, with Fräulein Wolf for an audience, we both discovered that our liking for each other was of the very coolest order, and that it was wiser to let the acquaintance end?"

"You might feel that, but I would never believe it of Brian. Why, he raved about you; he was passionately in love. He told me there was no sacrifice he would not make to call you his wife."

"He had so much to sacrifice," said Ida, with a cynical air.

"Don't be unkind, Ida. Of course I know that he has his fortune to make; but he is so thoroughly nice —so full of fun."

"Did you ever know him do anything good or great, anything worth being remembered—anything that proved the depth and nobility of his nature?" asked Ida, earnestly.

"Good gracious! no, not that I can remember. He is always nice, and amusing. He doesn't like carrying a basket, or skates, and things; but of course, where there are younger boys one couldn't expect him to do that; and he hates plain girls and old women; but I suppose that is natural, for even father does it, in his secret soul, though he is always so utterly sweet to the poor things. But I am sure Brian Walford has a tender heart, because he is so fond of kittens."

"I didn't mean to insinuate that he was a modern Domitian," answered Ida, smiling at Bessie's childish earnestness. "What I mean is that there is no depth in his nature, no nobility in his character. He is shallow, and, I fear, selfish. But, Bessie, my pet, I am going to ask you a favour."

"Ask away," cried Bessie, cheerfully; "I can't give you the moon, but anything which I really do possess is yours this instant."

"Don't let us ever talk of Brian Walford. I can never get over the feeling of humiliation which Miss Rylance's practical joke caused me; and my only chance of forgetting it is to forget your cousin's existence."

"Oh, but he will come to The Knoll, I hope, at Christmas, and then you will think better of him."

"If he should come I—I hope I shall not see him."

"Has he offended you so deeply?"

"Don't let us talk about him, Bess. Tell me all about your Bournemouth triumphs. I hear you were the belle of the place."

"Then you have heard a most egregious fib. There were dozens of girls with nineteen-inch waists, before whom I felt myself a monster of dumpiness. But I got on pretty well. I don't pretend to be a good dancer, but I can generally adapt myself to the badness of other people's steps, and that goes for something."

And now having got away from all painful subjects, Bessie rattled on at a tremendous pace, describing girls and gowns, and partners, and tennis tournaments, and yachting excursions, all in a breath, as she sat in front of the fire sipping her tea, and devouring a particular kind of buttered bun for which Miss Wendover's cook was famous.

"Aunt Betsy's tea is always nicer than any one else's; and so are her buns and her butter; in fact everything in this house is nicer than it is anywhere else," said Bessie, pausing in her reminiscences. "You are in clover here, Ida."

"Thanks to your goodness, Bess."

"To mine? But I have positively nothing to do with it."

"Yes, you have. It is from the wish to please her warm-hearted little niece that Miss Wendover has been so good to me."

"But if you had been plain or stupid she would have only been kind to you at a distance. Aunt Betsy has her idiosyncrasies, and one of them is a liking for beauty in individuals, as well as in chairs and tables and cups and saucers. You will see that all her servants are pretty. She picks them for their good looks, I believe, and trains them afterwards. She would not have so much as a bad-looking stable boy."

"Hard upon ugliness to be shut out of this paradise," said Ida.

"Oh, but she finds places for the ugly boys and girls, with people whose teeth are not so easily set on edge, she says herself. And now I must be off, to change my frock for dinner. You know the back way to The Knoll, across the fields to the little door in the kitchen-garden. You will always come that way, of course. When are you coming to see us? To-morrow?"

"You forget that my time is not my own. I will come whenever Miss Wendover can best spare me."

"Oh, you will have plenty of spare time, I am sure."

"I hope not too much, or I shall be too sharply reminded that Miss Wendover has taken me out of charity."

"Charity fiddlestick! A prize-winner like you! And now good-bye, pet, or I shall be late for dinner, which offends the Colonel beyond measure."

Bessie scampered off, Ida following her to the glass door, only in time to see her running across the lawn as fast as her feet could carry her. It was characteristic of Bessie to cut everything very fine in the way of time.

CHAPTER XII.
THE SWORD OF DAMOCLES.

AND now began for Ida a life of exceeding peacefulness, comfort, happiness even; for how could a girl

16*

fail to be happy among people who were so friendly
and kind, who so thoroughly respected her, and so
warmly admired her for gifts altogether independent of
fortune—who never, by word or look, reminded her that
she was in anywise of less importance than themselves?

Nor had the girl any cause to fear that she was a
useless member of Miss Wendover's household. That
lady found plenty of occupation for her young companion—varied and pleasant duties, which made the
days seem too short, and the leisure of the long winter
evenings an agreeable relief from the busy hours of
daylight.

That exquisite neatness which gave such a charm
to Miss Wendover's house was not attained without
labour. The polished surface of the old Chippendale
bureaus, the inlaid Sheraton chairs and tables, could
only be maintained by daily care. A housemaid's per-
functory dusting was not sufficient here; and Miss
Wendover, gloved and aproned, and armed with
leathers and brushes, gave at least half an hour every
morning to the care of her old furniture. Another
half hour was devoted to china; and the floral arrangements indoors, even in this wintry season, occupied half an hour more. This was all active work,
about which Aunt Betsy and Ida went merrily, talking tremendously as they polished and dusted, and
upon all possible subjects, for Miss Wendover's lonely
evenings had enabled her to read almost as much as
Southey, and she delighted in telling Ida the curious
out-of-the-way facts that were stored up in her memory.

Sometimes there was an hour or so given to
culinary matters — new dishes, new kickshaws, *hors
d'œuvres*, savouries—to be taught the young, teachable
cook-maid; for whenever Miss Wendover went to a

great dinner, her eagle eye was on the alert to discover some modern improvement in the dishes or the
table arrangements.

Then there was gardening, which absorbed a good
deal of time in fine weather; for Aunt Betsy held that
no gardener, however honestly inclined, would long
feel interested in a garden to which its owner was indifferent. Miss Wendover knew every flower that grew
—could bud, and graft, and pot, and prune, and do
everything that her youthful gardeners could do, besides being ever so much more learned in the science
of gardening.

Then there were inspections of piggery and poultry-
yard, medicines and particular foods to be prepared
for the poultry, hospitals to be established and looked
after in odd corners of the orchard, and the propaga-
tion of species to be carried on by mechanical con-
trivances.

On wet days there was art needlework, for which
Miss Wendover had what artists would call a great
deal of feeling, without being very skilful as an
executant. Under her direction, Ida began a mauresque
border for a tawny plush curtain, which was to be a
triumph of art when completed, and which was full of
interest in progress. She worked at this of an evening,
while Miss Wendover, who had a fine full voice, and
a perfect enunciation, read aloud to her. Then, when
Miss Wendover was tired, Ida went to the piano and
played for an hour or so, while the elder lady gave
herself up to rare idleness and dreamy thought.

These were home duties only. The two ladies had
occupations abroad of a more exacting nature. Miss
Wendover until now had given two botany lessons, and
one physical science lesson every week in the village

school. The botany lessons she now handed over to Ida, whom she coached for that purpose. Summer or winter these lessons were always given out of doors, in the course of an hour's ramble in field, lane, or wood. Then Miss Wendover had a weekly class for domestic economy, a class attended by all the most promising girls, from thirteen years old upwards, within five miles. This class was held in the kitchen, or housekeeper's room at the Homestead; and many were the savoury messes of broth or soup, cheap stews and meat puddings, and the jellies and custards compounded at these lessons, to be sent off next day to the sick poor upon Miss Wendover's list.

Then there was house to house visiting all over the widely-scattered parish, much talk with gaffers and goodies, in all of which Ida assisted. She would have hated the work had Miss Wendover been a person of the Pardiggle stamp; but as love was the governing principle of all Aunt Betsy's work, her presence was welcome as sunshine or balmy air; so welcome that her sharpest lectures (and she could lecture when there was need) were received with meekness and even gratitude. In these visits Ida learned to know a great deal about the ways and manners of the agricultural poor, all the weakness and all the nobility of the rural nature.

Every Saturday or half-holiday at the village school —blessed respite which gave the hard-worked mistress time to mend her clothes, and make herself bright and trim for Sunday, and opened for the master brilliant possibilities in the way of a jaunt to Romsey or Winchester—Miss Wendover gave a dinner to all the schoolchildren under twelve. She had taken up Victor Hugo's theory that a substantial meat dinner, even on one day out of seven, will do much to build up the youthful constitution and to prevent scrofulous diseases. Moved by these considerations, she had fitted up a disused barn as a rustic dining-hall, the walls plastered and whitewashed, or buff-washed, the massive cross timbers painted a dark red, a long deal table and a few forms the only furniture. Here, every Saturday, at half-past one o'clock, she provided a savoury meat dinner; and very strong must be that temptation or that necessity which would induce Aunt Betsy to abandon her duties as hostess at this weekly feast. It was she who said grace before and after meat—save when some suckling parson was admitted to the meal; it was she who surveyed and improved the manners of her guests by sarcastic hints or friendly admonitions; and it was she who furnished intellectual entertainment in the shape of anecdote, historical story, or excruciating conundrum.

Ida was allowed to assist at these banquets, and there was nothing in her new life which she enjoyed more than the sight of all those glad young faces round the board, or the sound of that frank, rustic laughter. Some there were naturally of a bovine dulness, in whom even Miss Wendover could not awaken a ray of intelligence; but these were few. The generality of the children were far above the average rustic in brightness of intellect, and this superiority might fairly be ascribed to Aunt Betsy's influence.

A fortnight before Christmas, by which time Ida had been at the Homestead more than a month, Miss Wendover suggested a drive to Winchester, and before starting she handed Ida a ten-pound note. "You may want some additional finery for Christmas" she said kindly. "Girls generally do. So you may as well buy it to-day."

"But, dear Aunt Betsy, I have only been with you a month."

"Never mind that, my dear. We will not be particular as to quarter-days. When I think you want money I shall give it to you, and we can make up our accounts at the end of the year."

"You are ever so much too good to me," said Ida, with a loving look that said a good deal more than words.

There was a light frost that whitened the hills, and the keen freshness of the air stimulated Brimstone to conduct of a somewhat riotous character, but Miss Wendover's firm hand held his spirits in check. Treacle was a sagacious beast, who never did more work than he was absolutely obliged to do, and who allowed Brimstone to drag the phaeton while he trotted complacently on the other side of the pole. But Miss Wendover would stand no nonsense, even from the amiable Treacle. She sent the pair across the hills at a splendid pace, and drove them under the old archway and down the stony street with a style which won the admiration of every experienced eye.

They drew up at the chief draper's of the town; and here Miss Wendover retired to hold a solemn conference with the head milliner, a judicious and accomplished person who made Aunt Betsy's gowns and bonnets—all of a solid and substantial architecture, as if modelled on the adjacent cathedral. Ida, left alone amidst all the fascinations of the chief shop in a smart county town, and feeling herself a Crœsus, had much need of fortitude and coolness of temper. Happily she remembered what a little way that five-pound note had gone in preparing her for her summer visit to

The Knoll, and this brought wisdom. Before spending sixpence upon herself she bought a gown—an olive merino gown, and velvet to trim it withal—for her stepmother.

"I don't think she gets a new gown much oftener than I do," she thought; "and even if this costs four or five shillings for carriage it will be worth the money, as a Christmas surprise."

The gown left only trifling change out of two sovereigns, so that by the time Ida had bought herself a dark brown cloth jacket and a brown cashmere gown there were only four sovereigns left out of the ten. She spent one of these upon some pale pink cashmere for an evening dress, and half a sovereign on gloves, as she knew Miss Wendover liked to see people neatly gloved. Ten shillings more were spent upon calico, and another sovereign went by-and-by at the boot-maker's, leaving the damsel with just twenty shillings out of her quarter's wage; but as the need of pocket-money at Kingthorpe, except for the Sunday offertory, was *nil*, she felt herself passing rich in the possession of that last remaining sovereign. She would have liked to spend it all upon Christmas gifts for her young friends at The Knoll; but this fond wish she relinquished with a sigh. Paupers could not be givers of gifts. Whatever she gave must be the fruit of her own labour—some delicate piece of handiwork made out of cheap materials.

"They are all too good to think meanly of me because I can only show my gratitude in words," she told herself.

As Christmas drew near Ida listened anxiously for any allusion to Brian Walford as a probable visitor: and to her infinite relief, just three days before the festival, she heard that he was not coming. He had been invited, and he had left his young cousins in suspense as to his intentions till the last moment, and then had written to say that he had accepted an invitation to Norfolk, where there would be shooting, and a probability of a stag-hunt on foot.

"Which I call horridly mean of him," protested Horatio, who had come across the fields expressly to announce this fact to Ida. "Why can't he come and shoot here? I don't mean to say that there is anything particular to shoot, but he and I could go out together and try our luck. Our hills are splendid for hares."

"Do you mean that there are plenty of hares?" inquired Ida.

"No, not exactly that. But it would be capital ground for them, don't you know, if there were any."

"And where is your other cousin Brian?" asked Ida, merely for the sake of conversation.

All interest, all idle dreaming about the unknown Brian was over with her since the fatal mistake which had marred her life. She could not conceive that anything save evil could ever arise to her henceforward out of that hated name.

"Oh, he is in Sweden, or Turkey, or Russia, or somewhere," replied Horatio, with a disgusted air; "always on the move, instead of keeping up the Abbey in proper style, and cultivating his cousins. A man with such an income is bound in duty to his fellow-creatures to keep a pack of foxhounds. What else was he sent into the world for, I should like to know."

"Perhaps to cultivate the knowledge of his fellow-creatures in distant countries, and to improve his mind."

"Rot!" exclaimed Horatio, who was not choice in his language. "What does he want with mind? or to make a walking Murray or Baedeker of himself? Society requires him to lay out his money to the local advantage. Here we are, with no foxhounds nearer than the New Forest, when we ought to have a pack at our door."

Ida could not enter into the keen sense of deprivation caused by a dearth of foxhounds, so she went on quietly with her work, shading the wing of the inevitable swallow flitting across the inevitable bulrushes which formed the design for a piano back.

Presently Bessie came bouncing in, her sealskin flung on anyhow, and the most disreputable thing in hats perched sideways on her bright brown curls.

"Mother is going to let us have a dance," she burst forth breathlessly, "on Twelfth Night. Won't that be too jolly? A regular party, don't you know, with a crumb-cloth, and a pianiste from Winchester, and perhaps a cornet. It's only another guinea, and if father's in a good temper he's sure to say yes. You must come over to The Knoll every evening to practise your waltzing. We shall have nothing but round dances in the programme. I'll take care of that!"

"But if there are any matrons who like to have a romp in the Lancers or the Caledonians, ain't it rather a shame to leave them out in the cold?" suggested Horatio. "You're so blessed selfish, Bess."

"We are not going to have any matrons. Mother will matronize the whole party. We are going to have the De Travers, and the Pococks, and the Ducies, and the Bullinghams over from Bournemouth."

"And where the deuce are you going to put 'em?"

"Oh, we can put up at least twenty—on spare mattresses, don't you know, in the old nursery, and in the dressing-rooms and bath-room; and as for us, why of course, *we* can sleep anywhere."

"Thank you," replied Horatio; "I hope you don't suppose I am going to turn out of my den, or to allow a pack of girls to ransack my drawers, and smoke my favourite pipe."

"I don't suppose any decent-minded girl would consent to sleep in such a loathsome hole," retorted Bessie. "She would prefer a pillow and a rug on the landing."

"My den is quite as tidy as that barrack of yours," said the Wykamite, "though I haven't yet risen to disfiguring my walls with kitchen plates and fourpenny fans. The cheap æsthetic is not my line."

"Don't pretend to be cantankerous, Horatio," said Ida, looking at him with the loveliest eyes, twinkling a little at his expense; "we all know that you are brimming over with good humour. Perhaps Aunt Betsy will take in some of your visitors, Bess. I am sure they shall be welcome to my room, if I have to sleep in the poultry yard."

"Happy thought," cried Bessie; "I'll sound the dear creature as to her views on the subject this very day."

Aunt Betsy was all goodness, and offered to accommodate half a dozen young ladies of neat and cleanly habits. She protested that she would have no candle-grease droppers or door-mat despisers in her house.

"The Homestead is the only toy I have," she said, "and I won't have it ill-used."

So six irreproachable young women, the pride of careful mothers, were billeted on Miss Wendover, while the more Bohemian damsels were to revel in the improvised accommodation of The Knoll.

That particular Christmas-tide at Kingthorpe was

a time of innocent mirth and youthful happiness which might have banished black care, for the nonce, from the oldest, weariest breast. For Ida, still young and fresh, loving and lovable, the contagion of that youthful mirth was irresistible.

She forgot by how fine a hair hung the sword that dangled over her guilty head—or began to think that the hair was tough enough to hold good for ever. And what mattered the existence of the sword provided it was never to fall? Sometimes it seemed to her in the pure and perfect happiness of this calm rural home, this useful, innocent life, as if that ill-advised act of hers had never been acted—as if that autumn morning, that one half-hour in the modern Gothic church, still smelling of mortar and pitch-pine, set in flat fields, from which October mists were rising ghostlike, was no more than a troubled dream—a dream that she had dreamed and done with for ever. Could it be that such an hour—so dim, so shadowy to look back upon from the substantial footing of her present existence— was to give colour to all the rest of her life? No, it was the dark dream of a troubled past, and she had nothing to do but to forget it as soon as possible.

Forgetfulness — or at least a temporary kind of forgetfulness—was tolerably easy while Brian Walford was civil enough to stay away from Kingthorpe; but the problem of life would be difficult were he to appear in the midst of that cordial circle—difficult to impossibility.

"It is evident that he doesn't mean to come while I am here," she told herself, "and that at least is kind. But in that case I must not stay here too long. It is not fair that I should shut him out of his uncle's house. It is I who am the interloper."

She thought with bitterest grief of any change from this peaceful life among friends who loved her, to service in the house of a stranger; but her conscience recognized the necessity for such a change.

She had no right to squat upon the family of the man she had married—to exclude him from his rightful heritage, she who refused to acknowledge his right as her husband. He had done her a deep wrong; he had deceived her cruelly; and she deemed that she had a right to repudiate a bond tainted by fraud; but she knew that she had no right to banish him from his family circle—to dwell, under false pretences, by the hearth of his kindred.

"I did wrong in coming here," she thought; "it was a mean thing to do. Yet how could I resist the temptation, when no other place offered, and when I knew I was such a burden at home?"

In the very midst of her happiness, therefore, there was always this corroding care, this remorseful sense of wrong doing. This present life of hers was all blissful, but it was bliss which could not, which must not, last. Yet what fortitude would be needed ere she could break this flowery bondage, loosen these dear fetters which love had laid upon her.

Once, during that jovial Christmas season, she hinted at a possible change in the future.

"What a happy day this has been!" she said, as she walked across the wintry fields with Miss Wendover on the verge of midnight, after a Christmas dinner and a long evening of Christmas games at The Knoll, Needham marching in front of them with an unnecessary lantern, and all the stars of heaven shining in blue frosty brilliance above their heads, "and what a happy home! I feel it is a privilege to have seen so much of it; and by-and-by, when I am among strangers——"

"What do you mean?" exclaimed Aunt Betsy, sharply; "there is to be no such by-and-by; or, if there ever be such a time, it will be your making, not mine. You suit me capitally; and I mean to keep you as long as ever I can, without absolute selfishness. If an eligible husband should want to carry you off, I must let you go; but I will part with you to no one less than a husband — unless, indeed," and here Betsy Wendover's voice took a colder and graver tone, "unless you should want to better yourself, as the servants say, and get more money than I can afford to give you. I know your accomplishments are worth much more; but it is not everybody to whom you would be as their own flesh and blood."

"Oh, Aunt Betsy, can you think that I should ever set money in the scale against your kindness—your infinite goodness to me?"

"When you talk of a change by-and-by, you set me thinking. Perhaps you are already beginning to tire of the rustic dulness."

"No, no, no; I never was so happy in my life— never since I was a child playing about on board the ship that brought my mother and me to England. Everybody was kind to me, and made much of me. My mother and I adored each other; and I did not know that she was dying. Soon after we landed she grew dangerously ill, and lay for weeks in a darkened room, which I was not allowed to enter. It was a dreary, miserable time; a lonely, friendless child pining in a furnished lodging, with no one but a servant and a sick-nurse to speak to; and then one dark November morning, the black hearse and coaches came to the

door, and I stood peeping behind a corner of the parlour blind, and saw my mother's coffin carried out of
the house. No; from the time we left the ship till I
came to The Knoll I had never known what perfect
happiness meant."

"Surely you must have had some happy days with
your father?" said Aunt Betsy.

"Very few. There was always a cloud. Papa is
not the kind of man who can be cheerful under difficulties. Besides, I have seen so little of him, poor
dear. He did not come home from India till I was
thirteen, and then he fell in love with my stepmother
and married her, and took her to France, where he
fancies it is cheaper to live than in England. Yet I
cannot help thinking there are corners of dear old
England where he might find a prettier home and live
quite as cheaply."

"Of course, if he were a sensible man; but I gather
from all you have told me that there is a gentlemanlike helplessness about him—as of a person who ought
to have inherited a handsome income, and is out of
his element as a struggler."

"That is quite true," answered Ida; "my father
was not born to wrestle with Fate."

They were at the glass door which opened into the
morning room by this time. The room was steeped in
rosy light—such a pretty room, with chintz curtains
and chintz-covered easy-chairs, low, luxurious, inviting;
the only ponderous piece of furniture an old Japanese
cabinet, rich in gold work upon black lacquer. On
the dainty little octagon table there was a large shallow brown glass vase full of Christmas roses; and there
was an odour of violets from the celadon china jars on
the chimney-piece. Aunt Betsy's favourite Persian cat,

a marvel of fluffy whiteness, rose from the hearth to welcome them. It was a delightful picture of home life.

Miss Wendover seemed in no hurry to go to bed. She seated herself in the low arm-chair by the fire, and allowed the Persian to rub its white head and arch its back against her dark brocade skirt. No one within twenty miles of Winchester wore such brocades or such velvets as Miss Wendover's. They were supposed to be woven on purpose for her. Her gowns were gowns of the old school, and lasted for years, smelling of the sandal or camphor wood chests in which they reposed for months at a stretch, yet, by virtue of some wonderful tact in the wearer, never looked dowdy or out of date.

"Now," said Miss Wendover, with a resolute air, "let us understand each other, my dear Ida. I don't quite like what you said just now; and I want to hear for certain that you are satisfied with your life here."

"I am utterly happy here, dear Aunt Betsy. Is that a sufficient answer? Only, when I came here, I felt that it was charity—an impulse of kindness for a friendless girl—that prompted you to offer me a home; that, in accepting your kindness, I had no right to become an encumbrance; that, having enjoyed your genial hospitality for a space, I ought to move on upon my journey, to go where I could be of more use."

"You too ridiculous girl, can you suppose that you are not useful to me?" exclaimed Aunt Betsy, impatiently. "Is there a single hour of your day unoccupied? Granted that my original motive was a desire to give a comfortable home to a dear girl who seemed in need of new surroundings, but that idea would hardly have occurred to me unless I had begun to feel the want of some energetic helpmate to lighten the load of my daily duties. The experiment has answered admirably, as far as I am concerned. But it is just possible you feel otherwise. You may think that you could make better use of your powers—earn double my poor salary, win distinction by your fine playing, dress better, see more of the world. I daresay to a girl of your age Kingthorpe seems a kind of living death."

"So far from that, I love Kingthorpe with all my heart, so much that I almost hate myself for not having been born here, for not being able to say these are my native fields, I was cradled among these hills."

"So be it. If you love Kingthorpe and love me, you have nothing to do but to stay here till the hero of your life-story comes to carry you off."

"There will be no such hero."

"Oh, yes, there will! Every story, however humble, has its hero; but yours is going to be a very magnificent personage, I hope."

The little clock on the chimney-piece chimed the half-hour after midnight, whereupon Aunt Betsy started up and called for her candle. She and Ida kissed as they wished each other good night on the threshold of the elder lady's room.

After this conversation, how could Ida ever again broach the subject of departure? and yet she felt that sooner or later she must depart. Honour, conscience, womanly feeling, forbade that she should remain at the cost of Brian Walford's banishment.

CHAPTER XIII.

KINGTHORPE SOCIETY.

On New Year's Eve Miss Wendover gave one of her famous dinner-parties; famous because it was always said that her dinners were, on their scale, better than anybody else's,—yea, even than Dr. Rylance's, although that gentleman spared no expense, and had been known to induce the French cook from the Dolphin at Southampton to come over and prepare the feast for him.

Miss Wendover's dinner was an excuse for the bringing forth of rich stores of old china, old glass, and older silver—the accumulations of aunts and uncles for past generations, and in some part of the lady herself, who had the true spirit of a collector, that special gift which the French connoisseur calls *le flair*. Ida and the lady of the house worked diligently all the morning in unpapering and polishing these treasures; and the dinner table, with its antique silver, Derby china, heavy diamond-cut glass, and white and scarlet exotics, was a picture to gladden the eyes of Aunt Betsy's guests.

The party consisted of Colonel and Mrs. Wendover, with their daughter Bessie, admitted to this sacred function for the first time in her young life, and duly impressed with the solemnity of the occasion; the Vicar and his wife; the new curate, an Oxford M.A., and a sprig of a good old family tree, altogether something very superior in the way of curates; Mr. and Mrs. Hildrop Havenant, the great people of a neighbouring settlement, with their eldest son, also an Oxonian; and Dr. and Miss Rylance.

"Be sure you two girls look your best to-night," said Miss Wendover, as she sat before the fire with Bessie and Ida, enjoying the free and easy luxury of a substantial afternoon tea, which would enable them all to be gracefully indifferent to the more solid features of dinner, and duly on the alert to make conversation. "We shall have three eligible men."

17*

"How do you make three, Aunt Betsy?" inquired her niece. "Of course we all know that young Hildrop Havenant is heir to nearly all the land between Havenant and Romsey; but he is such a mass of affectation that I can't imagine anybody wanting to marry him. And as for Mr. Jardine——"

"Is he a mass of affectation too, Bess?" inquired Aunt Betsy with intention, for Mr. Jardine, the curate, was supposed to have impressed the damsel's fancy more deeply than she would care to own. "He is an Oxford man."

"There is Oxford and Oxford," said Bess. "If all the Oxford men were like young Havenant, the only course open to the rest of the world would be to burn Oxford, just as Oxford burned the martyrs."

"Well, we may count Mr. Jardine as an eligible, I suppose?"

"But that only makes two. Who is your third?" asked Bessie.

"Dr. Rylance."

"Dr. Rylance an eligible!" cried Bessie, with girlhood's frank laughter at the absurd idea of middle age coming into the market to bid for youth. "Why, auntie, the man must be fifty."

"Five-and-forty at most, and very young-looking for his age; very polished, very well off. There are many girls who would be proud to win such a husband," said Miss Wendover, glancing at Ida in the firelight.

She wanted to test the girl's temper—to find out, were it possible, whether this girl, whom she so inclined to love, tried in the fierce furnace of poverty, had acquired mercenary instincts. She had heard from Urania of that reckless speech about marrying for money, and she wanted to know how much or how little that speech had implied.

Ida was silent. She had never told anyone of Dr. Rylance's offer. She would have deemed it dishonourable to let anyone into the secret of his humiliation—to let his little world know that he, so superior a person, could offer himself and be rejected.

"What do you think now, Bess," pursued Miss Wendover, "would it not be rather a nice thing if Dr. Rylance were to marry Ida? We all know how much he admires her."

"It would be a very horrid thing," cried the impetuous Bess. "I would ever so much rather Ida married poor Brian, although they had to pig in furnished lodgings for the first ten years of their life. Crabbed age and youth cannot dwell together."

"But Dr. Rylance is not crabbed, and he is not old."

"Let him marry a lady of the same doubtful age, which seems old to me, but young to you, and then no one will find fault with him," said Bess, savagely. "I feel an inward and spiritual conviction that Ida is doomed to marry Brian Walford. The poor fellow was so hopelessly in love with her when he left this place, that if she had not a stone inside her instead of a heart, she would have accepted him; but *magno est amor et prævalebit!*" concluded Bess, with a mighty effort, "I'm sure I hope that's right."

"I think it must be time for you to go home and dress, if you really wish to look nice to-night," said Ida, severely. "You know you generally find yourself without frilling, or something wrong, at the last moment."

"Heavens!" exclaimed Bessie, starting up and upsetting the petted Persian, which had been reposing in her lap, and which now skulked off resentfully, with a swollen tail, to hide its indignation under a chair, "you are as bad as an oracle. I have yards and yards of frilling to sew on before I dress—my sleeves—my neck —my sweeper."

"Shall I run over and sew the frills on for you?" asked Ida.

"You! when you are going to wear that lovely pink gown. You will want hours to dress. No: Blanche must make herself useful for once in her ridiculous life. *Au revoir*, auntie darling. Go, lovely rose"—to Ida—"and make yourself still lovelier in order to captivate Dr. Rylance."

The dinner was over. It had passed without a hitch, and the gentlemen were now enjoying their claret and conversation in a comfortable semicircle in front of Miss Wendover's roomy hearth.

The conversation was for the most part strictly local, Colonel Wendover and Mr. Hildrop Havenant leading, and the Vicar a good second; but now and then there was a brief diversion from the parish to European politics, when Dr. Rylance—who secretly abhorred parochial talk—dashed to the fore and talked with an authority which it was hard for the others to keep under. He spoke of the impending declaration of war—there is generally some such thing—as if he had been at the War Office that morning in confidential converse with the chief officials; but this was more than Squire Havenant could endure, and he flatly contradicted the physician on the strength of his morning's correspondence. Mr. Havenant always talked of his letters as if they contained all the law and the prophets. His correspondents were high in office, unimpeachable authorities, men who had the ear of the House, or who pulled the strings of the Government.

"I am told on the best authority that there will be no war," he said, swelling, or seeming to swell, as he spoke.

He was a large man, with a florid complexion and gray mutton-chop whiskers.

Dr. Rylance shrugged his shoulders and smiled blandly. It was the calm incredulous smile with which he encountered any rival medico who was bold enough to question his treatment.

"That is not the opinion of the War Office," he said quietly.

"But it is the opinion of men who dictate to the War Office," replied Mr. Havenant.

"We couldn't have a better place for the working men's club than old Parker's cottage," said the Vicar, addressing himself to Colonel Wendover.

"If Russia advances a foot farther there must be war in Beloochistan," said Dr. Rylance; "and if England is blind to the exigencies of the situation, I should like to know how you are going to get your troops through the Bolan Pass."

"A single line to Romsey would send up the value of land fifty per cent.," said the Colonel, who cared much more about Hampshire than Hindostan, although the best years of his life had been spent under Indian skies.

Hildrop Havenant pricked up his ears, and forgot all about the War Office.

"If the railway company had any pluck they ought to get that Bill through next Session," he said, meaning a Bill for a loop between Winchester and Romsey.

While the elder gentlemen prosed over their wine

the two younger men had found their way, first to the garden, for a cigar under the frosty moon, then back to Miss Wendover's pretty drawing-room, where Ida was playing Schumann's "Träumerei" at one end of the room with Bessie for her only audience, while Miss Rylance, Miss Wendover, and the three matrons made a stately group around and about the fire-place.

Urania was providing the greater part of the conversation. She had spent a delightful fortnight in Cavendish Square at the end of November, and had been everywhere and seen everything—winter exhibitions—new plays.

"I had no idea there could be so many nice people in town out of the season," she said with a grand air. "But then my father knows all the nicest people; he cultivates no Philistines."

The Vicar's wife required to have this last remark explained to her. She only knew the Philistines of Scripture, an unfortunate people who seem always to have been in the wrong.

"And you saw some good pictures?" inquired Aunt Betsy.

"A few good ones and acres of daubs," replied Urania. "Why will so many people paint? There are pictures which are an affliction to the eye—an outrage upon common sense. Instead of a huge gallery lined from floor to ceiling with commonplace, why cannot we have a Temple with a single Watts, or Burne Jones, or Dante Rossetti, which one could go in and worship quietly in a subdued light?"

"That is a horridly expensive way of seeing pictures," said the Vicar's wife; "I hate paying a shilling for seeing a single picture. If it is ever so good one feels one has had so little for one's money. Now at the Academy there are always at least fifty pictures which delight me."

"You must be very easy to please," said Urania.

"I am," replied the Vicar's wife, curtly, "and that is one of the blessings for which I am thankful to God. I hate your *nil admiraris*," added the lady, as if it were the name of a species.

After this Urania became suddenly interested in Schumann, and glided across the room to see what the music meant.

"That is very sweet," she murmured, sinking into a seat by Bessie; "classical, of course?"

"Schumann," answered Ida, briefly.

"I thought so. It has that delicious vagueness one only finds in German music—a half-developed meaning —leaving wide horizons of melodious uncertainty."

This was a conversational style which Miss Rylance had cultivated since her entrance into the small world of Kingthorpe, and the larger world of Cavendish Square, as a grown-up young woman. She had seen a good deal of a semi-artistic, quasi-literary circle, in which her father was the medical oracle, attending actresses and singers without any more substantial guerdon than free admittance to the best theatres on the best nights; prescribing for newspaper-men and literary lions, who sang his praises wherever they went.

Urania had fallen at once into all the tricks and manners of the new school. She had taken to short waists and broad sashes, and a style of drapery which accentuated the elegant slimness of her figure. She affected out-of-the-way colours, and quaint combinations—pale pinks and olive greens, tawny yellow and faded russet—and bought her gowns at a Japanese warehouse, where limp lengths of flimsy cashmere were mixed in artistic confusion with sixpenny teapots and paper umbrellas. In a word, Miss Rylance had become a disciple of the peacock-feather school of art, and affected to despise every other development of intellect or beauty.

This was the first time that she and Ida had met since the latter's return to Kingthorpe, except indeed for briefest greetings in the churchyard after morning service. Ida had not yet upbraided her for the trick of which she was the author and originator, but Urania was in no wise grateful for this forbearance. She had acted with deliberate maliciousness; and she wanted to know that her malice had given pain. The whole thing was a failure if it had not hurt the girl who had been audacious enough to outshine Miss Rylance, and to fascinate Miss Rylance's father. Urania had no idea that the physician had offered himself and his two houses to Ida Palliser, nay, had even pledged himself to sacrifice his daughter at the shrine of his new love. She knew that he admired Miss Palliser more than he had ever admired anyone else within her knowledge, and this was more than enough to make Ida hateful.

Ida was particularly obnoxious this evening, in that pale pink cashmere gown, with a falling collar of fine old Brussels point, a Christmas gift from Mrs. Wendover. The gown might not be the highest development of the Grosvenor Gallery school, but it was at once picturesque and becoming, and Ida was looking her loveliest.

"Why have you never come to see me since your return?" inquired Urania, with languid graciousness.

"I did not think you wanted me," Ida answered, coolly.

"I am always glad to see my friends. I stop at home on Thursday afternoons on purpose; but perhaps you have not quite forgiven Bess and me for that little bit of fun we indulged in last September," said Urania.

"I have quite forgiven Bess her share of the joke," answered Ida, scanning Miss Rylance's smiling countenance with dark, scornful eyes, "because I know she had no idea of giving me pain."

"But won't you forgive me too? Are you going to leave me out in the cold?"

"I don't think you care a straw whether I forgive or do not forgive you. You wanted to wound me— to humiliate me—and you succeeded—to a certain degree. But you see I have survived the humiliation. You did not hurt me quite so much as you intended, perhaps."

"What a too absurd view to take of the thing," cried Urania, with an injured air. "An innocent practical joke, not involving harm of any kind; a little girlish prank played on the spur of the moment. I thought you were more sensible than to be offended —much less seriously angry—at any such nonsense."

Ida contemplated her enemy silently for a few moments, as her hands wandered softly through one of those Kinderscenen which she knew by heart.

"If I am mistaken in your motives it is I who have to apologise," she said, quietly. "Perhaps I am inclined to make too much of what is really nothing. But I detest all practical jokes, and I should have thought you were the very last person to indulge in one, Miss Rylance. Sportiveness is hardly in your line."

"Nobody is always wise," murmured Urania, with her disagreeable simper.

"Not even Miss Rylance?" questioned Ida, without looking up from the keys.

"Please don't quarrel," pleaded Bessie, piteously; "such a bad use for the last night of the year. It was more my fault than anyone else's, though the suggestion did certainly come from Urania—but no harm has come of it—nor good either, I am sorry to say—and I have repented in sackcloth and ashes. Why should the dismal failure be raked up to-night?"

"I should not have spoken of it if Miss Rylance had been silent," said Ida; and here, happily, the two young men came in, and made at once for the group of girls by the piano, whereupon Urania had an opportunity of parading her newest ideas, all second, third, or even fourth-hand, before the young Oxonians. One young Oxonian was chillingly indifferent to the later developments of modern thought, and had eyes for no one but Bessie, whose childish face beamed with smiles as he talked to her, although his homely theme was old Sam Jones's rheumatics, and the Providence which had preserved Martha Morris's boy from instant death when he tumbled into the fire. It was only parish talk, but Bessie felt as happy as if one of the saints of old had condescended to converse with her—proud and pleased, too, when Mr. Jardine told her how grateful old Jones was for her occasional visits, and how her goodness to Mrs. Morris had made a deep impression upon that personage, commonly reported to have "a temper" and to be altogether a difficult subject.

The conversation drifted not unnaturally from parochial to more personal topics, and Mr. Jardine showed himself interested in Bessie's pursuits, studies, and amusements.

"I hear so much of you from those two brothers

of yours," said the curate—"fine, frank fellows. They often join me in my walks."

"I'm sure it is very good of you to have anything to say to them," replied Bessie, feeling, like other girls of eighteen, that there could hardly be anything more despicable—from a Society point of view—than her two brothers. "They are laboriously idle all through the holidays."

"Well, I daresay they might work a little more, with ultimate advantage," said Mr. Jardine, smiling; "but it is pleasant to see boys enjoy life so thoroughly. They are fond of all open-air amusements, and they are keen observers, and I find that they think a good deal, which is a stage towards work."

"They are not utterly idiotic," sighed Bessie; "but they never read, and they break things in a dreadful way. The legs of our chairs snap under those two boys as if old oak were touchwood; and Blanche and Eva, who ought to know better, devote all their energies to imitating them."

The other gentlemen had come in by this time, and Dr. Rylance came gliding across the room with his gentlemanly but somewhat cat-like tread, and planted himself behind Ida, bending down to question her about her music, and letting her see that he admired her as much as ever, and had even forgiven her for refusing him. But she rose as soon as she decently could, and left the piano.

"Miss Rylance will sing, I hope," she said, politely.

Miss Wendover came over to make the same request, and Urania sang the last fashionable ballad, "Blind Man's Holiday," in a hard chilly voice which was as unpleasant as a voice well could be without being actually out of tune.

After this Bessie sang "Darby and Joan," in a sweet contralto, but with a doleful slowness which hung heavily upon the spirits of the company, and a duly dismal effect having been produced, the young ladies were cordially thanked for—leaving off.

A pair of whist-tables were now started for the elders, while the three girls and the two Oxonians still clustered round the piano, and seemed to find plenty to talk about, till sweetly and suddenly upon the still night air came the silver tones of the church bells.

Miss Wendover started up from the card-table with a solemn look, as the curate opened a window and let in a flood of sound. A silent hush fell upon everyone.

"The New Year is born," said Aunt Betsy; "may it spare us those we love, and end as peacefully for us as the year that is just dead!"

And then they all shook hands with each other and parted.

The dance at The Knoll was a success, and Ida danced with the best men in the room, and was as much courted and admired as if she had been the greatest heiress in that part of Hampshire. Urania Rylance went simpering about the room telling everybody, in the kindest way, who Miss Palliser was, and how she had been an ill-used drudge at a suburban finishing school, before that dear good Miss Wendover took her as a useful companion; but even that crushing phrase, "useful companion," did not degrade Ida in the eyes of her admirers.

"Palliser's a good name," said one youth. "There's a Sir Vernon Palliser—knew him and his brother at Cambridge—members of the Alpine Club—great athletes. Any relation?"

"Very distant, I should think, from what I know of Miss Palliser's circumstances;" answered Miss Rylance, with an incredulous sneer.

But Urania failed in making youth and beauty contemptible, and was fain to admit to herself that Ida Palliser was the belle of the room. Dr. Rylance, who had not been invited, but who looked so well and so young that no one could be angry with him for coming, hung upon Miss Palliser's steps, and tortured her with his politeness.

For Ida the festivity was not all happiness. She would have been happier at the Homestead, sitting by the fire reading aloud to Miss Wendover—happier almost anywhere—for she had not only to endure a kind of gentlemanly persecution from Dr. Rylance, but she was tormented by an ever present dread of Brian Walford's appearance. Bessie had sent him a telegram only that morning, imploring him, as a personal favour, to be present at her ball, vowing that she would be deeply offended with him if he did not come; and more than once in the course of the evening Bessie had told Ida that there was still time, there was a train now just due at Winchester, and that might have brought him. Ida breathed more freely after midnight, when it was obviously too late for any one else to arrive.

"It is your fault," said Bessie, pettishly. "If you had not treated him very unkindly at Mauleverer he would be here to-night. He never failed me before."

Ida reddened, and then grew very pale.

"I see," she said, "you think I deprive you of your cousin's society. I will ask Miss Wendover to let me go back to France."

"No, no, no, you inhuman creature! how can you talk like that? You know that I love you ever so much

better than Brian, though he is my own kith and kin.
I would not lose you for worlds.   I don't care a straw
about his coming, for my own sake.   Only I should so
like you to marry him, and be one of us.   Oh, here's
that odious Dr. Rylance stealing after you.   Aunt Betsy
is quite right—the man would like to marry you—but
you won't accept him, will you, darling?—not even to
have your own house in Cavendish Square, a victoria
and brougham, and all those blessings we hear so
much about from Urania.   Remember, you would have
her for a step-daughter into the bargain."

"Be assured, dear Bess, I shall never be Urania's
stepmother.   And now, darling, put all thoughts of
matrimony out of your head;   for me, at least."

That brief flash of Christmas and New Year's gaiety
was soon over.   The Knoll resumed its wonted domestic calm.   Dr. Rylance went back to Cavendish
Square, and only emerged occasionally from the London vortex to spend a peaceful day or two at Kingthorpe.   His daughter was not installed as mistress of
his town house, as she had fondly hoped would be the
case.   She was permitted to spend an occasional week,
sometimes stretched to ten days or a fortnight, in Cavendish Square;   but the cook-housekeeper and the
clever German servant, half valet, half butler, still
reigned supreme in that well-ordered establishment;
and Urania felt that she had no more authority than
a visitor.   She dared not find fault with servants who
had lived ten years in her father's service, and who
suited him perfectly—even had there been any legiti-
mate reason for fault-finding, which there was not.

Dr. Rylance having got on so comfortably during

the last twelve years of his life without a mistress for his town house, was disinclined to surrender his freedom to a daughter who had more than once ventured to question his actions, to hint that he was not all wise. He considered it a duty to introduce his daughter into the pleasant circles where he was petted and made much of; and he fondly hoped she would speedily find a husband sufficiently eligible to be allowed the privilege of taking her off her father's hands. But in the meanwhile, Urania in London was somewhat of a bore; and Dr. Rylance was never more cheerful than when driving her to Waterloo Station.

Miss Rylance's life, therefore, during this period alternated between rural seclusion and London gaiety. She came back to the pastoral phase of her existence with the feelings and demeanour of a martyr; and her only consolation was found in those calm airs of superiority which seemed justified by her intimate acquaintance with society, and her free use of a kind of jargon which she called modern thought.

"How you can manage to exist here all the year round without going out of your mind, is more than I can understand," she told Bessie.

"Well, I know Kingthorpe is dull," replied Bess, meekly, "but it's a dear old hole, and I never find the days too long, especially when those odious boys are at home."

"But really now, Bessie, don't you think it is time you should leave off playing with boys, and begin wearing gloves?" sneered Urania.

"I did wear gloves at Bournemouth, religiously—mousquetaires, up to my elbows; never went out without them. No, Ranie, I am never dull at old Kingthorpe; and then there is always a hope of Bournemouth."

"Bournemouth is worse than this," exclaimed Urania. "There is nothing so laboriously dismal as a
semi-fashionable watering-place."

Talk as she might, Miss Rylance could not sour
Bessie's happy disposition with the vinegar of discontent. Hers was a sweet, joyous soul; and just now,
had she dared to speak the truth, she would have said
that this pastoral village of Kingthorpe, this cluster of
fine old houses and comfortable cottages, grouped
around an ancient parish church, was to her the central point of the universe, to leave which would be as
Eve's banishment from Eden. The pure and tender
heart had found its shrine, and laid down its offering
of reverent devotion. Mr. Jardine had said nothing as
yet, but he had sedulously cultivated Bessie Wendover's
society, and had made himself eminently agreeable to
her parents, who could find no fault with a man who
was at once a scholar and a gentleman, and who had
an income which made him comfortably independent
of immediate preferment.

He was enthusiastic, and he could afford to give
his enthusiasm full scope. Kingthorpe suited him admirably. It was a parish rich in sweet associations.
The present Vicar was a good, easy-going man, a High
Churchman of the old school rather than the new, yet
able to sympathize with men of more advanced opinions
and fiercer energies.

Thus it was that while Miss Rylance found her
bower at Kingthorpe a place of dullness and discontent, Bessie rose every morning to a new day of joy
and gladness, which began, oh, so sweetly, in the early
morning service, in which John Jardine's deep musical
voice gave new force and meaning to the daily lessons,
new melody to the Psalms. Ida was always present at

this morning service; and the two girls used to walk home together through the dewy fields, sometimes one, sometimes the other going out of her way to accompany her friend. Bessie poured all her innocent secrets into Ida's ear, expatiating with sweet girlish folly upon every look and tone of Mr. Jardine's, asking Ida again and again if she thought that he cared, ever so little, for her.

"You never tell me any of your secrets, Ida," she said, reproachfully, after one of these lengthy discussions. "I am always prosing about my affairs, until I must seem a lump of egotism. Why don't you make me listen sometimes? I should be deeply interested in any dream of yours, if it were ever so wild."

"My darling, I have no dreams, wild or tame," said Ida.

She could not say that she had no secret, having that one dreadful secret hanging over her and overshadowing her life.

"And have you never been in love?"

"Never. I once thought—almost thought—that I was in love. It was like drifting away in a frail, dancing little boat over an unknown sea—all very well while the sun shone and the boat went gaily—suddenly the boat fell to pieces, and I found myself in the cold, cruel water."

"Horrid!" cried Bess, with a shudder. "That could not have been real love."

"No, dear, it was a will-o'-the-wisp, not the true light."

"And you have got over it?"

"Quite. I am perfectly happy in the life I lead now."

This was the truth. There are these calm pauses in most lives—blessed intervals of bliss without pas-

18*

sion—a period in which heart and mind are both at rest, and yet growing and becoming nobler and purer in the time of repose, just as the body grows during sleep.

And thus Ida's life, full and useful, glided on, and the days went by only too swiftly; for it was never out of her mind that these days of tranquil happiness were numbered, that she was bound in honour to leave Kingthorpe before Brian Walford could feel the oppression of banishment from his kindred. At present Brian Walford was living in Paris, with an old college friend, both these youths being supposed to be studying the French language and literature, with a view to making themselves more valuable at the English bar. He had given up his chambers in Verulam Buildings, as too expensive for a man living from hand to mouth. He was understood to be contributing to the English magazines, and to be getting his living decently, but with no immediate prospect of briefs.

CHAPTER XIV.

THE TRUE KNIGHT.

KINGTHORPE, beautiful even in the winter, with its noble panorama of hills and woods, was now looking its loveliest in the leafy month of June. Ida had been living with Miss Wendover nearly eight months, and had become to her as a daughter, waiting upon her with faithful and loving service, always a bright and cheerful companion, joining with heart and hand in all good works. Her active life, her freedom from daily cares, had brightened her proud young beauty. She was lovelier than she had ever been as the belle of Mauleverer Manor, for that defiant look which had been the outcome of oppression had now given place to softness and smiles. The light of happiness beamed in her dark eyes. Between December and June this tranquil existence had scarcely been rippled by anything that could be called an event, save the one grand event of Bessie Wendover's life—her engagement to John Jardine, who had proposed quite unexpectedly, as Bessie declared, one evening in May, when the two had gone into a certain copse at the back of The Knoll gardens, famous as the immemorial resort of nightingales. Here, instead of listening to the nightingales, or silently awaiting a gush of melody from those pensive birds, Mr. Jardine had poured out his own melodious strain, which took the form of an ardent declaration. Bessie, who had been doing "He loves me, loves me not," with every flower in the garden—forgetting that from a botanical point of view the result was considerably influenced by the nature of the flower—pretended to be intensely surprised; made believe there was nothing further from her thoughts; and then, when her emboldened lover folded her to his breast, owned shyly, and with tears, that she had loved him desperately ever since Christmas, and that she would have been heartbroken had he married anyone else.

Colonel and Mrs. Wendover received the Curate's declaration with the coolness which is so aggravating in parents, who would hardly be elated if the sons of God came down once more to propose for the daughters of men.

They both considered that Bessie was ridiculously young—much too young to receive an offer of marriage. They consented, ultimately, to an engagement; but Bessie was not to be married till after her twenty-first birthday. This meant two years from next Sep-

tember, and Mr. Jardine pleaded hard for a milder
sentence. Surely one year would be long enough to
wait, when Bessie and he were so sure of their own
minds.

"Bessie is too young to be sure of anything," said
the Colonel; "and two years will only give you time
to find a living and a nice cosy vicarage, or rectory,
as the case may be."

Mr. Jardine did not venture to remind Colonel
Wendover that for him the cosiness of vicarage or
rectory was a mere detail as compared with a worthy
field for his labours. He meant to spend his life
where it would be of most use to his fellow-creatures;
even although the call of duty should come to him
from the smokiest of manufacturing towns, or in the
flat, dull fields of Lincolnshire, among pitmen and
stockingers. He was not the kind of man to consider
the snug rectory houses or fat glebes, but rather the
kind of man to take upon himself some long-neglected
parish, and ruin himself in building church and schools.

Fortunately for Bessie's hopes, however, Colonel
Wendover did not know this.

The Curate complained to Aunt Betsy of her
brother's hardness.

"Why cannot we be married at the end of this
year?" he said. "We have pledged ourselves to spend
our lives together. Why should we not begin that
bright new life—bright and new, at least to me—in a
few months? That would be ample time for the
Colonel and Mrs. Wendover to get accustomed to the
idea of Bessie's marriage."

"But a few months will not make her old enough
or wise enough for a clergyman's wife," said Miss
Wendover.

"She has plenty of wisdom—the wisdom of a generous and tender heart—the best kind of wisdom. All her instincts, all her impulses, are pure, and true, and noble. What can age give her better than that? Girl as she is, my parish will be the better for her sweet influence. She will be the sunshine of my people's life as well as of mine. How will she grow wiser by living two years longer, and reading novels, and dancing at Bournemouth? I don't want her to be worldly-wise; and the better kind of wisdom comes from above. She will learn that in the quiet of her married home."

"I see," said Miss Wendover, smiling at him; "you don't quite like the afternoon dances and tennis parties at Bournemouth."

"Pray don't suppose I am jealous," said the Curate. "My trust in my darling's goodness and purity is the strongest part of my love. But I don't want to see the best years of her youth, her freshness, her girlish energy and enthusiasm, frittered away upon dances, and tennis, and dress, which has lately been elevated into an art. I want her help, I want her sympathy, I want her for my own—the better part of myself—going hand in hand with me in all my hopes and acts."

"Two years sounds a long time," said Miss Wendover, musingly, "and I suppose, at your age and Bessie's, it *is* a long time; though at mine the years flow onward with such a gliding motion that it is only one's looking-glass, and the quarterly accounts, that tell one time is moving. However, I have seen a good many of these two-year engagements——"

"Yes."

"And I have seldom seen one of them last a twelvemonth."

"They have ended unhappily?"

"Quite the contrary. They have ended in a premature wedding. The young people have put their heads together, and have talked over the flinty-hearted parents; and some bright morning when the father and mother have been in a good temper the order for the trousseau has been given, the bridesmaids have received notice, and in six weeks the whole business was over, and the old people rather glad to have got rid of a love-sick damsel and her attendant swain. There is no greater nuisance in a house than engaged sweethearts. Who knows whether you and Bessie may not be equally fortunate!"

"I hope we may be so," said the Curate; "but I don't think we shall make ourselves obnoxious."

"Oh, of course you think not. Every man believes himself superior to every form of silliness, but I never saw a lover yet who did not lapse sooner or later into mild idiocy."

"*Amare et sapere vix deo conceditur.*"

"Of course. Indeed, with the gods of Olympus it was quite the other way. Nothing could be more absurd than their goings on."

Ida was delighted at her friend's happiness, and was never tired of hearing about Mr. Jardine's virtues. Love had already begun to exercise a sobering influence upon Bessie. She no longer romped with the boys, and she wore gloves. She had become very studious of her appearance, but all those little coquettish arts of the toilet which she had learned last autumn at Bournemouth, the cluster of flowers pinned on her shoulder, the laces and frivolities, were eschewed; lest Mr. Jardine should be reminded of the wanton eyed daughters of Zion, with their tinkling ornaments, and chains, and bracelets, and mufflers, and rings, and nose-jewels. She began to read with a view to improving her mind, and plodded laboriously through certain books of the advanced Anglican school which her lover had told her were good. But she learnt a great deal more from Mr. Jardine's oral instructions than from any books, and when the Winchester boys came home for an occasional Sunday they found her brimful of ecclesiastical knowledge, and at once nicknamed her the Perambulating Rubric, or by the name of any feminine saint which their limited learning suggested. Fortunately for Bessie, however, their jests were not unkindly meant, and they liked Mr. Jardine, whose knowledge of natural history, the ways and manners of every creature that flew, or walked, or crawled, or swam in that region of hill and valley, made him respectable in their eyes.

"He's not half a bad fellow—for a parson," said Horatio, condescendingly.

"And wouldn't he make a jolly schoolmaster?" exclaimed Reginald. "Boys would get on capitally with Jardine. They'd never try to bosh *him*."

"Schoolmaster, indeed!" echoed Bessie, with an offended air.

"I suppose you think it wouldn't be good enough for him? You expect him to be made an archbishop off-hand, without being educated up to his work by the rising generation. No doubt you forget that there have been such men as Arnold, and Temple, and Moberly. Pray what higher office can a man hold in this world than to form the minds of the rising generation?"

"I wish your master would form your manners," said Bessie, "for they are simply detestable."

It was nearly the end of June, and the song of the nightingales was growing rarer in the twilight woods.

Ida started early one heavenly midsummer morning with her book and her luncheon in a little basket, to see the old lodgekeeper at Wendover Abbey, who had nursed the elder Wendovers when they were babies in the nurseries at the Abbey, and who had lived in a gothic cottage at the gate—built on purpose for her by the last squire—ever since her retirement from active service. This walk to the Abbey was one of Ida's favourite rambles, and on this June morning the common, the wood, the corn-fields, and distant hills were glorious with that fleeting beauty of summer which gives a glamour to the most commonplace scenery.

She had a long idle morning before her, a thing which happened rarely. Miss Wendover had driven to Romsey with the Colonel and his wife, to lunch with some old friends in the neighbourhood of that quiet town, and was not likely to be home till afternoon tea. Bessie was left in charge of the younger members of the household, and was further deeply engaged in an elaborate piece of ecclesiastical embroidery, all crimson and gold, and peacock floss, which she hoped to finish before All Saints' Day.

Old Mrs. Rowse, the gatekeeper, was delighted to see Miss Palliser. The young lady was a frequent visitor, for the old woman was entitled to particular attention as a sufferer from chronic rheumatism, unable to do more than just crawl into her little patch of garden, or to the grass-plat before her door on a sunny afternoon. Her days were spent, for the most part, in an arm-chair in front of the neat little grate, where a handful of fire burnt, winter and summer, diffusing a turfy odour.

Ida liked to hear the old woman talk of the past. She had been a bright young girl, under-nurse, when the old squire was born; and now the squire had been lying at rest in the family vault for nigh upon fifteen years, and here she was still, without kith or kin, or a friend in the world except the Wendovers.

She liked to hold forth upon the remarkable events of her life—from her birth in a labourer's cottage, about half a mile from the Abbey, to the last time she had been able to walk as far as the parish church, now five years ago. She was cheerful, yet made the most of her afflictions, and seemed to think that chronic rheumatism of her particular type was a social distinction. She was also proud of her advanced age, and had hopes of living into the nineties, and having her death recorded in the county papers.

That romantic feeling about the Abbey which had taken possession of Ida's mind on her first visit, had hardly been lessened by familiarity with the place, or even by those painful associations which made the spot fatal to her. The time-old deserted mansion was still to her fancy a poem in stone; and although she could not think about its unknown master without a shudder, recalling her miserable delusion, she could not banish his image from her thoughts, when she roamed about the park, or explored the house, where the few old servants had grown fond of her and suffered her to wander at will.

When she had spent an hour with Mrs. Rowse, she walked on to the Abbey, and seated herself to eat her sandwiches and read her beloved Shelley under the cedar beneath which she and the Wendover party had picnicked so gaily on the day of her first visit. Shelley harmonised with her thoughtful moods, for with most of his longer poems there is interwoven that sense of wrong and sorrow, that idea of a life spoiled and blighted by the oppression of stern social laws, which could but remind Ida of her own entanglement. She had bound herself by a chain that could never be broken, and here she read of how all noblest and grandest impulses are above the law, and refuse to be so bound; and how, in such cases, it is noble to defy and trample upon the law. A kind of heroic lawlessness, spiritualised and diffused in a cloud of exquisite poetry, was what she found in her Shelley; and it comforted her to know that before her time there had been lofty souls caught in the web of their own folly.

When she was tired of reading she went into the Abbey. The great hall door stood open to admit the summer air and sunshine. Ida wandered from one room to another as freely as if she had been in her own house, knowing that any servant she met would be pleased to see her there. The old housekeeper was a devoted admirer of Miss Palliser; the two young housemaids were her pupils in a class which met every Sunday afternoon for study of the Scriptures. She had no fear of being considered an intruder. Many of the casements stood open, and there was the scent of flowers in the silent old rooms, where all was neat and prim, albeit a little faded and gray.

Ida loved to explore the library, where the books were for the most part quaint and old, original editions of seventeenth and eighteenth century books, in sober substantial bindings. It was pleasant to take out a volume of one of the old poets, or the eighteenth century essayists, and to read a few stanzas, or a paper of Addison's or Steele's, standing by the open window in the air and sunlight.

The rooms in which she roamed at will were the public apartments of the Abbey, and although beautiful in her eyes, they had the stiffness and solemnity of rooms which are not for the common uses of daily life.

But on one occasion Mrs. Mawley, the housekeeper, in a particularly communicative mood, showed her the suite of rooms in which Mr. Wendover lived when he was alone; and here, in the study where he read, and wrote, and smoked, and brooded in the long quiet days, she saw those personal belongings which gave at least some clue to the character of the man. Here on shelves which lined the room from floor to ceiling, she saw the books which Brian Wendover had collected for his own especial pleasure, and the neatness of their arrangement and classification told her that the master of Wendover Abbey was a man of calm temper and orderly habits.

"You'll never see a book out of place when he leaves the room," said Mrs. Mawley. "I've seen him take down fifty volumes of a morning, when he's at his studies. "I've seen the table covered with books, and books piled up on the carpet at each side of his chair, but they'd all be back on their shelves as neat as a new pin, when I went to tidy up the room after him. I never allow no butter-fingered girls in this room, except to sweep or scrub under my own eye. There's not many ornaments, but what there is is precious, and the apple of master's eye."

It was a lovely room, with a panelled oak ceiling, and a fine old oak mantel-piece, on which were three or four pieces of Oriental crackle. The large oak writing-table was neatly arranged with crimson leather blotting-book, despatch-box, old silver inkstand, and a pair of exquisite bronze statuettes of Apollo and Mercury, which seemed the presiding geniuses of the place.

"I don't believe Mr. Wendover could get on with his studies if those two figures weren't there," said Mrs. Mawley.

The rooms were kept always aired and ready—no one knew at what hour the master might return. He was a good master, honoured and beloved by the old servants, who had known him from his infancy; and his lightest whim was respected. The fact that he should have given the best part of his life since he left Oxford to roving about foreign countries was lamented; but this roving temper was regarded as only an eccentric manner of sowing those wild oats which youth must in some wise scatter; and it was hoped that with ripening years he would settle down and spend his days in the home of his ancestors. He might come home at any time, he had informed Mrs. Mawley in his last letter, received six weeks ago.

That glimpse of the room in which he lived gave Ida a vivid idea of the man—the calm, orderly student who had won high honours at the University, and was never happier than when absorbed in books that took him back to the past—to that very past which was presided over by the two pagan gods on the writing table. She noted that the wide block of books nearest Mr. Wendover's chair were all Greek and Latin; and straying round the room, she found Homers and Horaces, Greek playwrights and historians, repeating themselves many times, in various quaint costly editions. A scholar evidently—perhaps pragmatical and priggish. Bessie's coolness about her cousin implied that he was not altogether agreeable.

"Perhaps I should have liked him no better than the false Brian," she said to herself to-day, as she stood musing before the old brown books in the library, thinking of that more individual collection which she had been allowed to inspect on her last visit.

She shuddered at the image of that other Brian, remembering but too vividly how she had last seen him, kneeling to her, claiming her as his own. God! could he so claim her? Was she verily his, to summon at his will?—his by the law of heaven and earth, and only enjoying her liberty by his sufferance?

The thought was horrible. She snatched a book from the shelf—anything to distract her mind. Happily, the book was Shakespeare, and she was soon lost in Lear's woes, wilder, deeper than any sorrow she had ever tasted.

She read for an hour, the soft air fanning her, the sun shining upon her, the scent of roses and lilies breathing gently round her as she sat in the deep oak window seat. Then the clock struck three, and it was time to think of leaving this enchanted castle, where no princess of fairy tale ever came.

There was no need for haste. She might depart at her leisure, and dawdle as much as she pleased on her homeward way. All she wanted was to be seated neat and trim in a carefully-arranged room, ready to pour out Aunt Betsy's afternoon tea, when the cobs returned from Romsey. She put Lear back in his place, and strolled slowly through the rooms, opening one into another, to the hall, where she stopped idly to look at her favourite picture, that portrait of Sir Tristram Wendover which was attributed to Vandyke—a noble portrait, and with much of Vandyke's manner, whoever the painter. It occupied the place of honour in a richly-carved panel above the wide chimney-piece, a trophy of arms arranged on each side.

Ida stood gazing dreamily at that picture—the

dark, earnest eyes, under strongly marked brows, the commanding features, somewhat ruggedly modelled, but fine in their general effect—a Rembrandt face— every line telling; a face in which manhood and intellect predominated over physical beauty; and yet to Ida's fancy the face was the finest she had ever seen. It was her ideal of the knightly countenance, the face of the man who has won many a hard fight over all comers, and has beaten that last and worst enemy, his own lower nature, leaving the lofty soul paramount over the world, the flesh, and the devil. So must Lancelot have looked, Ida thought, towards the close of life, when conscience had conquered passion. It was a face that showed the traces of sorrows lived down and temptations overcome—a face which must have been a living reproof to the butterfly sybarites of Charles the Second's Court. Ida knew no more of Sir Tristram's history than that he had been a brave soldier and a faithful servant of the Stuarts in evil and good fortune; that he had married somewhat late in life, to become the father of an only son, from whom the present race of Wendovers were descended. Ida had tried in vain to discover any resemblance to this pictured face in the Colonel or his sister; but it was only to be supposed that the characteristics of the loyal knight had dwindled and vanished from the Wendover countenance with the passage of two centuries.

"No, there is not one of them has that noble look," murmured Ida, thinking aloud, as she turned to leave the hall.

She found herself face to face with a man, who stood looking at her with friendly eyes, which in their earnest expression and grave dark brows curiously resembled the eyes of the picture. Her heart gave one leap, and then seemed to stand still. There could be only one man in the world with such a face as that, and in that house. Yet, it was a modified copy of the portrait—younger, the features less rugged, the skin paler and less tawny, the expression less intense. Yet even here, despite the friendly smile, there was a gravity, a look of determination which verged upon severity.

This time she was not deceived. This was that very Brian Wendover whom she had thought of in her foolish day-dreams, the first romantic fancy of her girlhood, last year; and now, in the flush and glory of summer, he stood before her, smiling at her with eyes which seemed to invite her friendship.

"I am glad you like my ancestor's portrait," he said. "I could not resist watching you for the last five minutes, as you stood in rapt contemplation of the hero of our race; so unlike the manner of most visitors to the Abbey, who give Sir Tristram a casual glance, and go on to the next feature in the housekeeper's catalogue."

She stood with burning cheeks, looking downward, like a guilty thing, and for a moment or two could hardly speak. Then she said, faltering—

"It is a very interesting portrait," after which brilliant remark she stood looking helplessly towards the open door, which she could not reach without passing the stranger.

"I think I have the pleasure of speaking to Miss Palliser," he said. "Old Mrs. Rowse told me you were here. I am Brian Wendover."

Ida made him a little curtsey, so fluttering, so uncertain, as to have elicited the most severe reproof from Madame Rigolette could she have seen her pupil at this moment.

"I hope you do not mind," she said, hesitatingly. "Bessie and I have roamed about the Abbey often while you were away, and to-day I came alone and have been reading in the library for an hour or so."

"I am delighted that the old house should not be quite abandoned."

How different his tone in speaking of the Abbey from the false Brian's! There was tenderness and pride of race in every word.

"And I hope that my return will not scare either you or Bessie away; that you will come here as often as you feel inclined. I am something of a recluse when I am at home."

"You are very kind," said Ida, moving a little way towards the door. "Have you been to The Knoll yet?"

"I have only just come from Winchester. I landed at Hull yesterday afternoon, and I have been travelling ever since. But I am very anxious to see my aunts and cousins, especially Aunt Betsy. If you will allow me I will walk back to Kingthorpe with you."

Ida looked miserable at the suggestion.

"I—I—don't think Miss Wendover will be at home just yet," she said. "She has gone to the Grange, near Romsey, you know, to luncheon."

"But a luncheon doesn't last for ever. What time do you expect her back?"

"Not till five, at the earliest."

"And it is nearly half-past three. If you'll allow me to come with you I can lounge in that dear old orchard till Aunt Betsy comes home to give me some tea."

What could Ida say to this very simple proposition? To object would have been prudish in the last
degree. Brian Wendover could not know what manifold and guilty reasons she had for shrinking from any
association with him. He could not know that for
her there was something akin to terror in his name,
that a sense of shame mingled with her every thought
of him. For him she must needs be as other women,
and it was her business to make him believe that he
was to her as other men.

"I shall be very happy," she said, and then, with
a final effort, she added, "but are you not tired after
your journey? Would it not be wiser to rest, and go
to the Homestead a little later, at half-past seven,
when you are sure of finding Miss Wendover at home."

"I had rather risk it, and go now. I am only
tired of railway travelling, smoke and sulphur, dust
and heat. A quiet walk across the common and
through the wood will be absolute refreshment and
repose."

After this there was nothing to be said, and they
went out into the carriage-way in front of the Abbey,
side by side, and across the broad expanse of turf,
on which the cedars flung their wide stretching
shadows, and so by the Park to the corn-fields, where
the corn waved green and tall, and to the open common, above which the skylarks were soaring and singing as if the whole world were wild with joy.

They had not much to talk about, being such utter
strangers to each other, and Brian Wendover naturally
reserved and inclined to silence; but the little he did
say was made agreeable by a voice of singular rich-
ness and melody—just such a voice as that deep and
thrilling organ which Canon Mozley has described in

19*

the famous Provost of Oriel, and which was a marked characteristic of at least one of Bishop Coplestone's nephews—a voice which gives weight and significance to mere commonplace.

Ida, not prone to shyness, was to-day as one stricken dumb. She could not think of this man walking by her side, so unconscious of evil, without unutterable humiliation. If he had been an altogether commonplace man—pompous, underbred, ridiculous in any way—the situation would have been a shade less tragic. But he came too near her ideal. This was the kind of man she had dreamed of, and she had accepted in his stead the first frivolous, foppish youth whom chance had presented to her, under a borrowed name. Her own instinct, her own imagination, had told her the kind of man Brian of the Abbey must needs be, and, in her sordid craving for wealth and social status, she had allowed herself to be fobbed off with so poor a counterfeit. And now her very ideal— the dark-browed knight, with quiet dignity of manner, and that deep, earnest voice—had come upon the scene; and she thought of her folly with a keener shame than had touched her yet.

Brian walked at her side, saying very little, but not unobservant. He knew a good deal about this Miss Palliser from Bessie's letters, which had given him a detailed account of her chosen friend. He knew that the damsel had carried on a clandestine flirtation with his cousin, and had been expelled from Maul- everer Manor in consequence; and these facts, albeit Bessie had pictured her friend as the innocent victim of tyranny and wrong, had not given him a favourable opinion of his cousin's chosen companion. A girl who would meet a lover on the sly, a girl who was ignominiously ejected from a boarding-school, although clever and useful there, could not be a proper person for his cousin to know. He was sorry that Aunt Betsy's good nature had been stronger than her judgment, and that she had brought such a girl to Kingthorpe as a permanent resident. He had imagined her a flashy damsel, underbred, with a vulgar style of beauty, a superficial cleverness, and all those baser arts by which the needy sometimes ingratiate themselves into the favour of the rich. Nothing could be more different from his fancy picture than the girl by whose side he was walking, under that cloudless sky, where the larks were singing high up in the blue.

What did he see, as he gravely contemplated the lady by his side? A perfect profile, in which refinement was as distinctly marked as beauty of line. Darkly fringed lids drooping over lovely eyes, which looked at him shyly, shrinkingly, with unaffected modesty, when compelled to look. A tall and beautifully modelled figure, set off by a simple white gown; glorious dark hair, crowned with the plainest of straw hats. There was nothing flashy or vulgar here, no trace of bad breeding in tone or manner. Was this a girl to carry on illicit flirtations, to be mean or underhand, to do anything meriting expulsion from a genteel boarding-school? A thousand times no! He began to think that Bessie was right, that Aunt Betsy's judgment, face to face with the actual facts, had been wiser than his own view of the case at a distance. And then, suddenly remembering upon what grounds he was arriving at this more liberal view, he began to feel scornful of himself, after the manner of your thinking man, given to metaphysics.

"Heaven help me! I am as weak as the rest of

my sex," he said to himself. "Because she is lovely
I am ready to think she is good—ready to fall into
the old, old trap which has snapped its wicked jaws
upon so many victims. However, be she what she
may, at the worst she is not vulgar. I am glad of
that, for Bessie's sake."

He tried to make a little conversation during the
rest of the way, asking about different members of the
Wendover family, and telling Ida some stray facts
about his late wanderings. But she did not encourage
him to talk. Her answers were faltering, her manner
absent-minded. He began to think her stupid; and
yet he had been told that she was a wonder of cleverness.

"I daresay her talent all lies in her finger's ends,"
he thought. "She plays Beethoven and works in
crewels. That is a girl's idea of feminine genius. Perhaps she makes her own gowns, which is a higher
flight, since it involves usefulness."

It was only four o'clock when they went in at the
little orchard gate, and Miss Wendover could hardly
be expected for an hour. What was Ida to do with
her guest, unless he kept his word and stayed in the
orchard?

"Shall I send you out the newspapers, or any refreshment?" she asked.

There were rustic tables and chairs, a huge Japanese
umbrella, every accommodation for lounging, in that
prettiest bit of the spacious old orchard which ad-
joined the garden, and here Ida made this polite offer
of refreshment for mind or body.

"No, thank you; I'll stay here and smoke a cigarette.
I can get on very well without newspapers, having
lived so long beyond easy reach of them."

She left him, but glancing back at the garden gate she saw him take a book from his pocket and settle himself in one of the basket chairs, with a luxurious air, like a man perfectly content. This was a kind of thing quite new to her in her experience of the Wendovers, who were not a bookish race.

She went into the house, and made all her little preparations for afternoon tea, filling the vases with freshly-cut flowers, drawing up blinds, arranging booktables, work-baskets, curtains—all the details of the prettiest drawing-room in Kingthorpe, but walking to and fro all the while like a creature in a dream. She had not half recovered from her surprise, her painful wonder at Brian Wendover's appearance, at his strange likeness to her ideal knight—strange to her, but not miraculous, since such hereditary faces are to be found after the lapse of centuries.

When all her small duties had been performed she went up to her room, bathed her face and brushed her hair, and put on a fresher gown, and then sat down to read, trying to lose herself in the thoughts of another mind, trying to forget this embarrassment, this sense of humiliation, which had come upon her. She sat thus for half an hour or so, reading "The Caxtons," one of her favourite novels, and felt a little more composed and philosophical when the rhythmical beat of Brimstone and Treacle's eight iron shoes told her that Miss Wendover had returned.

She ran to the gate to welcome that kind friend, looking so fresh and bright in her clean white gown that Aunt Betsy saw no sign of the past struggle.

"Mr. Wendover is here," she said, shyly, when Aunt Betsy had kissed her and given her some brief

account of the day's adventures. The rest of the party
had been deposited at The Knoll.

"Whom do you mean by Mr. Wendover, child?"

"Mr. Wendover of the Abbey. He is reading in
the orchard."

"Of course, I never saw him without a book in his
hand. So he has come back at last. I am very glad.
He is a good fellow, a little too reserved and self-
contained, too fond of brooding over some beautiful
truism of Plato's when he ought to be thinking of deep
drainage and a new school-house; but a good fellow
for all that, and always ready with his cheque-book.
Let us go and look for him."

"You will find him in the orchard," said Ida. "I
will go and hurry on the tea. You must want some
tea after your dusty drive."

"Dusty!" exclaimed Miss Wendover; "we are
positively smothered. Yes. I am dying for my tea;
but I must see this nephew of mine first."

Ida went back to the drawing-room, where everything was perfectly ready, as she knew very well
beforehand; but she shrank with a sickly dread from
any further acquaintance with the master of Wendover
Abbey. She hoped that he and his aunt might say
all they had to say to each other in the orchard, and
that he would go on to The Knoll to pay his respects
to the rest of his relations.

In this she was disappointed. Scarcely had she
seated herself before the tea-table when Aunt Betsy
and her nephew entered through the open window.

"You two young people have contrived to get
acquainted without my aid," said Miss Wendover,
cheerily, "so there's no necessity for any introduction.
Now, Brian, sit down and make yourself comfortable.

Give him some tea, Ida. I believe he is just civilised enough to like tea, in spite of his wanderings."

"On account of them, you might as well say, Aunt Betsy. I drank nothing but tea in Scandinavia. It was the easiest thing to get."

Ida's occupation at the table gave her an excuse for silence. She had only to attend to her cups and saucers, and to listen to Miss Wendover and her nephew, who had plenty to talk about. To hear that deep full voice, with its perfect intonation, was in itself a pleasure—pleasant, also, to discover that Brian Wendover, albeit a famous Balliol man and a Greek scholar after the Porsonian ideal, could still be warmly interested in simple things and lowly folk. She began to feel at ease in his presence; she began to perceive that here was a thoroughly noble nature, a mind so lofty and liberal that even had the man known her pitiful sordid story he would have been more inclined to compassionate than to condemn.

Having recovered her favourite nephew, after so long a severance, Aunt Betsy was in no wise disposed to let him go. She insisted upon his staying to dinner; and before the evening was over Ida found herself quite at home with the dreaded master of the Abbey. At Miss Wendover's request she played for nearly an hour, and Brian listened with evident appreciation, sitting at his ease just outside the open window, among the roses and lilies of June, under a moonlit sky. It was a calm, peaceful, rational kind of evening, and Ida's mind was tranquillised by the time it was over; and when she went to her room, after a friendly parting with Miss Wendover's nephew, she told herself that she was not likely to be often troubled with his society. He was too much a lover of learned solitude to be likely to be interested in the small amusements and occupations of the family at The Knoll—too much in the clouds to concern himself with Aunt Betsy's various endeavours to improve her poorer neighbours in themselves and their surroundings.

She did not long remain under this delusion. She was busy in the garden, with basket and scissors, trimming away fading roses and cankered buds from the luxuriance of bush and standard, arch and trellis, at eleven o'clock next morning, when she heard the garden gate open, and beheld Mr. Wendover, Bessie, and Urania coming across the lawn.

"We are going for a botanical prowl in the woods," said Bessie, "and we want you to come with us. You are always anxious to improve your mind, and here is a grand opportunity for you. Brian is a tremendous botanist, and Mr. Jardine is not an ignoramus in that line."

"Oh, then Mr. Jardine is going to prowl too?" said Ida, smiling at her.

"Yes, he is going to give himself a holiday, for once in a way. Blanche is packing a basket. She and Eva are to have the car, but the rest of us are going to walk. Come along, Ida, just as you are. We are going to grovel and grub after club-mosses and toad-stools. Your oldest gown is too good."

"Please wear a white gown, as you did yesterday," said Brian. "White has such a lovely effect amidst the lights and shadows of a wood."

"Isn't it rather too violent a contrast?" argued Urania. "A faint sage-green, or a pale gray—or even that too lovely terra-cotta red——"

"Flower-pot colour!" screamed Bessie. "Horrid!"

"I should like to go," faltered Ida, "but I have so

much to do—an afternoon class—no, it is quite impossible. Thank you very much for thinking of me, all the same."

"You utterly disagreeable thing!" exclaimed Bessie; and at this moment Miss Wendover came upon the scene, from an adjacent green-house, where she had been working diligently with sponge and watering-pot. She heard the rights and wrongs of the case, and insisted that Ida should go.

"Never mind the afternoon class—I'll take that. You work hard enough, child; you must have a holiday sometimes."

"I had a holiday yesterday, Aunt Betsy; and really I had rather not go. The day is so very warm, and I have a slight headache already."

"Go and lose it in the wood, where Rosalind lost her heart-ache. Nothing like a long ramble when one is a little out of sorts. Go and get rid of your basket, and get your sunshade. Where are you going for your botanising?"

"All over the world," said Bessie; "just as fancy leads us. If you will promise to meet us anywhere, we'll be there."

"So be it," replied Aunt Betsy. "Suppose we arrange a tea-meeting. I will be ready for you by the Queen Beech, in Framleigh Wood, as the clock strikes five, and we will all come home together. And now run away, before the day gets old. Glad to see you unbending for once in a way, Urania."

Miss Rylance had been curiously willing to unbend this morning, when Bessie ran in and surprised her at her morning practice with the wonderful tidings of Brian's return. She appeared delighted at the idea of a botanising expedition, though she cared as little

for botany as she did for Hebrew. But when a young
lady of large aspirations is compelled to vegetate in a
village—even after her presentation at court and introduction into society—she is naturally avid for the
society of the one eligible man in the parish.

"Mr. Jardine is coming with us," Bessie told her,
as a further temptation.

Urania gave her hand a little squeeze, and murmured, "Yes, darling, I'll come; Mr. Jardine is so nice.
Will my frock do?"

The frock was of the pre-Raffaelite or Bedford-
Parkian order, short-waisted, flowing, and flabby, colour
the foliage of a lavender bush, relieved by a broad
brick-dust sash. An amber necklace, a large limp
Leghorn hat with a sunflower in it, and a pair of long
yellow gloves completed Urania's costume.

"Your frock will be spoilt in the woods," said
Bessie; but Urania did not mean to do much botanical
work, and was not afraid of spoiling her frock.

They found Mr. Jardine waiting for them at the
churchyard gate, and to him Bessie presented her
cousin, somewhat reversing the ceremonial order of
things, since Brian Wendover was the patron of the
living, and could have made John Jardine vicar on
the arising of a vacancy.

Brian and the Curate walked on ahead with Miss
Rylance, who seemed bent upon keeping them both
in conversation, and Bessie fell back a little way with
Ida.

"You dearest darling," she exclaimed, squeezing
her arm rapturously.

"What has happened, Bess? Why such unusual
radiance?"

"Do you suppose I am not glad of Brian's return?"

"I thought you liked the other one best?"

"Well, yes; one is more at home with him, don't you see. This one was a double-first—got the Ireland Scholarship. Why Ireland, when it was at Oxford he got it? He is awfully learned; knows Greek plays by heart, just as that sweet Mr. Brandram who came last winter to read for the new school-house knows Shakespeare. But I am very fond of him, all the same; and oh, Ida, what a too heavenly thing it would be if he were to fall in love with you!"

"Bessie!" exclaimed Ida, with an indignant frown.

"Don't look so angry. You should have heard how he spoke of you this morning at breakfast; such praise! Approbation from Sir Hubert What's-his-name is praise indeed, don't you know. There's Shakespeare for you!" added Bessie, whose knowledge of polite literature had its limits.

"Bessie, you contrived once—meaning no harm, of course—to give me great pain, to humiliate me to the very dust," said Ida, seriously. "Let us have no more such fooling. Your cousin is—your cousin—quite out of my sphere. However civil he may be to me, however kindly he may speak of me, he can never be any more to me than he is at this moment."

"Very well," said Bess, meekly, "I will be as silent as the grave. I don't think I said anything very offensive, but—I apologise. Do you think you would very much mind kissing me, just as if nothing had happened?"

Ida clasped the lovable damsel in her arms and kissed her warmly. And now Mr. Jardine turned back and joined them, at the entrance to a wood supposed to be particularly rich in mosses, flowers, and fungi. Urania still absorbed the attention of Mr. Wendover,

who strolled by her side and listened somewhat
languidly to her disquisitions upon various phases of
modern thought.

"What a beautiful girl Bessie has discovered for
her bosom friend," he said, presently.

"Miss Palliser; yes, she is quite too lovely, is she
not?" said Urania, with that air of heartiness which
every well-trained young woman assumes when she
discusses a rival beauty; "but she has not the purity
of the early Italian manner. It is a Carlo-Dolci face
—the beauty of the Florentine decadence. I was at
school with her."

"So I understood. Were you great friends?"

"No," replied Miss Rylance, decisively; "if we had
been at school for as many years as it took to evolve
man from the lowest of the vertebrata we should not
have been friends."

"I understand. The thousandth part of an inch,
unbridged, is as metaphysically impassable as the gulf
which divides us from the farthest nebula. In your
case there was no conveying medium, no sympathy to
draw you together," said Brian, answering the young
lady in her own coin.

She glanced at him doubtfully, rather inclined to
think he was laughing at her, if any one could laugh
at Miss Rylance.

"She was frankly detestable," said Urania. "I
endure her here for Bessie's sake; just as I would
endure the ungraceful curves of a Dachshund if Bess
took it into her head to make a pet of one; but at
school I could keep her at a distance."

"What has she done to offend you?"

"Done? nothing. She exists, that is quite enough.
Her whole nature—her moral being—is antagonistic

to mine. What is your opinion of a young woman who declares in cold blood that she means to marry for money?"

"Not a pleasant avowal from such lips, certainly," said Brian. "She may have been only joking."

"After events showed that she was in earnest."

"How so? Has she married for money? I thought she was still Miss Palliser?"

"She is; but that is not her fault. She tried her hardest to secure a husband whom she supposed to be rich."

And then Miss Rylance told how in frolic mood his penniless cousin had been palmed upon Miss Palliser as the owner of the Abbey; how she had fallen readily into the trap, and had carried on a clandestine acquaintance which had resulted in her expulsion from the school where she had filled the subordinate position of pupil-teacher.

"I have heard most of this before, from Bessie, but not the full particulars of the practical joke which put Brian Walford in my shoes," said Mr. Wendover.

He felt more shocked, more wounded than there was need for him to feel, perhaps; but the girl's beauty had charmed him, and he was prepared to think her a goddess.

"How do you know that Miss Palliser did not like my cousin for his own sake?" he speculated presently. "Brian Walford is a very nice fellow."

"She did not like him well enough to marry him when she knew the truth," replied Urania. "I believe the poor fellow was passionately in love with her. She encouraged him, fooled him to the top of his bent, and then flung him over directly she found he was not the rich Mr. Wendover. He has never been to Kingthorpe since. That would show how deeply he was wounded."

"The fooling was not all on her side," said Mr. Wendover. "She had a right to resent the trick that had been played upon her. I am surprised that Bessie could lend herself to such a mean attempt to put her friend at a disadvantage."

"Oh, I am sure Bessie meant only the most innocent fun; her tremendous animal spirits carry her away sometimes, don't you know! And then, again, she thinks her chosen friend perfection. She could not understand that Miss Palliser could really marry a man for the sake of his houses and lands. *I* knew her better."

"And it was you who hatched the plot, I think," said Brian.

Miss Rylance had not been prepared to admit as much. She intended Bessie to bear whatever blame there might be attached to the escapade in Mr. Wendover's mind; but it seemed from this remark of his that Bessie had betrayed her.

"I may have thrown out the idea when your cousin suddenly appeared upon the scene. We were all in wild spirits that day. And really Miss Palliser had made herself very absurd by her romantic admiration of the Abbey."

"Well, I hope this young lady-like conspiracy did no harm," said Brian; "but I have a hearty abhorrence of all practical jokes."

They were in a deep, rutty lane by this time, a lane with banks rich in ferns and floral growth, and here came Blanche and Eva and the youngest boy, released from Latin grammar and Greek delectus at an earlier hour than usual. The car was sent on to the wood, and Bessie and her two sisters produced their fern trowels, and began digging and delving for rare specimens—real or imaginary—assisted by Mr. Jardine, who had more knowledge but less enthusiasm than the girls.

"I can't think what you can want with more ferns," said Urania, disdainfully; "every corner at The Knoll has its fernery."

"Oh, but one can't have too much of a good thing; and then there is the pleasure of looking for them. Aren't you going to hunt for anything?"

"Thanks, no. It is a day for basking rather than work. Shall we go to the end of the lane—there is a lovely view from there—and sit and bask?"

"With all my heart," replied Mr. Wendover. "Come, Miss Palliser, of course you'll join the basking detachment."

Urania would have liked to leave Ida out of the business, but she smiled sweetly at Mr. Wendover's speech, and they all three strolled to the end of the lane, which ascended all the way, till they found themselves upon a fine upland, with a lovely view of woodland and valley stretching away towards Alresford. Here in the warm June sunshine they seated themselves on a ferny bank to wait for the diggers and delvers below. It was verily weather in which to bask was quite the most rapturous employment. The orchestral harmonies of summer insects made a low drowsy music round them. There was just enough air to faintly stir the petals of the dog-roses without blowing them from their frail stems. The dazzling light above, the cool verdure around, made a delicious contrast. Ida looked dreamily across the bold grassy downs, with here and there a patch of white, which shone like a jewel in the sun. It was very pleasant to sit here—very pleasant to listen to Brian Wendover's description of Norway and the Norwegians. A book of travels might have been ever so much better, perhaps; but there was a charm in these vivid pictures of recent experiences which no printed page could have conveyed. And then the talk was delightfully desultory, now touching upon literature, now upon art, now even descending to family reminiscences, stories of the time when Brian had been a Winchester boy, as his cousins were now, and his happy hunting grounds had been among these hills.

Ida talked very little. She was disposed to be silent, but had it been otherwise she would have found slight opportunity for conversation. Miss Rylance, educated up to the standard of good professional society, was ready to give her opinions upon anything between heaven and earth, from the spectrum analysis of the sun's rays to the latest discovery in the habits of ants. She did not mean Ida to shine, and she so usurped the conversation that Miss Palliser's opinions and ideas remained a blank to Mr. Wendover.

Yet a glance at Ida's face now and then told him that she was not unintelligent, and by the time that summer day was over, and they all sat round the gipsy tea-kettle in the wood, with Aunt Betsy presiding over the feast, Mr. Wendover felt as if he knew a good deal about Miss Palliser. They had talked, and walked, and botanised together in the wood, in spite of Miss Rylance; and Urania felt somehow that the day had been a failure. She had made up her mind long ago that Mr. Wendover of the Abbey was just the one person in Hampshire whom she could allow herself to marry. Anyone else in that locality was impossible.

Under these circumstances it was trying to behold Mr. Wendover laying himself, as it were, at the feet of a poor dependent and hanger-on of his family, merely because that young person happened to be handsome. He could have no ulterior views; he was only revealing that innate shallowness and frivolity of the masculine mind which allows even the wisest man to be caught by a pair of fine eyes, a Grecian nose, and a brilliant complexion. Mr. Wendover was no doubt a great deal too wise to have any serious ideas about such a person as Ida Palliser; but he liked to talk to her, he liked to watch the sensitive colour come and go upon the perfect oval of her cheek, while the dark eye brightened or clouded with every change of feeling; and while he was yielding to these vulgar distractions there was no chance of his falling in love with Urania Rylance.

It was a crushing blow to Miss Rylance when a little conversation at tea-time showed that Mr. Wendover was not disposed to think Miss Palliser altogether a nobody, and that a young woman who earned a salary as a useful companion might belong to a better family than Miss Rylance could boast.

"I have heard your name before to-day, Miss Palliser," said Brian. "Is your father any relation to Sir Vernon Palliser?"

"Sir Vernon is my father's nephew."

"Indeed. Then your father is the Captain Palliser of whom I've heard Vernon and Peter Palliser talk sometimes. Your cousins are members of the Alpine

Club, and of the Travellers', and we have often met. Capital fellows, both of them."

"I have never seen them," said Ida, "so much of my life has been spent at school. Sir Vernon and his brother went to see my father and stepmother last October, and made a very good impression. But that is all I know of them."

A baronet for a first cousin, and she had never mentioned the fact at Mauleverer, where it would have scored high. What an unaccountable kind of girl, and quite wanting in human feeling, thought Urania, listening intently, though pretending to be interested in a vehement discussion between Blanche and Bessie as to whether a certain puffy excrescence was or was not a beefsteak fungus, and should or should not be cooked for dinner.

"Do you know your cousin's Sussex property? Have you ever been at Wimperfield?" inquired Brian.

"Never. I have heard my father say it is a lovely place, a little way beyond Petersfield."

"Yes, I know every inch of the country round. It is charming."

"It cannot be prettier than this," said Ida, with conviction.

"I hardly agree with you there. It is a wilder and more varied landscape. Hampshire has nothing so picturesque on this side of the New Forest. If Sir Vernon and his brother are at Wimperfield this summer, we might make up a party and drive over to see the place. I know he would give us a hearty welcome."

Ida was silent, but Aunt Betsy and her niece declared that it was a splendid idea of Brian's, and must certainly be carried out.

"Fancy Brian introducing Ida to her cousin!" exclaimed Bessie. "Would it not be quite too deliciously absurd? Sir Vernon Palliser, permit me to introduce you to your first cousin!"

And then Bessie, who was an incorrigible match-maker where Ida was concerned, began to think what a happy thing it would be if Sir Vernon Palliser were to fall in love with his cousin, and incontinently propose to make her mistress of this delightful place near Petersfield.

They all walked back to Kingthorpe together, and parted at the Homestead gate.

Miss Rylance, who hated woods, wild-flowers, ferns, and toadstools, and all the accompaniments of rustic life, went back to her æsthetic drawing-room in a savage humour, albeit that fine training which comes of advanced civilisation enabled her to part from her friends with endearing smiles.

She expected her father that evening, and she was looking forward to the refreshment of hearing of that metropolis which suited her so much better than Hampshire hills and woods; nay, there was even the possibility that he might bring someone down with him, as it was his custom to do now and then. But instead of Dr. Rylance she found an orange-coloured envelope upon the hall table containing an apologetic message.

"Sorry to disappoint you. Have been persuaded to go to first representation of new play at Lyceum, with Lady Jinks and the Titmarshes. All London will be there."

"And I am buried alive in this loathsome hole, where nobody cares a straw about me," cried Urania, banging her bed-room door, and flinging herself upon

her luxurious sofa in as despairing an attitude as if it
had been the straw pallet of a condemned cell.

From the very beginning of things she had hated
Ida Palliser, with the jealous hatred of conscious in-
feriority. She who had made up her mind to go
through life as a superior being, to be always on the
top rung of the social ladder, found herself easily
distanced by the penniless pupil-teacher. This had
been bitter to bear even at Mauleverer, where that
snobbish feeling which prevails among schoolgirls had
allowed the fashionable physician's daughter a certain
superiority over the penniless beauty. But here, at
Kingthorpe, where rustic ignorance was ready to worship
beauty and talent for their own sakes, it was still harder
for Urania to assert her superiority; while in the depths
of her inner consciousness lurked the uncomfortable
conviction that she was in many ways inferior to her
rival. And now that she discovered Ida Palliser's near
relationship to a baronet of old family, owner of a
fine property within thirty miles of Kingthorpe, Urania
began to feel that she must needs be distanced in the
race. She might have held her own against the shabby
half-pay captain's daughter, but Sir Vernon Palliser's
first cousin was quite a different person. If Brian
Wendover admired Ida, her lack of fortune was hardly
likely to influence him, seeing that in family she was
his equal. Such a man might have shrunk from ally-
ing himself with a woman of obscure parentage and
vulgar associations; but to a man of Brian Wendover's
liberal mind and ample fortune Ida Palliser would no
doubt seem as suitable a match as the daughter of a
duke.

Miss Rylance had grown worldly-wise since her
introduction to London society, that particular and

agreeable section of upper-middle class life which
prides itself upon cleverness rather than wealth, and
which spices its conversation with a good deal of
smart personality. She had formed a more correct
estimate of life in general, and her father's position in
particular, and had acquired a keener sense of proportion than she had learnt at Mauleverer Manor. She had
learnt that Dr. Rylance, of Cavendish Square, was not
quite such a great man as she had supposed in the
ignorant faith of her girlhood. She had discovered
that his greatness was at best a kind of lap-dog or
tame cat distinction; that he was better known as the
caressed and petted adviser of patrician dowagers and
effeminate old gentlemen, of fashionable beauties and
hysterical matrons, than as one of the lights of his
profession. He was a clever specialist, who had made
his fortune by half-a-dozen prescriptions as harmless as
Morrison's pills, and who owed more to the grace of
his manner and the excellence of his laundress and
his tailor, than to his original discoveries in the
grandest science of the age. Other people made discoveries, and Dr. Rylance talked about them; and he
was so quick in his absorption of every new idea, so
glib in his exposition of every new theory, that his
patients swore by him as a man in the front rank of
modern thought and scientific development. He was a
clever man, and he had a large belief in the great
healer Nature, so he rarely did much harm; while his
careful consideration of every word his patients said
to him, his earnest countenance and thoughtful brow,
taken in conjunction with his immaculate shirt-front
and shapely white hand, rarely failed to make a favourable impression.

He was a comfortable physician, lenient in the

article of diet, exacting only moderate sacrifices from the high liver. His Hygeia was not a severe goddess —rather a friendly matron of the monthly-nurse type, who adapted herself to circumstances.

"We have been taking a pint of Cliquot every day at luncheon, and we don't feel that we could eat any luncheon without it. Well, well, suppose we try about half the quantity, very dry, and make an effort to eat a cutlet or a little bit of plain roast mutton," Dr. Rylance would murmur tenderly to a stout middle-aged lady who had confessed that her appetite was inferior to her powers of absorption. Men who were drinking themselves to death in a gentlemanly manner always went to Dr. Rylance. He did not make their lives a burden to them by an impossible regimen: he kept them alive as long as he could, and made departure as gradual and as easy as possible; but his was no kill-or-cure system; he was not a man for heroic remedies. And now Urania had found that her father was not a great man—that he was praised and petted, and had made his nest in the purple and velvet of this world, but that he was not looked up to or pointed at as one of the beacon-lights on the coast-line of the age—and that he being so small a Somebody, she his daughter was very little more than Nobody. Knowing this, she had made up her mind that whenever Brian Wendover of the Abbey should appear upon the scene, she would do her uttermost to make him her captive.

END OF VOL. I.

PRINTING OFFICE OF THE PUBLISHER.